A
Poisonous
Page

Also available by Kitt Crowe

The Sweet Fiction Bookshop Mysteries
Digging Up Trouble

A
Poisonous
Page

A SWEET FICTION
BOOKSHOP MYSTERY

Kitt Crowe

CROOKED
LANE

NEW YORK

Copyright © 2022 by Stephanie Jacobson

Published in the United States by Crooked Lane Books, an imprint of The Quick Brown Fox & Company LLC.

Crooked Lane Books and its logo are trademarks of The Quick Brown Fox & Company LLC.

Library of Congress Catalog-in-Publication data available upon request.

ISBN (hardcover): 978-1-64385-920-0
ISBN (ebook): 978-1-64385-921-7

Cover design by Ben Perini

Printed in the United States.

www.crookedlanebooks.com

Crooked Lane Books
34 West 27th St., 10th Floor
New York, NY 10001

First Edition: July 2022

10 9 8 7 6 5 4 3 2 1

To my family and friends, especially to Cat for keeping me motivated and teasing with baked goods she never mailed. To my boys who refuse to read, I hope when the zombie apocalypse hits, you're stuck in a library. And of course, I dedicate this book to Cookie, without whom this story would not be possible.

Chapter One

Death is good for business.

Yes, I know. Just saying that makes me sound morbid. But ever since I helped solve a murder a little over two months ago, my bookshop has seen a steady uptick in sales. Apparently, Confection, Oregon—the best little tourist town in Oregon (just ask us)—was seeing an unprecedented increase in retail sales, tourism, and hotel stays, more than it had in the past two years combined. Our local news guy said so last night on TV, so it must be true.

I finished ringing up a customer who'd purchased a stack of thrillers on sale and turned to the next fellow in line with a smile. "Hi. What can I do for you?"

"Hello. Do you have anything on organic gardening? I checked the gardening section but didn't see anything."

"I have to order some more books then, because we had some just yesterday." I nodded to one of my coworkers—the human one, not the lazy canine snoozing under the counter. "Hey, Cat, can you man the register while I look for a book?"

"Sure." The six-foot-two Amazon I called my best friend smiled and took my place behind the register. She flipped her shoulder-length, wavy red hair over her shoulder—she'd been growing it out since her new boyfriend seemed to like it—and got down to business.

Meanwhile, I did nothing with my blond hair, which was artfully pulled back in a ponytail. I had no boyfriend and kept my hair long because I liked it that way. Lately, I'd begun to wonder if dating was an idea I should revisit, what with all my friends getting coupled up. But between the bookshop, my dog, and finishing the book I'd been writing, I had little time for a social life.

Or so I kept telling myself.

I skirted the counter, sidestepped several book enthusiasts, and checked over the bookcase, finding a title that had been misplaced. I held it out to the customer. "This one looks like it might help."

He nodded and perused the book. "Looks interesting." Not a for-sure sale yet. I'd give him time to think it over.

"Let me know if I can help with anything else. And don't hesitate to use our laptop over there if you need to." I pointed to the store laptop secured to a tall table under the Information sign overhead.

"I will, thanks."

I walked back to the register, watching my dog (an adorable border collie/pit mix) give a huge yawn before crawling out from under the main counter to sit and enjoy the attention of two cute kids while their mother chatted with a friend nearby. I recognized them as locals and smiled, feeling good today.

I glanced around, pleased to see so many customers on a late Thursday afternoon. We typically closed by five, but I'd been keeping the store open an hour later to truly appreciate the late summer as well as the final festival of the season, appropriately named the End of Summer Celebration.

Confection is a cute tourist town that believes in celebrating *everything*. We're nestled between the eastern edge of the Cascade Mountains and the Deschutes River. Life in the high desert is always confusing. Hot during a summer day yet cold enough to freeze your tush off at night. So you can never pack away your jeans and jackets.

At close to seven thousand strong, our town's main economy is tourism, especially during the summer and ski seasons. We're as well known for our charming homes and incredible gardening community as we are for our cutesy businesses and street names. I live on Peppermint Way. We also have a Nutmeg Avenue. Sweet Fiction is our main bookshop. We have stores named Cookie Crumbles, Eats 'n' Treats, and Taffy Toys. You get the picture.

And of course, our chamber of commerce is always hard at work with one festival or another to keep the cheerful feel of our town alive. Something all of us business owners—well, not me, but my parents, surely—appreciated.

The bell over the door jangled, and another local stepped inside. Although this one I could have done without. At times I disliked him, while at other times I found myself wondering about him during the day. What must it be like to work as a police detective? Did it feel good to be taller and stronger than most people? Did that contribute to his superiority complex? Or had his looks given him a leg up all his life and left him plain irritating?

I chalked up my fascination to a crime fixation and left it at that.

Irritation, thy name be Detective Chad Berg.

I swear, without fail, Berg liked to pop into my shop to give me "the eye" on a weekly basis. I wasn't the only one who'd noticed.

Cat gave a subtle nod his way, then winked at me before returning to business.

She liked to pretend he had a romantic interest in me, but Berg and I both knew he kept an eye on me *and* my dog, ready to throw us in the slammer for the smallest infraction.

Avoiding him would only work for so long, until it became obvious I was dodging the law in our small storefront. Instead, I put on a bright smile and clasped my hands in front of me . . . so I wouldn't be tempted to strangle the man.

"Well, Detective Berg. What a pleasure. What can we do for you today?"

He grunted, which was his form of a greeting. As usual, he was dressed in his summer finest—khaki trousers, a dark-blue, short-sleeve polo with the word "POLICE" stretched across his broad chest and back, and a Confection PD ballcap he'd removed upon entering the store. Berg served as part of the foundation for my detective character in the suspense novel I was writing, though I'd given my lead a nicer disposition and kinder attitude toward my intrepid heroine.

He looked to the dog at my side and offered a rare smile.

Whoa boy, did that expression work in his favor. Normally, he looked like a stone-faced killer, with short, dark hair, a granite jaw, and light-gray eyes as cold as ice. Berg possessed the build of a linebacker, far bigger than me, and always seemed tense, as if poised to tackle someone for breaking the law.

He focused his gaze on my dog, Cookie. "Keeping out of trouble?"

Cookie took a delicate step forward to sniff his outstretched hand. She licked him once, then darted back to my side.

"I take it that's a yes." He nodded, then looked back at me. His smile faded. "And you . . ."

I swallowed a sigh. "And I . . . what?" My reply came out a little snappier than I'd intended. No matter how hard I tried, I couldn't be pleasant with the man for more than a few minutes at a time. I wasn't sure why.

Then again, Berg did have a tendency to cite me for violations of town ordinances I'd never even heard of. Six months on the force and he seemed to be everywhere, watching me and my dog break the law, which we never did on purpose, but which he didn't seem to believe.

"I was just going to say you look good without the cast."

I glanced at my left arm, noting how much scrawnier my forearm looked compared to my right one. It felt weaker, too, but had healed well thanks to seven weeks spent in a cast. "Oh, thanks. I still feel funny since my other arm is tan and this one is nearly white. But it's freeing to finally have the cast off."

We both paused, remembering what caused my injury—a killer doing his utter best to make sure I never told any tales.

"Yeah." Berg frowned. "You need some strength training to build back your endurance and strengthen the bone."

"Thanks, Doctor."

He ignored my sarcasm, as usual. "You're most welcome." He glanced at Cookie again.

I could almost see him itching to write us up for something and couldn't believe it when he actually took that blasted notepad out of his back pocket.

"Ms. Jones, I need to ask—"

"Oh my gosh!" I lowered my voice when a few people looked over at me, but I couldn't help my seething reaction. "First of all, how many times do I need to tell you to call me *Lexi*, not Ms. Jones? Second, Cookie doesn't need to be on a leash in the store, Detective Berg. And we haven't broken any laws since last

Tuesday, when you cited us for jaywalking." I sniffed. "Which was a totally trumped up charge, since we only raced across the street to avoid Tommy Showalter's water gun."

"And almost got hit by the mayor on Main Street. Not a good look for our town."

"He was doing forty in a twenty-mile-per-hour zone," I muttered.

"More like a few miles *under* the speed limit showing off his brand-new car." He looked down at his notepad then back up at me. Was he trying to bite back a smile? The jerk. "I need to—"

I blurted, "You can't possibly write me another ticket for something I didn't do!" Geez. What was this guy's problem with me anyway? I glanced at Cookie. Make that, problem with *us*. Cookie was adorable! And smart. And amazing. Why the heck couldn't he see that by now?

"I was going to ask you about a book, actually." He read from his notepad, "*The Art of the Criminal Catch* by A. Jonesboro." He glanced back up and lifted a brow.

"I . . . oh." I swallowed and prayed my face didn't look as red as it felt. His smirk didn't help any. I got the sense he enjoyed seeing me wound up. "We ordered two copies last week and sold one." To one of his officers, if I wasn't mistaken.

"I know. Roger told me I should grab a copy. Thought I'd like it."

My cheeks felt hotter than hades. "Sure, sure."

"Although if you really wanted me to write you up, I'm positive I could think of something."

I grimaced. "I'm positive you could."

I walked him over to the crime section and plucked the title from the shelf. "Here you go."

"Thanks, *Lexi*." He gave me a super-fake smile, beaming.

"You're welcome, *Chad*." I beamed right back.

Locked in a cheery, dazzling duel, we might have stayed that way forever if his radio hadn't squawked. He turned down the volume as he answered, still staring at me. "Berg here."

"We've got a 10-54.," The caller then rattled off an address.

Berg's eyes narrowed, his excitement diamond-bright. "Roger that." Before I could say a word, he handed me the book. "Keep this for me, would you? And *stay*."

Cookie sat and didn't so much as twitch next to me. Berg didn't bother to hide his smile.

I glared at his back as he hustled out the door and said, "I'm not a dog, you know."

Then I realized what I'd heard.

I hurried over to Cat and whispered, "Berg left on a 10-54. Does that mean what I think it means?" I'd been doing a lot of research into murder for my suspense novel.

Cat was dating a police officer, and she'd been doing her own research into crime. And punishment, but that was another discussion I planned never to have with her.

Her eyes grew wide. "10-54?"

I nodded, and together we whispered, "Possible dead body?"

Oh boy. Not this again.

Chapter Two

I spent the rest of my time at the bookstore gossiping with Cat as we wondered who might have died. By six, we hadn't heard anything from anyone about a dead body, and we wrapped up and headed out. Cat waved and left for the apartment she shared with Teri—my other best friend—and I walked with Cookie toward home.

I'd been back in Confection for close to two years now, and I couldn't believe I'd ever been gone. Life in Seattle, editing for a big-name publishing house, had nothing on selling books in a small town in Central Oregon.

I no longer worked sixty hours a week, didn't have a growing ulcer, and knew a lot of the people I passed on my walk home. The sun still shone brightly through meandering clouds overhead, and the cool breeze brought the rich smell of roses, lavender, and peonies.

With Cookie on her mandatory leash, I walked with her past the Confection Rose, our town's most famous rosebush, located in Central Garden, and continued down Cinnamon Avenue to Court Street, taking the long way home.

Every house I passed had well-tended lawns and glorious displays of flowers. I enjoyed my walk with Cookie and, spotting no one nearby, took off her leash.

"There. All better."

She grinned at me and kept by my side as we continued toward home. I waved to a few folks I recognized from the bookstore, stopped so a little boy could pet Cookie, then continued past Ed Mullins's house.

I walked fast, and Cookie trotted to keep up. Ed, president of the Confection Garden Club, CGC for short, didn't particularly like me. The feeling was mutual. He hated dogs and lived for his flowers. I hated his attitude and lived for my dog. We agreed to disagree, mostly, but I liked keeping off his radar.

An older man who had once worked—I only know because he tells everyone within five seconds of meeting them—at the International Rose Test Garden in Portland, Ed had opinions on how people should garden. He also involved himself in everything in town, from the CGC to the chamber of commerce to the Confection Historic Homes committee.

He'd been pretty congenial lately—meaning he ignored us—since we'd solved the murder of my neighbor. Cookie had been awarded a baked key to the city—peanut butter flavor—by our mayor. Even Detective Berg had given thanks, handing over the many citations I'd accrued since he'd moved to town. A few of those citations had been complaints on Ed's behalf, accusations that Cookie defecated on his lawn at night, under the cover of dark.

Yeah, right. She preferred the park west of us for her deposits, but there was no telling Ed that. Still, I knew better than to keep Cookie's doggie door unlocked at night, since she had been known to escape the backyard on occasion.

I eyed Ed's yard as we passed, saw that Cookie did the same, and warned her to behave. I had no idea how long my detente with Ed would last.

Not chancing it, I hurried Cookie along and continued to the charming little Craftsman cottage I called home.

The three bedroom, two bath house was perfect for my needs. I had enough lawn to kill if I wasn't careful, cheerful if sloppily planted flowers in the front and back, a nice front porch, and a back patio. And the most important part of the place—a backyard big enough for Cookie to run around, play, and fight with Mr. Peabody and his gang of cutthroat squirrels.

As we walked toward the front porch, my new neighbor greeted me. "Hey, Lexi. Hi, Cookie. You guys want to come over for some lemonade?"

A total one-eighty from my old neighbor, Abe Cloutier had moved in a month ago and had been doing a bang-up job clearing out the older home of all the junk his dad had collected. He'd also taken to upgrading the award-winning garden out back in addition to planting new flowers out front.

When Gil Cloutier had been alive, he'd yelled at me and Cookie for everything, including—and I'm not making this up—breathing too loud. The fence between our backyards kept us private, and since I'd never been invited over, I'd had no idea how amazing Gil's backyard garden was. After Gil's untimely death, Abe had inherited, and boy, what a difference a friendly neighbor could make. Cookie and I had been over a few times to share a drink, help with weeds, and enjoy a nice evening under the stars.

A few years older than me, Abe was a recovering alcoholic and the new manager of the smoothie shop in town. A pretty nice guy, actually, and his lemonade had the proper balance of tart to sweet, so I never said no to a glass.

"Sure, Abe. Thanks." I crossed into his yard and walked with him and Cookie along the side into the back. I whistled. "Oh, wow. You've outdone yourself."

He'd added a pergola over the back deck he'd re-stained, which provided a nice view of the garden. Prize-winning vegetables in raised beds took up prime sun space, and the many flowers he'd planted along the border of the fence in the back looked lovely. In a few new, large pots, clusters of red flowers crowded and trailed over the sides toward lush, green grass.

"Yeah, I'm feeling a blue, purple, yellow buzz lately." Abe grinned. "So the phlox, lilies, and delphinium work. But I added some red petunias in pots to add a shock of warmth."

Petunias. Right. I'd been thinking pansies. And now I had no idea what pansies looked like.

"You really do have your dad's green thumb."

He smiled, not looking so sad at mention of his dad anymore. "Thanks. Here's that drink I promised." He poured two glasses of pink lemonade, and I took one.

"That's perfect." Icy cold and clear. I took a sip and added *magnificent* to my description. It had a hint of something delicious I couldn't put my finger on. Man, I had to learn his recipe.

Cookie wandered around, sniffing.

"Don't even think about digging, missy," I called.

She gave me a disdainful huff and continued looking around.

"Sometimes she seems almost human." Abe watched her as he sipped. He sat at his patio table and nodded for me to join him. "It's like she understands when I talk to her."

"She probably does." I sat next to him and sighed, pleased to be off my feet. "I found her wandering around a side road on my drive to Confection when I moved back from Seattle. She was such a cutie, and she'd look at me when I talked to her, as if she could actually understand me. She still does that. It's weird, but that's Cookie." I paused. "I'm really glad you moved in. You're a great neighbor, Abe."

He flushed. "Thanks. You too. I can't understand why my dad was always complaining about you. I never hear you guys unless Cookie's barking at Mr. Peabody."

The tree in the corner of my backyard hung over his yard as well. Mr. Peabody spared no one when on a squirrel rant.

"They have a hate-hate relationship going on," I said to Abe.

He grinned. "Yeah, well, anytime Cookie wants to come over and defend my dad's, I mean, *my* potatoes, she can."

Cookie rejoined us and sat by Abe's side, calmly looking over the yard.

"Thanks. And we'll use *the gate,*" I said more for her benefit than Abe's. "No digging under the fence." I'd caught her last week trying to peek at Abe under the fence separating our yards.

She nudged Abe's hand and put her chin on his leg.

He laughed and petted her. "Don't worry, Cookie. I know you won't dig again." His grin faded. "So, um, did you hear?"

"About?"

"The dead body they found."

"Oh, yeah. Detective Berg was in the store when he got the call."

"Do you know who died?"

"No idea." And it was killing me . . . so to speak.

"I was grabbing dinner to go from Eats 'n' Treats and saw a lady crying. I moved closer and overheard her talking about her dead boss."

"No kidding." I sat forward in my chair. "Do you know who she was, or who she worked for?"

He shook his head. "I didn't recognize her. I'd planned to ask if she needed help when I noticed Officer Halston walking up to her. He sat with her and talked in a low voice. I didn't want to intrude."

My excitement spiked. Cat happened to be dating Officer Roger Halston. I thought she'd mentioned a date with him tonight. So maybe I'd get some answers tomorrow.

"I didn't hear her say who specifically had died," Abe continued, "but I'd swear the lady said 'she' a few times in regards to her boss."

"Hmm." Interesting.

Abe swallowed. "Do you think whoever they found was murdered?"

"I sure hope not." I finished my lemonade, wondering if it would be rude to ask for more. "But I doubt it. What are the odds someone else was murdered in our small town just after what happened with your dad?"

He looked relieved. "True. And Dad's case was an odd one. Not like we have a serial killer offing locals."

Wasn't that a lovely thought? "Now I'm going to have a hard time sleeping tonight."

He grimaced. "Me too. Sorry I mentioned it." He finished his drink.

I rose with Cookie. "Guess I'll head home. Thanks again for the lemonade." I had to know. "What makes it pink? Strawberries?"

"Watermelon. I tried strawberries and raspberries, but berries can be overpowering."

"Ah. Got it. Hey, if you need any more painter's tape, let me know. I still have a few rolls left over."

"Thanks, Lexi." Abe stood and watched us leave with a wave.

We exited through a side gate and walked to my house, where the ugliest garden gnome in existence stood watch by the front porch. The ceramic statue stood two feet tall and had to weigh over ten pounds. The hideous little bearded guy had green pants, a blue shirt, and a red hat.

"Hey, Humperdink. Everything calm on the home front?"

Dinkie didn't answer, but Cookie licked him on our way inside.

I shut and locked the door behind me, relaxing once we stepped into the living area. Painted a cheery but neutral "roasted sesame" (buttery-yellow), the place comforted me like nothing else. Inherited from my grandma, completely paid for, and full of my things and my dog.

I took the purse over my shoulder and hung it on a peg by the door, where I also hoisted Cookie's leash. I slipped off my shoes and headed for the kitchen.

After feeding the beast, I made myself a ham and cheese sandwich and small salad and went out back. Cookie took her time sniffing around the yard, no doubt making note of where Mr. Peabody and his minions had trespassed. Overhead, the sun cast orange and purple shadows in the clouds, and the temperature dropped with the sun's departure.

Two things I especially loved about summers in Central Oregon—warm days and cold nights.

The welcome chill eventually forced me inside, and Cookie and I enjoyed a quiet evening, turning in early.

The next morning, I woke to several texts I ignored. I yawned, let Cookie out to do her business, and made a small pot of coffee before indulging in eggs and toast. After a shower and a fretful decision on what to wear—a pink or red T-shirt to go with white capris—I settled on red and dressed.

Finally feeling awake, I checked my phone.

Two texts from Uncle Elvis, one from Uncle Jimmy, three from Cat, two from Teri, and one from Dash, Teri's older brother. To call Dash my frenemy would be inflating his importance in my life. I considered him a pest, as only a best friend's older brother can be, as well as a grudging friend of mine. Cookie loved the ground he walked on, which only cemented the truth of his good-guyness. It didn't help that he still saw me as his little sister's pesky friend. Or that I'd had a secret crush on him in high school, because he was incredibly good-looking.

He also knew exactly how good-looking he was, which had helped lessen my infatuation as the years wore on.

After scrolling through all the texts, I finally let myself digest them.

Holy schmolly, we had a name.

Marilyn Freeman, the chair of the Confection Chamber of Commerce, had passed away. She had been a hot-shot real estate agent. Pretty much everyone who ran a business in Confection knew her, or at least knew her name. A beautiful woman in her mid-thirties, she seemed too young to die. My uncles didn't know more than that she'd been found by her cleaning lady.

Teri, who works at the DA's office as a file clerk, heard a rumor that Marilyn died of a heart attack.

Cat, dating Officer Halston, offered little more, with hints about how wonderful her date had been.

Dash, late to the game, also mentioned Marilyn by name but had nothing else to offer.

While I felt badly for Marilyn's family, I didn't know her personally. Since I'm not an owner but only manage the bookstore, I'd never joined the chamber of commerce. From what I'd heard, they mostly talked about gardening and fishing, and the petty feuds between chamber members could get messy.

I had enough gossip mongering thanks to my uncles, my friends, and Sweet Fiction's book club—the Macaroons. I figured I didn't need to add to any drama.

We'd no doubt talk about Marilyn and her death Monday night, when the Macaroons met. My mother had started the club years ago. But when she and my father turned over managing the bookshop to me so they could travel across the country in their RV, I'd done my best to keep everyone focused on quality reads. And then I'd been accused of murder, and somehow we'd morphed from book lovers to crime solvers.

Fortunately, Detective Berg didn't know about the book club's new side mission, or I'm sure he would have cited me for that too.

I grunted with displeasure at the thought, grabbed Cookie and her leash, and left for work, careful to keep a lookout for Mr. Law and Order.

Oddly, I didn't pass many people on the way to the bookshop. Perhaps the clouds overhead were to blame, but I didn't mind. I liked walking to clear my thoughts. And I couldn't help wondering about Marilyn's life, and how easy it was to be here one moment and gone the next.

The clouds shifted, and a shadow ghosted over me. I shivered, more from the cold than an imagined portent of doom. Yet I couldn't shake the notion something bad was coming.

When Cookie looked up and cocked her head at me, I knew to pay attention.

"What do you think, Cookie? Is Marilyn someone we need to worry about? Or did she die of natural causes?"

"Woof."

I knew what that meant.

Well, not really, but I imagined Cookie agreed.

Best to be on the lookout for murder.

Chapter Three

Friday passed quickly, the number of out-of-towners growing as the weekend neared, our festival ramping up with musical guests and a closed-off downtown, full of craft and food stalls.

I'd heard more than one local talking about Marilyn, speculation into her death a rabid topic of conversation.

"Well, she never did stop to smell the roses, always busy making one deal or another."

"So sad. Did you know she was only thirty-five?"

"Just like her mother, although Judy died in her late forties. Like Marilyn. Heart failure."

The rumors kept circulating, and by closing time, I was more than ready to relax with friends, where we could discuss our own theories about the dead woman.

I met up with Cat and Teri at the Ripe Raisin, a popular downtown bar that offered pub-style food. Dash Hagen, Teri's brother, co-owned the place and had been doing a fantastic job bringing in more customers, making the Ripe Raisin *the* place to be in the evenings, especially during festivities.

I found my friends huddled in a corner booth. The three of us together looked like a patchwork quilt of companions. A tall, athletic redhead with a goofy grin; a petite, gorgeous pixie with glossy black hair and an ever-present suspicion shining in her eyes; and me, an average blond with a nice tan who fit perfectly between Muscles McGee and the delicate conspiracy theorist that was Teri.

They perked up as I neared and held out beers to toast my tardiness.

"Late, as usual." Cat grinned.

"Crap. I bet you'd be early for once," Teri groused and handed Cat a five dollar bill.

I groaned. "Sorry. But you should know better, Teri. Anyway, I had to go back home to drop off Cookie, who was not pleased at being left behind. Then my mom called, and I had to reassure her I wasn't under arrest for Marilyn's death."

"So far no one is," Teri said. "Seems like it was a heart attack."

I nodded. "That's what we've been hearing at Sweet Fiction. Once I reassured Mom the shop and everything was fine, I freshened up and hurried over."

They gave my T-shirt a once-over.

"Dressed up for tonight, huh?" Teri snorted.

"Hey, it's clean. I did spray on some perfume though. Just for you ladies."

"Aw, how charming," a deep voice said from over my shoulder. "Three knuckleheads all in a row."

I turned to see Dash grinning down at us, a half apron tied at his trim waist, his arms crossed over his muscular chest, showcasing an impressive set of biceps. He saw me noticing and winked. Anyone seeing him with Teri would not think they were related. Their parents had married each other after their spouses had both passed. And while Dash looked like his dad, tall and boy-next-door handsome with light tan skin and sandy brown hair, Teri took after her mom, a gorgeous, petite woman from Guam.

Genetics aside, I swear, both Teri and Dash had the same snarky sense of humor.

"Bulking up, I see." I shook my head at him. "You know what they say, when a guy spends a lot of time at the gym, he's typically compensating."

Teri snickered, and Cat coughed to muffle laughter.

Dash didn't take the bait. He smirked. "Nice try. I don't have any problems with my life, and especially not with the ladies." He chuckled. "Hell, who wouldn't want to date this fine hunk of manliness?" He pointed to his chest with his thumb.

I rolled my eyes and saw Teri do the same.

Behind him, our server arrived.

"Hey, Mike," Cat said. "We'll have the usual."

"Right. Three of our cheapest drafts and a hot, baked pretzel with beer-cheese sauce."

"Yum." Teri licked her lips. "I'm starved."

"Coming right up." Mike winked at us before leaving.

Dash sat next to his sister and bodily moved her over.

Teri frowned. "Hey."

"So what do you guys think about Marilyn?" he asked.

Perfect. I'd been wanting to talk about her. "I didn't know her very well. Did any of you?"

Teri glanced at her brother. "Ask Dash. He dated her."

We all stared at Dash, who flushed. "Hey, it was a long time ago."

Teri snorted. "Try last year."

"Which is a long time ago," Dash said. "Marilyn had looks and money and wasn't afraid to flaunt either. She had a decent sense of humor and could be a lot of fun." He sighed. "I can't believe she's dead. She was a pretty lively woman."

Cat said, "She commanded the housing market in town. SunSweet Realty made a ton of money. My aunt bought through her, and Marilyn got her a heck of a deal."

"Plus she was president of the chamber of commerce," I said. "She had a lot of power in town." And with power came enemies. "And a lot of stress, I'll bet."

"Yeah." Dash ran a finger over the table. "She used to tell me she wanted to slow down, but she had to close just one more deal. She always had just one more deal."

"Is that why you broke up?" Teri asked.

"Well, uh, we weren't really dating." He kept his gaze on the table. "We were just friends, if you know what I mean."

"With benefits," Cat added, as if the rest of us didn't know what he meant.

"Right." Dash glanced up. "I liked her. I'm sorry she's gone. But hey, at least it was quick."

"How do you know?" I asked.

"If she had a heart attack, it wouldn't have taken long, would it?"

"How do you know it was a heart attack?"

Teri answered, "From what I heard at work today—and it's all anyone can talk about—there was nothing suspicious at her house. A table set for two that never got used. She was lying on the floor, dressed up for company and wearing heels, looking pretty peaceful, according to the first officer on the scene."

"Berg?" I asked, though technically he was a detective, not a police officer.

"No, Officer Brown, I think." Teri pursed her lips. "He arrived before Berg. But their consensus is that Marilyn died of heart failure." She leaned in closer, so we did the same. "I heard Berg say he noticed a letter from her doctor wanting to do more tests. She had high cholesterol. My mom was friends with Judy Freeman, Marilyn's mom, who also died of heart failure. Apparently, it's a family problem."

"Oh, that's sad." I forced myself to stop being disappointed that we had no murder to investigate. What kind of person was I? A woman had died.

Mike returned with our drinks and appetizer. "Man, Marilyn is all anyone's talking about tonight," he said, having overheard us. "You know, she sold me and Sherry the house we just bought. Was super nice about it too." He shook his head. "I wonder what will happen with her business. Far as I know, she didn't have any family in town, just an ex-husband who moved to the East Coast a few years ago."

"Yeah." Dash shrugged. "But I think she has distant cousins or family down south. If she didn't leave a will, that's going to be a massive headache for the lawyers to figure out." He glanced past Mike. "Shoot. Noah's waving me down. Gotta go." He dragged Teri close and kissed her on the head, ignoring her shoving and grumbling. "Don't get into any trouble, you three." He had the nerve to stare me in the eye. "And yeah, I'm talking to you, Blondie."

"Oh please. I'm not the troublemaking type. And I didn't even know Marilyn."

Mike left, his attention taken by the booth behind us.

"I'm not talking about her," Dash said. "I'm talking about all the single tourists in town looking to get lucky. You three look like fresh bait."

Not the nicest description I'd ever gotten. Teri frowned at him, apparently in agreement with me.

Cat gave him a wide grin. "Aw, thanks, Dash."

He chuckled. "Keep them in line, Cat. Just threaten anyone who comes too close with your boyfriend."

She turned as red as her hair.

We waited for Dash to leave before talk returned to Marilyn.

Teri motioned for us to move closer and shared, "That's not all I heard about Marilyn. Supposedly, she was a man-magnet. She didn't care about wives or girlfriends. If she saw a man she wanted, she went after him."

"Oh, wow." I thought that a terrific motive for murder. Jealousy provided real conflict. At least, it did in the story I'd written.

"Yeah." Teri's eyes glittered. "I overheard Connie Oliver earlier when I went to the bathroom. You know, when we were waiting for *you*." I ignored that tidbit, pretending to be fascinated by my beer. "Anyhow, Connie was complaining to a girlfriend about Marilyn getting what she deserved. Then her friend asked what she was talking about, and Connie said she just knew Marilyn had once slept with her husband, though Tad always denied it."

I knew Connie and Tad because they owned the toy shop next to Sweet Fiction.

"No kidding?" Cat blinked. "But I've been into Taffy Toys a bunch of times, and Tad and Connie always seem so happy together."

I wondered what my uncles thought of Marilyn. Between Uncle Jimmy and Uncle Elvis, the pair knew everything about everyone. Our town is small and kind of boring. Someone popular dying was bound to be talked about ad nauseum. Or so I told myself so as to not feel bad about gossiping. But I was only talking with Teri and Cat. And Dash. But that was it. It wasn't really gossip, just talk with friends, right?

"Is it wrong that I want this to be a murder?" The question popped out before I could stop myself.

My friends paused and then, at the same time, sighed.

"Same," Cat said.

Teri nodded. "I feel horrible because I'm disappointed. I'm a bad person."

We all considered our terrible personalities before digging into the hot baked pretzel.

"It's human nature to be curious about death," I said, trying to put a positive spin on it. "And it was exciting to solve Gil's murder. It makes sense we'd want to solve another mystery."

"Well, there is the mystery of who Marilyn had set that table for," Cat added. "Teri, you said it was set for two."

I frowned. "It took Marilyn's housekeeper to call in to the police. Not her would-be dinner guest?"

Teri bit off a chunk of pretzel and set it on her plate. "Yeah, but if you were sleeping around on your wife with Marilyn, and you found her dead, would you want to be caught up in all that?"

"Oh, I guess that makes sense." I needed to stop trying to make Marilyn's death into more than it was.

Cat nodded. "Roger let it slip that nothing seemed suspicious about the scene. He didn't actually get to see it, but he heard from the officers who were there. After what happened with Gil, the police are suspicious of anyone dying. They were all over it, and it looks normal. Sad, but normal."

That capped it.

"We need to put this non-mystery to rest." I held up my glass. "Let's eat, drink, and be glad we're still alive and kicking."

We all held up our glasses and toasted a good life.

Later, I made a pit stop at the restroom and was returning to the table when a crowd forced me to stop and circle around a rowdy group of middle-aged men.

"Marilyn is dead, Sherry," Mike was saying into his cell phone, standing to the side of the bar. He paused and frowned. "I know. That's why. Just forget it, okay?"

I could feel his frustration from here. Hmm. Had Mike been one of Marilyn's men? I couldn't see it. He and Sherry had been on again, off again for too long. And Sherry definitely wasn't the type to let anyone flirting with Mike go publicly unpunished.

Mike wrapped up his call. "I can't. I have to get back to work. Love you."

I skirted another crowded table and saw, to my surprise, Pastor Nestor Donahue sitting with Ed Mullins, the men deep in discussion about something. It wasn't a big deal to see Pastor Nestor drinking a beer, but that he was out and about without his wife attached at the hip did surprise me.

Peggy Donahue was an older white woman with clear judgments about what she considered proper and decent. I considered her a pain in the A, but she had pull in the community. She wouldn't mind her husband chatting with Ed. They were all members of the CGC, of course. But I didn't think Peggy would have liked Marilyn, especially if those rumors about Marilyn sleeping around turned out to be true.

Again, not my business.

Yet as I passed their table, I heard Marilyn's name come up.

"Peggy was giving me grief about having the memorial at the church," Pastor Nestor was saying. "But Marilyn was a church member and a generous donor. It would be a sin *not* to have it there."

Ed agreed. "You're right. Peggy's just upset because Marilyn could get flirty. We all know it."

"Yeah, she was one handsome woman." Pastor Nestor shrugged. "Not her fault she was gifted with beauty and grace."

"And a contrary attitude," Ed muttered. "She was a tyrant in the chamber, Nestor. You know what she could be like."

"I do, but I hate to speak ill of the dead."

"I have no such problems." Ed huffed. "She and Rachel butted heads at work and brought that animosity into the chamber. Marilyn and Connie never got along either. And don't get me started on Cathy."

"Cathy Salter?"

"Yeah. Apparently, Cathy accused Marilyn of illegally involving herself in some questionable real estate bids. I don't know the details, but it sounded shady as heck."

"Huh. I guess with the way the real estate market has been heading, with few houses in town for sale and great demand, things could get ugly. But you know Cathy's just as sly and competitive as Marilyn is. Was, I mean."

"Too bad." Ed sighed. "Should have made them best friends, not best rivals."

"So says the former chair of the chamber of commerce. Why weren't you and Marilyn better friends?"

Ed said something I couldn't make out because a drunken woman nearly doused me with what remained in her wine glass. And yeah, it was a deep red. I managed to avoid her, only to have her toss her wine up into the face behind me.

Into Detective Chad Berg.

He wiped his face. No more than a splash of wine found its way to his collar and shoulder. Fortunately, the inebriated young woman hadn't had a full glass to begin with.

Berg stared from her to me and shook his head.

"I had nothing to do with it," I said quickly, staring in shock at the woman giggling hysterically at his feet. She'd fallen in slow motion, clinging to the tower of Berg as she slowly slid to her knees and remained there, laughing and hugging his legs.

I tried not to laugh, but his resigned expression had me cracking up.

"Sorry, s-studly." The woman laughed harder. "Oh my God. I'm sitting at the foot of Mt. Bachelor. Get it?" She laughed again before sobering enough to ask, "Are you a bachelor? Asking for a friend."

"No," Berg growled before carefully lifting the woman to her feet and putting her back in the arms of her friends, who were trying to escort her back to their table.

Amid a cacophony of apologies, they dispersed, leaving me staring at the wine staining Berg's collar. The poor guy had made a bad decision to wear light yellow tonight. He scowled down at me, as if any of that had been my doing.

"You know, if you keep making that face and someone slaps you on the back, you'll be stuck like that for life." I paused. "Is that what happened to you a long time ago?"

"Ha ha. Not only does she run a bookstore, she's a comedian." Berg accepted a clutch of napkins from a nearby table and finished wiping his face and neck dry.

I totally felt for him, despite him living his life to annoy me. Hey, I'd been there. I was the master of staining light-colored clothing.

"Come on." I nodded for Berg to follow me and headed back to the corner booth, where my friends watched with wide eyes as I led "Mt. Bachelor" to our table.

"Ladies," Berg said, his voice deep, like something from the bowels of the underworld.

"Detective," Cat chirped. "What brings you here?"

Teri just stared. "Oh my God. Did you try to ticket her in the bar?"

"What?" he asked, sounding confused.

"Is that why Lexi threw wine in your face?"

I felt myself blushing as I rummaged through my purse for a stain-removal stick. "Got it." I motioned for Berg to lower himself.

He stared at me with suspicion.

"Oh my gosh. I'm not going to poison you." I waved my magic stick at him. "It's for stains. I get them all the time. Trust me, this works."

"She's a klutz with food," Teri agreed, now grinning so hard her dimples threatened to do her in. "And a sloppy drunk."

"Enough out of you," I warned her. "Or I'll be telling tales to Randy."

Randy was Teri's maybe-boyfriend, a cutie who had the hots for her, but for whom she was holding back. Only because she liked him so much. Teri was a living mass of contradictions, but she never bored me.

She twisted a pretend key over her mouth. "My lips are sealed, lady of the shaken orange soda. That's what prompted you to start carrying a stain deterrent in your purse, remember?"

Berg didn't even pretend not to listen. "Who shook the soda?"

"My bet is Dash, but he never copped to it," I muttered as I ran the stain remover over Berg's collar and part of his shoulder. I had to put my hand under the material to get a good rubbing, not wanting to grind the detergent into his skin. For a guy nicknamed Iceberg, he sure radiated heat.

He just stood there, bent close, his face way too near mine, and let me work on his wine-stained shirt.

My friends were too quiet, and it started to feel awkward.

"Seriously, Lexi, manhandle your date in private, would you? This is a family bar." Dash's obnoxious voice didn't help matters.

Berg's raised brow didn't either.

I narrowed my eyes on the growly detective, which only made him start to smile.

"I—Oh, it's you," Dash said, his voice no longer so congenial. "What are you doing here, Berg? Got a warrant out for Lexi?"

"I wanted a beer but got waylaid by a drunk woman who does not need any more wine."

Dash lost his attitude. "Oh, I bet that was Rachel. She just sold a big property today, and her friends took her out for a drink." He turned and yelled, "Yo, Rachel. Slow down, girl."

"What-ever! The witch is dead, I'm drinking!"

"Witch? What witch?" I asked, but I thought I knew.

Dash sounded embarrassed for her. "I think she means Marilyn. Rachel's number two in SunSweet Realty, and she and Marilyn had some issues. But now that Marilyn's dead, Rachel won't be having office problems anymore."

Yet another motive for murder.

I met Berg's gaze, and I swear he read my mind because he scowled at me.

I let him go and patted his rock-hard shoulder. "No worries, Chad. It shouldn't stain. Now I'm going to sit here with my friends and gossip about Mt. Bachelor."

He reddened.

And my night was made.

Teri glanced from him to me and asked, "What about Mt. Bachelor? Are you going hiking or something?"

Berg mumbled an excuse and left. Dash followed, doing his best to get Rachel and her friends to tone it down.

I explained to my friends about the Mt. Bachelor comment, and they exploded with laughter.

"Lucky I refrained from punching Rachel in the nose. She almost got me with that wine," I said. "But because I'm wearing red, naturally, she hit someone else instead."

"Always happens that way." Teri nodded.

"What?" Cat asked.

"You wear something light, you get hit with stains. You wear something that blends, nothing can touch you."

My shirt was blood-red.

An odd thought struck me.

I wondered what Marilyn had been wearing when she died.

Chapter Four

S aturday passed in a blur. I spent the morning doing chores, the afternoon walking around the festival, and the evening watching a movie at the theater.

Alone.

I went by myself because I like to be entertained. I normally don't watch with Cat because she talks through movies, which drives me batty. I wouldn't have minded seeing one with Teri, but she had a date with hunky Randy.

Teri has always had the ability to make me laugh. She's super pretty and knows it but isn't conceited and often makes fun of herself. She's loyal to a fault, and I know I can trust her completely with my secrets. She's also kookier than a canine circus clown when it comes to conspiracies and a mistrust of authority in general.

Which made her work at the district attorney's office—a mainstay of authority figures—so weird. She got to read files about people in town, and was thus privy to a lot of secrets she'd always been good enough to share with her best friends. But it also caused a lack of trust when it came to her relationships. Seeing the ugly underbelly of supposedly upstanding citizens had an impact on her love life.

Frankly, I didn't have those problems. Cookie loved me because I fed her, housed her, and because she thought I was better than Stefanie Connett's peanut butter cookies. Yeah, my dog loves me something fierce. And I love her right back . . . even if she is getting a little neurotic about Mr. Peabody.

So it was Sunday morning around ten as I broke up yet another fight over a dropped peanut in the backyard.

"Cookie, geez, let him have it. We have places to be." When she continued to growl, I stopped her with five words. "Uncle Jimmy. Uncle Elvis. Brunch."

She immediately turned and trotted into the house, where she tugged her leash off the hook and held it in her mouth, waiting by the front door.

With a grin, I slipped on my shoes and jacket to combat the sudden chill, and we headed toward my uncles' house. My uncles live on the south side, like me, except they have a house on Lemon Loop, the upper-crust area of town.

They bought when prices were low, and with Uncle Elvis doing all the woodwork and Uncle Jimmy taking care of everything else, their aging Victorian looked like a reigning queen among their neighbors. Cookie and I cut through Central Park, walking on one of the many manmade trails through the fourteen acre woodland surrounding Soda Creek.

We call them honey trails, though I've never understood why, as we don't have a plethora of bees or apiaries in Central Park. In any case, plenty of people wandered through the woods. Families with children, joggers, walkers, and the like. And as we passed, they all said hello and smiled.

I really loved my town. It had taken me years away to realize leaving home had been, not a mistake, but a lesson I'd needed to learn. Confection was now home. Smiling with neighbors, welcoming friendly faces, and enjoying a sense of community had been lacking when I'd lived in a big city. And that wasn't to say people in Seattle didn't have ties to each other, but it hadn't been the city for me.

I liked my small town. Despite that, ahem, *murder* back in June, Confection still gleamed like the gem I knew it to be.

Cookie continued to carry her leash in her mouth as we walked over the Soda Creek bridge toward Lemon Loop. I walked south so as to pass the mayor's house. According to Uncle Elvis, who does a lot of work around town, the mayor had recently added on to his front porch.

It looked lovely. Red roses climbed black trellises built along the sides of the grand front porch, the aging Victorian home filled with character and detail. Lavender scalloped shingles complemented a darker purple siding below, which covered the first two floors of the home, ending in a nearly black siding up to a black tiled roof. A sculpted hedge ran up the length of the walkway from the sidewalk to the front porch, the lavender and blue stone calming against a sea of green and variety of color— the many flowers of the front yard all in shades of red and purple.

I slowed down and glanced at the mayor's driveway, not spotting his new Charger, which meant his family was no doubt attending church that morning. Something I typically avoided unless the holidays neared, my parents were in town, or a special occasion arose. My last visit had seen the church packed with those present to support Gil Cloutier's family, in a devotion dedicated to his memory.

I admit I'd attended out of curiosity rather than any love for my dead neighbor.

Since Marilyn's service had been slotted for next weekend—something I'd overheard before leaving the bar last night—I figured I'd go back to church next Sunday.

Cookie grunted at me to pay attention, and we picked up the pace toward my uncles' house.

I reached the front screen door and knocked.

"Come in," Uncle Elvis called.

Cookie perked up upon hearing his voice. Elvis had earned her love upon first meeting with a peanut butter biscuit—my pup's kryptonite. Anytime we visited, he gave her oodles of attention and treats, some of which she wasn't supposed to have. Unfortunately, food seemed unable to stay on my uncle's plate whenever Cookie visited.

We entered, and she made a beeline for Elvis in the kitchen, the scrabble of her claws against the hardwood floors telling. I soon heard loud, canine crunching.

I sighed. "Uncle Elvis! She just ate breakfast at home."

"I have no idea what you're talking about."

"You know, the vet is going to blame *me* if she arrives five pounds heavier for her next checkup."

"Cookie, she's so mean. Of course you need your vitamin bacon," I heard him rumbling.

I continued inside and found Uncle Jimmy sitting at the round dining table, reading the local paper. When my uncles had company, they opened that round table up to seat a dozen people easily. A refined sideboard with a matching rectangular mirror, chandelier, and lovely flower arrangement in the middle of the sideboard added to the glamour of brunch with my relatives.

However, today it was just me, Cookie, and the uncles.

The youngest of the Jones boys, Uncle Jimmy had the trademark Jones blond hair, pulled back in a ponytail, his goatee carefully maintained, the slant of his brows screaming *attitude*. He had the build of a pro wrestler and looked like a motorcycle gang member, with tough features and mean green eyes. Until he smiled. Then he looked like my lovable Uncle Jimmy.

His husband, Uncle Elvis, had been known to make the ladies in town swoon. He was lean, with a dark-tan skin tone, and handsome. His brilliant blue eyes didn't miss a trick. He'd been committed to my uncle for twenty years, married for the last ten. My cousin, Collin, their son, worked for me part-time in the store. He was a chip off both blocks: funny, intelligent, and good-looking. But a little more humble than his parents.

"Collin not coming today?" I asked as I grabbed a cup of coffee and sat with Jimmy at the table, noticing only three place settings.

"Nope. He's hiking with Lee-Ann up at Mt. Bachelor."

That reminded me of the comment about Berg from last night, so I laughingly recounted it to my uncles, who also found it amusing.

"Detective Berg's been pretty busy since coming to Confection six months ago," Uncle Jimmy said. "First time in over twenty years we've had a murder here. But he solved it, with our help of course."

"Yep." I sipped the coffee, in love with the faint flavors of molasses and chocolate bleeding through. "Couldn't have done it without Cookie, though."

We paused to hear Elvis crooning to her. Personally, as much as I loved Cookie, we both knew she wasn't the "best girl ever, ever, ever and so sweet." More like clever, cute, and devious with whiskers.

"At least Marilyn's death seems normal. Sad, but nothing more than a heart attack." Jimmy smiled up at Elvis, who carried a covered plate stacked high with pancakes. I waited, knowing better than to offer to help or interrupt service, and inhaled with pleasure as Elvis returned twice more, once with eggs and toast for each of us, and then again with a plate of bacon.

Cookie hovered next to him, eager to help should Elvis grow clumsy and drop *more* bacon on the floor.

He sat, finally, and we all dug into our plates.

"Shoot. Hold on." Jimmy got up this time and returned with a carafe of orange juice.

"It's a wonder you two aren't huge with all this good food you're constantly eating."

"A real wonder," Elvis repeated. He shot Jimmy a critical once-over but said nothing.

"I saw that," Jimmy growled.

Elvis snickered, and I chuckled, used to their snarky banter. We ate and teased and talked about Mom and Dad and their current trek through Wyoming. I loved my parents using their well-earned retirement to do what they'd been talking about for years. Touring the United States in their RV, visiting friends, with no timeline and no limits, was their idea of the good life.

I changed the subject to my version of a good life. "So, Uncle Elvis, are you coming to book club tomorrow night?" Sweet Fiction's book club met twice a month.

He nodded. "Can't wait. This will only be my third book club since I had to miss the others." He'd been working on a remodel that needed his attention and had missed all of last month while working.

"Did you read the book?" Our club had selected *The Girl with the Dragon Tattoo* by Stieg Larsson this time, an older title but one that merited discussion. I'd loved the book, personally, and was surprised it had taken me this long to finally read it.

"I watched the movie." Elvis held up a finger to silence me. "Both movies. The Swedish version with Noomi Rapace and the American one with Rooney Mara. I can't say for sure which one I like more, but we can discuss that tomorrow night, right?"

I shared a glance with Uncle Jimmy, mine aggrieved, his amused.

"You're supposed to *read the book*, Uncle Elvis."

He shrugged. "It was ruined for me already. I mean, one movie I might have avoided, but two? I had to watch them to compare."

Jimmy didn't even bother to hide his laughter.

I groaned. "Fine. But pretend you read it, okay? You don't want to get on Darcy's bad side."

"Ugh. That's right. She's back from vacation."

Darcy Mason, in her early thirties, was a bit of a know-it-all. She'd been crowned Mrs. Confection a few years ago, a beautiful blond mother of two and wife to a successful banker. She had an English degree (she never let us forget it), lived in a big house, and had big dreams of being in charge of her entire world. Except *I* ran book club, and I had no intention of letting her or our other more aggressive members take charge.

"Yep, Darcy makes nine. We'll have a full house tomorrow." I was excited. Attendance had been spotty for a bit while our members indulged in summer vacations, missing meetings.

"No problem. I can pretend with the best of them." Elvis paused. "Will there be treats?"

Jimmy laughed out loud. "His real motivation for joining the Macaroons."

"Yes, there will be treats. But I'm not going to Nadine's to pick up the coffee." Nadine Kim—owner of Confection Coffee, was my nemesis. We loved loathing each other, and I saw no reason not to continue tradition. "Why don't you pick up the coffee order tomorrow?"

Elvis smirked. "Is this punishment for not reading the book?"

"Yes."

"Fine." He huffed. "But that means everyone has to read my selection when it's my turn to choose. I'm thinking an original *Walking Dead* or maybe *Watchmen*. Oh, no, wait. I know. We'll read some Thor. *Ages of Thunder* is a classic."

A classic comic.

I wondered if it was too late to uninvite my uncle to book club.

"Right. Well." I coughed and avoided looking at Uncle Jimmy, who had warned me about his husband's reading habits weeks ago. "Brunch was wonderful, as usual. Thanks, guys. When you see Collin, could you let him know I've updated the schedule? I texted him, but he doesn't always respond."

"Try him on Snapchat," Jimmy volunteered.

Shocked, because my uncle typically viewed his cell phone as evil incarnate, I could only nod.

"You know you're going to have to cut back his hours once the fall term starts."

"I already talked to him and Lee-Ann about that. They have another friend I plan to hire to fill in the gaps." My college-age help had been a godsend this past summer. I didn't want to be glued to the store during such beautiful days when I could be out with Cookie, playing in a lake. Or eating ice cream while we sunned in the backyard.

Plus, my broken arm had hurt something fierce and left me tired and crabby for a few weeks this past July. Collin, Lee-Ann, and Cat, of course, had been awesome about helping out more.

"Who's Collin's friend you're thinking of hiring?" Jimmy asked.

"Um, Neil, I think."

Elvis nodded. "Neil Forsythe is a good kid. We know his parents."

"Great." I'd already interviewed the young guy and liked him. He had a cute-college-nerdy vibe that went great with books for sale. From what I gathered, he was majoring in engineering at the OSU campus in Bend, where my cousin and Lee-Ann also went to school.

"Yeah, he and Collin are in a lot of the same classes."

"They are? I thought Collin was going for mechanical engineering."

Jimmy shrugged. "He was. He's switched to computer engineering with an applied option in software entrepreneurship."

Elvis nodded. "We have no idea what that actually means, but it sounds impressive when we tell all our friends."

I laughed. "Well, I'm just glad I have help I can count on."

Jimmy looked at me. "Are you going to buy the store?"

Something I'd been considering.

"You know your parents want you to." Elvis nodded. "Your dad brags about how you're increasing revenue, and your mom keeps harping on me to fix up the sign to whatever colors *you* want for Sweet Fiction."

I chafed at the unintended pressure. "I know. But I love just managing the store for now, because I'm not stressed about ownership." Or tied down, though I had no intention of moving anytime soon. "The managing gig is giving me time to write."

"Aren't you done with that book yet?" Jimmy frowned. "I thought you finished it already."

"With my arm in a cast? Um, no. I pretty much finished my rough draft though. But it takes more than that before the book is complete." And I still had issues with my lead detective character. An amalgam of Chad Berg and Dash Hagen, my fictional detective had turned into a sexy, sardonic foil for my amateur sleuth, an independent woman determined to find out who killed her brother. At first I'd offed her father, but my brother had been pretty annoying on our last Zoom chat, so I decided to kill the heroine's brother instead.

"Well, whenever it's done, Elvis and I want to read it."

I blushed. "Yeah, sure." I hurried to dump my dishes in the sink, kissed both uncles on the cheek, and left with Cookie, offering the excuse of not wanting to miss a musical group downtown.

They let me leave without the third degree about my book, which I appreciated. So I figured I might as well make good on my lie.

I wandered downtown with Cookie, and we purchased a home-baked bag of molasses doggie treats for her and a cute hair doohickey for me.

As the crowd surged, I moved us back, away from all the people. I stepped up onto a sidewalk and bumped into someone. I turned to apologize. "Oh, I'm so sorry."

"My fault, I'm sure." The woman looked closer to my age, with an infectious smile and deep brown eyes. At the end of the leash she held, a pug glared up at me with a haughty sneer. Cookie, I noticed, ignored the dog in favor of the woman, who laughed. "You don't know who I am, do you?"

"I'm so sorry. You look so familiar too."

She grinned. "It's me, Sherry. Mike's girlfriend. I mean, fiancée. Just got my hair colored a few days ago. What do you think?"

She looked fabulous, her once dark brown hair now a light brown with red highlights. "Wow. You look like a model!" I noticed her ring and *ooh*ed and *ahh*ed over it. A round cut marquis diamond gleamed in the sunlight, looking pricey. "That ring is gorgeous. Man, I feel underdressed."

Sherry beamed. "Mike's too good to me. We're getting married next summer, and we just moved into our amazing new place. I'm working on improving myself before the wedding."

"Not much to improve."

She blushed. "You're so sweet. I need to get back into Sweet Fiction. Not only to catch up with you but also to buy a few bridal magazines."

"We have the latest, so come on in." I nodded. "Seriously, Sherry. You look incredible."

"Thanks." She fluffed her hair and grinned. "Hey, I'm with Dr. Ryan now at Sassy Pets Veterinary. So maybe I'll see you there when you bring Cookie in for her next appointment."

The vet had put Cookie's picture up on the wall to commemorate her heroic efforts in apprehending a murderer. He was one of my dog's favorite people. Dr Ryan, a smart man, regularly bribed her with Cheez Whiz and dog biscuits.

Sherry waved past me, and I turned to see Mike walking toward us with a big smile. He held a plate of food and looked a lot more relaxed than he'd been Friday night.

"Nice to see Dash lets you have time off," I teased when he joined us.

"He sure does love cracking the whip."

Sherry snorted. "He can crack all he wants. Mike came home with huge tips on Friday."

"He earned it," I said. "The Ripe Raisin was packed Friday night."

Mike nodded. "And all anyone could talk about was Marilyn Freeman."

Sherry's lips tightened. Or it seemed like they did. But she was glaring at someone in the crowd, so I couldn't be sure if the topic of Marilyn had annoyed her or the object of her current wrath had. Sherry had a reputation for flying off the handle pretty easily.

She fumed. "Seriously? I can't believe she's wearing that! Can you believe Josie Letford thinks she should be wearing a tube top in public? With that body?"

Ouch. Judgy much? I liked Josie, a middle-aged woman with a sense of humor. She also liked to drink. A lot. And she'd been known to date Mike during his off-again periods with Sherry.

Either on again or off again, Mike didn't have many qualms about spending time with other women, something everyone who hung out at the Ripe Raisin knew because Mike didn't believe in keeping his private life private. He'd always been nice to me, but I just didn't understand how he could treat Sherry so badly, or why she tolerated it. Yet they *both* seemed to feed off arguing in public. Talk about dysfunctional.

The way Sherry stared at Josie didn't bode well.

Cookie did me a huge solid by sneering at Sherry's pug and letting out a little growl.

"Uh-oh. I think I need to get Cookie home. Too many people around."

Sherry turned back to me and Cookie, Josie forgotten, and gave me a bright smile. "So great seeing you again, Lexi. Have a nice walk home. See you soon, Cookie." She patted Cookie on the head.

Mike waved. "Later, Lexie. Cookie." He slung an arm around Sherry, who gave him lovey-dovey eyes.

Oy.

Cookie turned to walk *me* home, not the other way around, grabbing her leash in her mouth and tugging me after her. Several people pointed and laughed at us, and I laughed with them, enjoying my furry companion and a fitting end to the summer.

As we left, I heard one of the bands cover Blue Oyster Cult's "(Don't Fear) The Reaper," finally playing some decent music.

We left the crowd and turned onto Court Street toward home. Cookie let me take back the leash, content to saunter next to me without encumbrance. A glance showed us safe from the police, and I walked with confidence, humming with the sounds of the band I could still hear.

The breeze picked up, and the clouds shifted to obscure the sun. "(Don't Fear) The Reaper" still drifted on the wind.

I looked down at Cookie. "Do you think Marilyn's trying to tell us something?"

She cocked her head but didn't respond. Then the rain started, and we rushed home, arriving drenched. But before I could read into ominous weather as a sign of things to come, a rainbow appeared, and the sun shone down on us again.

"See, Cookie? You're letting your imagination run away with you."

She studied me for a moment, as if considering the weight of my words. Then she shook, drenched me all over again, and grinned at the rainbow overhead.

I sighed, slogging a hank of hair from my face. "You're going to pay for that, dog."

She lay down and rolled over, showing her belly.

If only everyone would show me the same deference, I thought as I spied Nadine snickering at me from under an umbrella as she walked on by.

Chapter Five

M onday morning, the clear sky promised a lovely day. Warm
yet not too hot thanks to the rain we'd had yesterday.

Cleanup from the festival was ongoing, but Cookie and I made
it to the bookstore, entering from the back. Lee-Ann and Collin
had left me a smiley faced note on the front counter thanking me
for the food coupons I'd left them. If they were smart, they'd have
visited the mini donut food truck. Yum with a capital Y.

I left Cookie to roam while I went into the back to gather
the new titles I'd planned to stack. After putting them in the
book cart, I wheeled them out and went around the store,
straightening and reorganizing titles, putting everything back
into its proper place.

Teri thinks it's weird how incredibly satisfying I find it to
make sure the books are stacked just so, certain covers face out,
others spine out. I also like to put personal recommendation
notes by noted Macaroon reads, in addition to sprucing up our
local author table. I include anyone in Central Oregon as a local,
and we're more than open to genre fiction.

It confounded me how some bookstores tried to bar the
more lucrative, popular genres like romance and crime fiction,

43

as if by being popular, those books didn't matter as much as literary novels.

First off, I used to edit genre fiction and still loved the heck out of it. Secondly, I was down for whatever readers wanted to buy, and the romance genre alone sold more than a billion dollars a year worldwide. I knew better than to argue with numbers.

We had a few writers from Bend and Redmond to add to our collection this week, I was happy to note, spurring me to think about when I'd be adding my own novel to the local author table. Soon, I hoped. With any luck, before I turned thirty.

In two and a half more years.

I continued puttering and heard the back door open.

"Whoa. What happened? You're early," Cat said, carrying a tray of treats. "You feeling okay?"

I'd been late *one day* and the woman never let me forget it. "What did you bring me?"

"You mean, what did I bring our lucky, lucky customers?" She set her covered tray down and pulled back the foil.

"Yes!" I started to drool, the scent of her S'more Books, Please cookies making the entire store smell heavenly.

"But wait, there's more." She left and returned with a tray of something delicate, sweet, and citrusy.

"What's that?" Intrigued, I leaned closer and saw a light orange glaze over triangular shaped baked goods flecked with red. Cherries? Cranberries?

"Orange cranberry scones." Cat stared at them critically. "I hope they're good. Roger liked them, but he's easy."

"Hmm. Someone's seeing an awful lot of the police lately."

Cat blushed. "Shut up."

I laughed and helped her set her baked goodies into the glass cabinet atop the coffee counter. Since adding coffee and treats to our menu of books and more books, we'd increased foot-traffic by a third. Cat was to thank, though she insisted she hadn't done much but do what she loved—bake.

By the time she'd set everything up to look pretty, the store smelled like fresh brewed coffee, and I turned the sign to open and unlocked the front door, pleased to find a few customers already outside waiting.

The morning passed by busily enough. I ordered books for customers, contacted a few distributors for some publications I'd sold out of this past weekend, and perused a few catalogues looking for new reads to add to our store.

Teri arrived at lunchtime, so I turned the sign to closed and set the clock hands on the sign to one o'clock, when we'd be back open. It didn't give us much time to eat, but a half hour was plenty with friends.

"So okay, did you hear about the fight yesterday?" Teri asked as she joined Cat, Cookie, and myself in the back kitchen. A small space filled with a kitchen sink, microwave, slender fridge, and oven, it also provided a table and chairs, a welcome respite when one stood on one's feet all day.

"What fight?" I asked as I ate my PB&J.

Cat grinned, her mouth full, and mumbled, "Tell her, Teri."

"Sherry Resnick decked Josie Letford at the festival yesterday."

"That had to be right after I left," I told them. "I was talking to Sherry when she spotted Josie in the crowd. No love lost there."

Teri grinned. "It was epic. No hair pulling or anything. But a lot of smack talk and fist action." She pounded a small fist into

45

her hand. "Randy and I took bets. I won." She wore smug like a second skin. "Josie was raging about the insults to her figure, so Sherry raged right on back then slapped her! Then Josie got up and bam, retaliation! The cops took them in for disturbing the peace, but the DA will likely fine them and let them go."

"I don't know," Cat said. "Roger had a tough time tearing them apart. Maybe some jail time would make them think twice about throwing punches."

"You mean, throwing punches at your man," Teri corrected. "Relax. Roger's a tough guy. He can take a hit."

"Not funny."

I listened to them bicker for a bit before Teri added more news. "I also saw Stefanie and Alison at the festival. They were arguing over who served the best barbecue."

"We have judges for that," I frowned. "Matter of fact, weren't Stefanie and Alison supposed to be on the barbecue judging panel?"

"They had too many people, so Alison and Stefanie agreed to share a seat. But then it turned into a 'Texas barbecue is better than any other barbecue' discussion. And, well, with Stefanie being from Texas, you know who she was voting for."

I laughed. Stefanie Connett and Alison Wills were two of our more vocal members of the Macaroons. Well, at least Stefanie was. A retired teacher born in Texas, who had spent the majority of her life in Oregon, the older Black woman had an opinion on everything. Her best friend, Alison, had pale skin, red hair going to white, and freckles and was constantly battling the scale. She didn't say much until you really knew her, and then look out. The retired librarian knew everything about everyone in town, and if she didn't know it, she could find out.

The pair had been instrumental in solving our murder mystery back in June. To my surprise, I looked forward to seeing them at book club. No matter that Stefanie had a tendency to try and take over, she felt more like a friend than a crabby book snob at meetings. Alison, too, had shown herself to be made of stern stuff. I really wanted to know what they'd make of Marilyn's death before putting her passing to rest.

So to speak.

"Anyway, Randy and I are getting along." Teri blushed. "We're going to that winery in Terrebonne this weekend. They have live music and appetizers and stuff."

I goggled. "Teri? You at a winery? Aw, you're all grown up, aren't you?" She flipped me off, and I had to laugh. "I'm kidding. You guys will have a great time."

Cat finished her lunch and pushed her plate away. "Yeah. Let me know how it is. Maybe I'll go one night with Roger."

"You do realize you'd need to dress up a little," Teri cautioned. "We all know how partial you are to Zombie Hello Kitty shirts and Converse sneakers, but a winery is a little more upscale."

Cat scowled. "I know how to dress up."

I patted her shoulder and shot her an uber kind smile. "Really?"

"I'd have help. You guys know stuff," she said, still acting as if it wouldn't be a huge chore to wear something nice. "I do have a few dresses in my closet, you know."

"Yeah, from ten years ago," Teri muttered.

My friends are both fun and pretty, but only one of them is super stoked about nice clothes. Cat is really into athletic wear, spending a fourth of her day in the gym or getting fit, the rest split between work, dating, and baking. Teri had practically been born in a dress and heels. Well, not really, but her mom was crowned Ms. Guam over thirty years ago, and Teri had inherited her good bones and love of fashion from her mom. But fortunately, she'd missed out on her mother's personality. Mrs. Hagen can be *mean*.

"Shoot. I have to get back to work. See you two slackers tonight for book club!" Teri left in a rush, and Cat and I reluctantly got to our feet.

"Hey, can I take Cookie out?" Cat asked. "It's so nice out, and I need to walk off this lunch."

"Sure. She'd love it." I patted Cookie, who'd been hopeful about scraps or dropped food and kept shooting me dirty looks, disappointed no crusts from my PB&J had been forthcoming. "Cookie, be nice to Cat. She's taking you out to water the grass."

Cookie chased after Cat and sat still while Cat put the harness on her before attaching the leash. Very rule-conscious, that girl. They left, and the store felt empty.

After turning the sign on the door back to open, I used the small bit of downtime before the afternoon rush hit to edit my book.

It was coming together nicely, but I needed to rework a few scenes.

Writing about crime and interesting protagonists had been more difficult than I'd imagined. In my old life, I'd edited romance and suspense novels, so I appreciated pacing and character. But I still had a tough time getting it all together, creating a story from scratch. Then I'd been involved in a *real* murder, an actual suspect of the crime. And it had turned my writing around completely.

Fortunately, I was getting past my reluctance to share my work. Any day now and I'd have the courage to give the draft to the Macaroons to see what they made of the book.

My stomach churned just thinking about it.

A rush of customers entered, seemingly all at once, and I gladly focused on Sweet Fiction and helping readers find books.

Cat returned with Cookie, and Cookie made her rounds, sniffing and licking every other person, until I reminded her not to maul the customers. None of them seemed to mind, everyone in love with my dog.

I mean, I loved her too, but she could be a glory hound sometimes.

Ha. I'd have to share that with her later. Glory *hound*. I chuckled.

The day passed, and as I moved through the store to help folks while Cat rang them up, I noticed a few books stacked on the floor. As I returned one to the shelf, I accidentally dropped the other. A book on craft beer, which was a hugely popular topic in this town. As I picked it up, a ripped piece of paper fell out with something typed on it.

Saw the wine. Nice vintage. Late to be out. CR 2am. Don't forget or el—

Hmm. The page had been torn. That last word felt like "else." Before I could think too hard about it, a crash behind me had me turning around. I rushed to a small child crying near a mini book tower that had fallen over. The little boy was mumbling to his mom in Korean, and I recognized that tearstained face, a mirror image of his mom's.

She said something back and gave him a hug.

"Hey, now, LJ, are you okay?" I asked.

Kay Mitchell, another of our Macaroons and a woman I really liked, sighed. "Sorry, about that." Kay knelt to collect the books with me. "Jay had the day off and is out fishing with Chris and Joe, so I decided to spend the day with LJ."

"And Soo?" I asked, not seeing her adorable toddler, the lone girl in a household of older brothers.

"My mom has her." Kay crossed her eyes as she and her six-year-old stacked the fallen books. "Grandma was insistent she needed some girl time."

I'd met Eun Jung Gim, and though she's always been super nice to me, I'd seen her light into Kay a time or two. You didn't need to speak the language to know when a mother was chastising her daughter. Some things were universal.

LJ handed his mom a book. "I'm sorry, Mom. Someone pushed me into it."

"Honey, it's okay," I said before anyone made this a bigger deal than it had to be. "Accidents happen. You know what? I think for helping us pick things up, you should go tell Cat to give you a cookie."

He brightened and disappeared, in search of the magic cookie lady. And speaking of Cookie, she'd waited for LJ to get closer before licking him into laughter.

"Sure, LJ, go ahead. It's fine. You can have a cookie," Kay said to thin air, making me laugh. "I swear, that kid. Dangle sugar in front of him and he forgets everything." Kay stood, and we put the remaining books back into the mini tower. She grabbed one. "Thanks for the cookie. I'm happy to buy it."

"No way. I like LJ. He's one of my best young customers."

"He's been a little trooper all day. And honestly, of all my hooligans, he's the easiest to handle."

I grinned. "Hey, you wanted four kids."

"What the heck was I thinking?" She ran a hand through her hair and chuckled. "Sometimes it's nice to do one on one with the kids. But I'm looking forward to book club tonight."

"Me too." I nodded.

I walked with her back to the register, chatting, and rang her up for the book. Then I rang up a few more customers. It took me a while to remember the note I'd seen on the ground, but when I looked over at the spot where I'd seen it fall, it was no longer there. Oh well.

I soon got slammed with a teen book club and forgot about everything but the joy of sharing good reads.

Before I knew it, the clock read five thirty, and Cookie was nudging my leg and glancing toward the back kitchen. Seeing no one ready to check out, I hurried into the back to feed her, returned to the front to check out more customers, and chatted with a smile on my face, pleased to have had such a busy day.

Then six o'clock arrived.

It was time to discuss a not-murder with the Macaroons.

Chapter Six

C at had gone home to take a small break and was the first to arrive for book club, which typically started at quarter after six. We had another ten minutes to go.

"Hey, can you hold the fort while I take Cookie out?" I asked her.

She nodded. "Oh, great. There's Elvis with the coffee."

I waved to my uncle walking down the sidewalk with two large brown beverage boxes in hand and hurried Cookie to Central Park a block away. A bunch of people were taking pictures of the Confection Rose, our town's unofficial mascot. The grand, blooming bush radiated health and vitality, its flowers a deep, blushing red surrounded by thick, dark green leaves and thorns. The scent was light but sweet, and I kept an eye on Cookie as she sniffed at a few petals.

"It's over a hundred years old," Ed said from behind me, standing with two of the Confection Garden Club members— or CGC mafia, as I liked to call them. The women with him kept an eye on my dog but didn't say anything. Behind them, I saw a few familiar faces as well as a host of new ones.

"Garden tour, Ed?" I asked.

He grunted, gave Cookie a sour look, then continued for his group's benefit, "We have a rotating group that cares for the Confection Rose year-round. The bush is officially a hundred and eight years old, believe it or not, from the original bush planted here. Typically a rosebush might live anywhere from ten to thirty-five years, depending on several factors: weather, rootstock, feeding, soil. But our hardy Confection Rose is in a class by itself."

Ed walked past me, at least a dozen or more following him, until finally I had a moment's peace. I gave the rosebush one final sniff and moved with Cookie toward the dog-approved area of grass some distance away.

"Do your thing," I told her.

She glanced at me, at the leash, and sat, waiting.

"Shoot. Come on." I looked around, waiting for Berg to jump out the moment I took off her leash. Or worse, some CGC mafia member snapping photographic proof of my misdeeds and forwarding it to the police.

Cookie just stared at me and gave a low grunt.

"I won't watch." Not like I wanted to see her take care of business.

She didn't move.

Time was ticking.

"Fine, but hurry up. You keep getting me in trouble." I took the leash off and out of the corner of my eye watched her search for the perfect spot to do her thing.

Cookie is an oddball for sure. I can take her out, on a leash, and she'll pee. Anything other than that, though, and she won't go unless she's free to be . . . free.

I waited, looking around and over my shoulder, obviously suspicious, and breathed a sigh of relief when she'd finished. Just as I tossed a bag of dog poop into a nearby receptacle, Berg was stalking toward me on a mission.

I swore under my breath and knelt, as if tying my shoe. "Cookie, come," I whispered harshly, then shielded her with my body while I fixed her leash to the harness.

"Ms. Jones, your dog—"

"Hey, Detective Berg." I stood and smiled at him, making sure he saw her leash in my hand. But the wattage of my smile must have been a little too bright because he stopped in his tracks. "Just letting Cookie do her thing before I go back to Sweet Fiction."

He still wore his uniform, but he looked more relaxed. Mentally off duty? I thought I might just escape unscathed.

"Actually, I was wondering if I could borrow you and your dog for a few moments."

I paused. "What?"

"I'm giving a class on police safety to a bunch of kids and wanted to use Cookie in my demonstration."

"They're letting you talk to children?" came out before I could stop myself.

His eyes narrowed.

I coughed. "I mean, that's awesome. You won't scare them at all."

He sighed. "I know. I'm tall and maybe a little imposing."

"A little?"

He growled, "Can I borrow her or not?"

"Sure. She loves kids and would love to help. Right, Cookie?" I looked down at her and saw her grinning. "When's the presentation?"

"Now."

I blinked. "I'm sorry, when?"

He flushed. "I had a golden doodle lined up, but the owner flaked on me. So can I borrow you and Cookie or what?"

"It'll have to just be Cookie." I handed him her leash. "I have book club in five minutes. Bring her back to Sweet Fiction when you're done, okay? But the front door will be locked, so text me and I'll come out to get her."

Berg stared at the pink leash in his hand, then at Cookie. "Will she be okay with me?"

I crouched and looked into her eyes. "Go with Detective Berg and make the kids feel safe. He's going to teach them about police stuff, and it's important they not be afraid of him. Work your charming doggie magic, okay?"

She licked my nose then sat next to Berg, attentive and ready for duty.

He stared from me to her in disbelief and tilted up his ballcap. "Do you really think she understood all that?"

"You'd be surprised what this genius dog can understand. Talk to her like you respect her and know she's smart. She'll do the rest."

"Um, okay." He tugged on the leash a little. "Cookie, let's go."

She stood and looked up at him, still smiling.

"You're such a menace for being so cute," he muttered.

She grinned.

"You treat her well or there'll be hel—eck to pay," I said as a few small kids skipped by, their mom and dad close behind.

"Yes, ma'am." Berg gave me a mock salute, looking big and imposing despite my sweet beast by his side.

"That's more like it. Cookie, see you later."

She gave a soft woof and walked away with Berg.

It was only as I walked back to Sweet Fiction that I realized I'd had no qualms about handing her off to a stranger. I mean, I knew the detective, but not well. Yet I felt, deep down, that he'd never put her in harm's way. Huh. I'd have to think about that later.

"Hey, slowpoke," Stefanie Connett yelled from the bookshop, her head hanging out the front door. "You coming to book club any time this year or what?" Like the boom of a cannon, her voice echoed down Main Street.

Yeah, I'd think about Berg and Cookie much later. I had no urge to suffer the wrath of the Macaroons.

* * *

Sitting in a circle of chairs an hour later, comfortably full on club sandwiches, iced tea, and now sipping coffee, I half-listened as Kay gave her thoughts on *The Girl with the Dragon Tattoo*.

A glance at everyone else showed them interested.

On one side of me, I had Cat, Teri, and Uncle Elvis. Next to him sat Kay, then Darcy and Alan, our only other male club member. A retired electrician by trade, Alan still did contract work when he felt like it for people in town. A sweet and likable fellow, he loved noir fiction and romances, surprisingly enough. He never missed a meeting if he could help it and was married to a photographer and CGC member, a lovely woman I had yet to sway to book club.

On my other side sat Stefanie and Alison, intent on what Kay was saying.

The nine of us had been keen to talk about the book, even Uncle Elvis doing his part by being vague enough about details but specific enough on plot and tone that everyone bought the notion he'd actually read the book.

As if he read my mind, my uncle met my gaze and gave a half-smile.

I rolled my eyes, not wanting to encourage his non-book reading, and tuned in to Kay.

"Yeah, the misogyny in this book is clear, from the way they treat the main character, shoving her from foster care to booting her out, to her rape at the hands of her state-appointed legal guardian. And the book is actually titled *Men Who Hate Women* in Swedish."

"I didn't know that," Stefanie said. "Huh. Still, I thought Lisbeth was one of the best woman characters I've read. She had to deal with a lot of trauma, and we still don't know a ton about her past, but she sure does kick butt in this book."

Next to her, Alison nodded. "I loved her intelligence. And her ability to stand up for what she believes in."

Darcy, Teri, and Cat agreed. So did I. "This was a great choice, Darcy."

Darcy smiled. "I know. I read this book when it was released, then went and read the following books. But Larsson died before book four could come out. It's good, but not as good as the ones he wrote, I don't think."

Alan frowned. "Really? I thought the fourth book was just as good if not better. Dealing with more of her past."

Elvis interrupted, "Didn't they make a movie of the fourth book?"

Cat nodded. "Yeah. And I'm torn, because having read the book, I want to watch the movie of *The Girl with the Dragon Tattoo*, but do I watch the original or the American version?"

Before Elvis could give himself away, I suggested, "Why not try both?"

Teri nodded. "We'll do a movie night."

"Good idea."

Then Stefanie said what we'd all been thinking about. "You know, this book was great and all, and I probably will read the other two Larsson wrote, not sure about the fourth and fifth written after his death by that other guy. But this murder—"

"There's a fifth book?" Darcy asked.

"Yes, but that's not the point," Stefanie said. "This town is small. We know a lot of the locals even as we're growing bigger. Gil Cloutier was murdered, and it threw the town on its head. And now we have a second suspicious death two months later with Marilyn Freeman."

"Not suspicious," Cat said. "Heart attack."

"Well, yes, but I'm not convinced," Stefanie said, her mouth set in a line, an aura of stubborn covering her from head to toe.

"I felt the same way for a while, but Stefanie, it really does seem like she died of heart failure, like her mom," I said, just to play devil's advocate.

"True," Alison said, her voice soft yet firm. "Stefanie and I talked about this. With what happened to Gil—"

"Which was clearly murder," Stefanie reminded her. Gil had been stabbed, after all.

"Yes, it was," Alison agreed, "but now we might be jumping to conclusions. Not every death is a murder."

Alan chimed in. "I think because she was so young and lively, it's taken the town aback."

"Lively, huh." Kay snorted. "She came on to Jay when we first moved here."

"Ha. That." Darcy pointed at Kay and nodded. "She tried to flirt with Dex too."

I hadn't realized Marilyn had flirted with not only every available man in town, she'd also hit on the not-so-available ones. "Are you guys sure about that? Maybe you're projecting from the rumors that have circulated about her. I mean, she couldn't have tried to flirt with *every* man in this town, could she?"

Kay, Darcy, and Stefanie eyed me with pity, and Stefanie said, "Honey, now, don't take this the wrong way. But you're single. And pretty. And if you'd had a man and had crossed paths with Marilyn, at some point she'd have tried to flirt with your guy just to prove a point."

"That's not nice," Alan said with a frown.

Elvis coughed. "Um, true, but I used to watch Marilyn work. I've done a ton of projects for her. And she just had a way with the male of the species."

Alan flushed. "I thought she was nice."

"She was," Elvis agreed. "But I wonder what Mandy would say about her."

Alan considered his wife and shrugged. "I don't know."

"Ha!" Stefanie crowed. "That right there tells us Mandy's already said something. Look, I liked the woman. She was a powerful lady with a head on her shoulders who knew her business. But I can't say I liked her friendliness all the time. With my Ralph gone, I didn't need to worry about that."

"I didn't worry," Kay said. "I trust Jay, and I know some women are more social than others. But I saw her come on to him then laugh it off when she saw me watching. She didn't care." Kay's eyes narrowed. "And that's a dangerous thing to be doing to the women in this town."

Darcy's eyes grew large, and she turned to me. "Motive, right, Lexi? Maybe Marilyn upset the wrong wife or girlfriend and they made it look like a heart attack."

I gave an apologetic look to Cat and Teri and repeated what I'd said earlier about her supposed dinner guest, concluding with, "It makes sense that the guy wouldn't step up to admit he found her dead. But it still bothers me that it took her cleaning person to find her."

"Maybe she got stood up," Teri offered. "Just because she set the table for him with fancy wine glasses and porcelain dinner plates doesn't mean he showed up. Maybe he ditched her, and that got her mad enough that she stroked out."

"Wait, she had a stroke?" Cat asked, looking confused. "Because a stroke and a heart attack are two different things."

Darcy explained what she knew of strokes, since her mother-in-law had had one last year. Then Alan told everyone about his father-in-law's arrhythmia. Which had the others all adding their knowledge and first- and secondhand experiences with medical issues.

Kay's eyes sparkled as she met mine, and she grinned and talked over Darcy about angina and blood pressure.

I sighed, having lost control of the discussion the moment Stefanie mentioned Marilyn. But I knew these people, and they were my people. We'd all been stuck on murder and mystery since Gil had been killed. Maybe this just needed to play out.

Distracted by a text, I made an excuse and wandered to the front door to grab Cookie from Berg. My gaze passed over the craft section, and I realized what had been lodged in my brain but hadn't jarred free until now.

Chapter Seven

Teri had mentioned wine glasses. That note on the ground earlier in the day had mentioned a fine vintage. But it had been typed. Odd. Had someone used it as a bookmark and stuck it in that book on craft beer? But why put it in a book that had been on the floor?

And why was I obsessing over every little thing lately? Had to be the Macaroons' fault. Just as I'd put Marilyn's demise to the back of my mind as not my business, they brought up their own suspicions and had me wondering all over again.

Not a smart thing to do with a detective at my door.

I opened it for Cookie, not expecting Berg to come through with her. The door closed behind him, the jingle of the overhead bell soft compared to the loud talk coming from the back room, where we had book club.

"She was outstanding," Berg said with a wide smile.

My heart raced, and I stood transfixed by the man looking . . . happy. Something I didn't often see on his face.

I should say something. "Oh, great."

"Yeah, Cookie sat and stood and did whatever I told her. It was amazing. I had no idea she'd been so well-trained." He had his hat off and scratched the back of his head, tucking his ball-cap over the radio clipped to the side of his belt. "So I wanted to ask if—"

"I think she was killed, that's why," Stefanie's voice sounded overly loud in the empty bookshop.

Berg's eyes narrowed.

"We're having book club," I said loudly, hoping one of the dunderheads in the back would overhear.

"Oh, come on," Stefanie blundered on. "She regularly slept around town. Of course she's a prime candidate for a killing."

"What exactly are you guys reading?" Berg asked, his eyes bright with suspicion as he stared down at me.

I stood as tall and straight as I could. And still came to the middle of his chest, dang it. "We're reading *The Girl with the Dragon Tattoo*, Detective Berg," I said as loudly as I could without looking as if I were deliberately shouting.

He stomped past me to the back room, entering to a quiet book club. "Well hello." He looked at everyone, ignoring Cookie who trotted behind him and made her way to Uncle Elvis. "What are you all discussing so heatedly?"

"Larsson's deal with women," Teri said quickly. "Did you know *The Girl with the Dragon Tattoo* was originally titled *Men Who Loathe Women*?"

Thank goodness for my fast-acting, mistrusting bestie.

Darcy frowned. "It was *Men Who Hate Women*, Teri."

"The point is, Stieg Larsson made a statement. You should read it, Detective," Teri said to Berg. "It's a heck of a crime novel."

"A crime novel that came out years ago. I saw the movie."

"Which one?" Elvis was quick to ask. "Just curious."

"The original," Berg said, eyeballing the table with all the treats.

Cat hurried to stand. "Hey, guys, let's take a break. Detective Berg, would you like something to eat or drink? We have plenty."

He gave her a half-smile. "Is this why you all come every other Monday? To eat and drink and pretend to talk about books?"

Cat flushed bright red. "P-pretend? Um, no. Not at all."

My best friend was so bad at lying. I shared a disgusted look with Teri, who smoothly sidled next to Cat and added, "We don't all watch the movie first, Cat. Now Detective, since you saw the movie—"

"And read the book." He took a sandwich and bit into it, devouring it in seconds.

In awe, Teri handed him another. "Please. We have more than we need."

"Thanks. I missed dinner." He ate it, added a soda and a mini cheesecake, and engaged in conversation with Teri about the merits of citizen ride-alongs with law enforcement and a neighborhood watch, especially for a small town like ours versus a behemoth city like Portland.

But crafty Teri had steered him neatly away from learning that we didn't always talk about books.

After a good twenty minutes, in which folks had more than enough time to use the restroom and get more dessert or coffee, we all sat down while Berg stood at the doorway, ready to leave, thank goodness.

"Appreciate the food and drink," he said. "And Cookie." He smiled. And man, he should do that more often. "Cookie was the real star of the show with my crime talk tonight."

"She's talented," my uncle agreed. "Nice that you can educate children about the police. Though isn't it a little late for a kid talk?"

He shrugged. "The mayor set it up with some of the chamber folks. It went well, and we had about two dozen children in attendance. It was at the library."

"Oh, nice." Alison smiled, good friends with our local librarian and not that far retired from her own job in a library. "The librarian's husband was a policeman, so she's got a soft spot for law enforcement."

"So she said." Berg nodded.

Elvis was talking about Cookie with Cat. "A heart of gold under all the fur. But she's sometimes a little too smart for her own good."

"A little too shifty, you mean," Stefanie muttered, apparently still miffed that Cookie had once stolen a tray of peanut butter cookies from Stefanie's backyard, where they'd been set out to cool.

That had been a year ago. Stefanie clearly held grudges.

We all glanced at my dog, guiltily chewing something under my chair. Her crunching could not be mistaken for anything other than something food-related.

Everyone laughed.

Berg laughed too, I noticed, and tried to pretend Teri wasn't watching *me* watch *him* and grinning like a goof.

"Anyway, thanks again." Berg grabbed his ballcap then paused, as if debating with himself. "Just so you know, the M.E. classified Marilyn Freeman's death as being of natural causes, and we've got an official death certificate to state as such."

You could hear a collective sigh—of disappointment? relief?—come from the room.

"I wouldn't normally be inclined to share this information, but since *some* of you have a penchant for putting your noses where they don't belong"—he stared from Cookie to me and refused to blink—"I just thought I'd let you know it's not murder. However, if we *are* inundated with suspicious deaths in the future, I'd advise you to please let the police handle them." He glared around the room. "Anyone interfering with a police investigation will be tossed in jail." He looked at me again. "Remember that."

"Sure thing, Detective." I waved and forced myself not to respond with gritted teeth and a death glare. "Great seeing you."

"Yeah, yeah. I'm watching you." He did that weird thing Dash and Teri's mom does, pointing two fingers at his eyes, then those same two fingers at me. He left, and none of us spoke until the bell over the door rang and the door snapped closed again.

"Whew. Well, it's clear Berg has his eyes on Lexi," Alison said with a nervous laugh. "Which leaves the rest of us free to inquire about Marilyn, if we want to. But I guess we don't, since the police ruled it not a homicide. That's a good thing, right?"

"I'm still not convinced." Stefanie harrumphed. "But I have even worse news."

"Oh?" Elvis leaned forward. "What is it?"

Stefanie sighed, looking older than her sixty-seven years. "Selma Livingston passed away in her sleep this afternoon."

Crap. Not Selma! I liked her. "Oh no. Was it expected?" The octogenarian had been coming into the bookshop for as long as it had been open. A steady customer who always had a kind word and a big wallet, she never left the store with less than four books in hand.

"She was in good health, but she was tired. Herman died just last year, and I think Selma was ready to go." Stefanie dabbed at her eyes and took the napkin Alison handed her. "We were friends."

"Shocking, I know," Alison teased, which made Stefanie laugh. "Selma was a wonder, all right. Her funeral will be the day after Marilyn's, which is on Monday, I believe. On Tuesday of next week, if anyone's interested in coming. I only know because Selma had me help her plan everything out after Herman passed. Her daughter and grandchildren have nothing to do but attend the funeral and sort out the will. Estate planning made easy," Alison said, looking sad.

Alan nodded. "That's smart. Something we did a few years ago for our boys."

Darcy looked worried. "You know, I think Dex and I should see a lawyer."

Kay appeared ill. "Yeah, me and Jay too."

The rest of us started talking about wills and how to handle the death of a loved one. I ignored the burn behind my eyes, not ready to worry about losing my uncles, my family, or my friends.

I stroked Cookie, who stood protectively by my side. "Yeah, I love you too, you furry fiend."

She licked my hand, a little more enthusiastically than was called for, and I had to laugh. She'd found a smear of cream cheese on the back of my hand from the mini-cheesecake.

"Never change, Cookie."

She gave a soft grumble and licked me once more.

Darcy broke the dour mood with a question. "So, if we're done with all the death talk, can we discuss our next book club read?" She glanced at Elvis. "The new guy needs a turn." She smiled, charmed by my jokester of an uncle.

I gave him a warning glance, which he ignored.

"In honor of Detective Berg"—he talked over my loud groan—"our own hometown superhero, I suggest *Thor: Ages of Thunder.* It's a comic."

Alan brightened. "I haven't read comics in ages. This should be fun."

Kay nodded. "Maybe I can get my boys into it."

"Well, make sure you read it over first. It can be pretty violent."

I looked around, surprised to see the enthusiasm, even from Stefanie and Alison, who had huddled together to whisper.

I cleared my throat. "Ahem. So we're all good with this?"

Elvis looked smug.

Alison gave me a thumbs-up and surprised everyone when she flushed and said, "I'm in. Have you seen those hunky heroes? The artists are incredible with detail. And who doesn't love Thor?"

"That's what I told Lexi! Who doesn't love the god of thunder?" Elvis soon had everyone laughing with stories about his Comic Con days.

After the group, minus Cat and Teri, had left, I made a note to order nine issues of *Ages of Thunder* the next day and locked up. As we all cut through Central Park toward our respective homes, my friends were talking among themselves.

"Did you see that back there, Cat?" Teri asked, her voice light, a little too casual.

Which put me immediately on edge. Cookie, however, ignored her in favor of sniffing everything in sight. Yeah, I had her off her leash and was proud of it.

"What do you mean?" Cat asked, her tone way too stilted to be real.

"I'm referring to the sizzle between Mt. Bachelor and our own Alexis Jones, the fine manager of Sweet Fiction Bookshop."

"Oh, *that* sizzle." Cat cupped her chin, as if in thought. "You know, I did catch some of that threateningly cute vibe between them. The way he glares into her soul and she does her best to pretend not to care while eyeballing his impressive biceps." Cat paused. "I wonder what he can bench-press."

"A five-three blond with no problem." Teri grinned.

"Try five-five," I snapped, glad for the shadows that hid my blush.

"Yeah, I bet he wants to bench you something fierce." Cat laughed with Teri, and when Cookie gave her garbled version of a laugh, even I chuckled.

"You guys are ridiculous."

"Are we?" Cat asked.

"He's in Sweet Fiction once a week," Teri pointed out.

"Harassing me," I said, not meaning it. I did like the police presence to remind folks to behave. And after that mess with Gil's murder, I liked knowing a cop was nearby for protection. "It wouldn't be so bad if he didn't keep ticketing me."

"You mean for letting your dog run around off leash?" Cat asked, pointedly staring at Cookie, who trotted in front of us on the sidewalk down Court Street.

"Come on. Cookie is fine."

"Really?" Cat just looked at me.

"She is. She listens." I turned and whistled. "Cookie, come here." She did . . . after taking a few detours to sniff around. "She's not hurting anything."

"True," Teri agreed. "Cat's just being a pain."

"My purpose in life," Cat deadpanned.

Cookie grinned up at her, and Cat bent to pet her. "I'm just kidding, Cookie. I like getting under Lexi's skin." Cat grinned at me, and I made a rude gesture that had her laughing.

"Well, I think that was an interesting meeting," Teri said.

"Me too. Sad though. I'll miss Selma."

"She was so nice." Cat sighed. "Always buying a few cookies to take back to her granddaughter. Kind of brings all our suspicions and mysterious thoughts about Marilyn back down to earth. I mean, sometimes people just die. It's a bummer, but it just is."

"Yeah," Teri and I said at the same time.

Cookie rumbled, not wanting to be left out. That was my dog.

I hugged my friends goodbye, parting as they continued down Court Street toward their apartment building while I turned right onto Peppermint Way.

Cookie and I arrived home as the darkness descended. The sun didn't set until closer to nine, but it was already eight thirty, and I felt tired.

I yawned and led us inside. Cookie danced around until I removed her harness—all for show anyway—and went out back to do her rounds. I poured myself some water and sat out back, enjoying the quiet. Crickets, a few chirping birds that had yet to bed down in their trees, and an occasional bark mixed with the wind fluttering through the leaves of the aspens next door.

The sweet scent of honeysuckle reached me, and I breathed it in, allowing the lively smell to counter the sadness of losing both Selma and Marilyn. Despite not knowing the real estate queen well, I grieved the town's loss.

And that got me missing my mom and dad. Even my brother, whom I loved even though he could be a little snot.

I promised myself I'd call my parents in the morning and went inside to write my brother a snarky note. I'd mail it on my way to work, giving him something to look forward to besides bills and junk mail.

Freed from the day, I watched a sitcom, joined by Cookie, and laughed at the silly onscreen antics. Then I locked up, took a bath, and let myself soak until my lids refused to stay open.

I finally slid into bed, Cookie at the foot of it, and enjoyed a peaceful slumber.

Until the phone rang at six in the morning, with Teri babbling something about a dead body.

Another dead body?

This one found in Dash's backyard.

And the police were calling it murder.

Chapter Eight

I rushed to Dash's house to see the flashing lights of police vehicles. A small crowd stood outside, watching as Dash talked to Detective Berg and Officer Halston. Plenty of law enforcement cordoned off the yard and house while rubberneckers waited for any sign of the unfolding drama.

Teri waved, and I hurried over to her and Cat, having left Cookie at home. I'd practically run over, dressed in a ratty T-shirt and shorts, not taking the time to shower, and found myself in like company. Most folks around us were dressed in robes or PJs.

Holy Hannah! A dead body found in Dash's backyard? Who had found it? Who was the dead body? Why were the police standing so close to Dash? The worried look on his face didn't bode well.

"Oh my gosh. They don't think Dash did it, do they?" I asked Teri in a low voice.

She shrugged. "It's what I would think. I mean, they found the body in his yard, after all."

"But who found it?" I looked around, seeing better as the sun started to rise.

"We don't know," Cat said. "Roger's busy, so I can't ask now. And I'm pretty sure Berg will be on him especially to keep it quiet. You know, because we're dating, and we"—she gestured to herself and Teri and I—"are friends."

"I get that." But it frustrated me. "Wait until Berg's not so keyed up about it. Give it a day or two. Then get Roger to tell you everything."

"I'm on it." She saluted me.

I would have grinned, but I was too stunned by the commotion. A dead body? In Dash's yard? That didn't make much sense. Because no way was Dash the kind of guy who would murder someone, and if he did, he was smart enough to hide any evidence. A corpse in the backyard was a surefire giveaway of something nefarious afoot.

Teri crept closer, so Cat and I followed her. Until Berg glanced up and spotted us.

Crap.

He made a beeline in our direction.

"Uh-oh," Teri said. "Detective Berg looks annoyed."

"You mean, he looks the way he always looks around us."

"Yep."

I waited, my senses buzzing. For some reason, I wanted to tie this back to Marilyn. And I had no idea who had been killed or why or with what. There I went, writing my own novel into reality.

"You three."

I gave him a weak wave. "Oh, er, hey, Chad."

He sighed. "It's way too early to deal with you."

"Hey."

"Sorry." He didn't sound sorry. "Can anyone vouch for Dash Hagen's whereabouts last night?"

"Seriously?" I goggled. "You think Dash murdered someone?"

"We don't know anything as yet, but—"

"Who died? And who found the body?"

Berg scowled. "That's for us to investigate, not you. Now, his whereabouts?"

The three of us looked at each other and shrugged.

Berg glanced around. "Where's Cookie?"

"At home."

"Good." He looked relieved. "Look, I can't discuss the case, but if rumor spreads as fast as it did the last time someone in town died, I'm sure you'll know all about it five seconds after opening your store. Now, please." He raised his voice. "Everyone, clear out. Go home. Let us do our jobs."

"Is that Rachel Nevis?" someone yelled.

Rachel, who had worked with Marilyn. I knew it!

"No comment." Berg's expression darkened. "Now go home."

A lot of grumbles as neighbors dispersed, until only Teri, Cat, and I remained.

"You three aren't special." Berg crossed his arms over his chest. "You need to leave."

Teri bolstered herself to an imposing five two. "I don't think so. That's my brother you're falsely accusing." Her eyes narrowed. "I'm sticking by to make sure you people don't plant any evidence."

"You people?" Berg blinked.

"The police. I know your type."

"Don't you work for the district attorney's office?"

"Don't change the subject." She yelled to her brother, "Don't worry, Dash. I'm getting all this on video." She whipped out her phone.

I didn't need to see Berg pinch the bridge of his nose to gauge his frustration. Teri worked for the DA yet distrusted the police and thought everything had a conspiracy behind it. Don't get me started on her stance on UFOs and the aliens living among us.

"She's just worried for her brother," I said as Cat joined them and Roger Halston.

"I know. And she should be." Berg shook his head. "An anonymous call from a concerned neighbor about a woman not moving in the back of Hagen's lawn came in. We thought it was a prank. Until Roger found the body. Now I don't know what to think."

Neither did I. "Rachel Nevis?" When he drew that mask of Serious Police Person over his face, I tugged on his sleeve. "Oh, come on. It's not going to be a secret, especially not after someone shouted out her name." I paused. "Pretty weird though, huh?"

"What? A murder in our lovely town? Yeah, that's weird."

"Well, yes, but I meant that it's Rachel. Who worked for Marilyn. Who also recently died."

"I knew you hadn't let that go." He just looked at me. "She died of natural causes. A heart attack."

"Or she was made *to look* as if she died of natural causes."

He sighed. "Selma Livingston passed away too. Who do you supposed killed her?"

"No, Selma passed after a good, long life. But Marilyn and Rachel worked together. Same office. Same place where Marilyn slept around and made shady real estate deals."

Now he looked both irritated and interested, an odd combination. "Where did you hear that?"

"I hear things."

"Name your source." He planted his hands on his hips and glowered at me. "If it's credible, I'll look into it."

"You'll look into it anyway because Rachel died, and it looks like murder."

"Not any kind of murder I've ever seen." He mused on what he'd said, and I wanted badly to know what that meant. "But finding her body in Hagen's yard puts a real twist in the works."

Someone yelled for him, and Berg ran a hand over his short hair, his ball cap nowhere in sight, though he wore his summer uniform. "Look, I need to get back to work. Do *not* put yourself anywhere near any of this."

"I won't. Trust me. I had my fill with Gil, and that was completely by accident." I frowned. "I was trying to keep myself out of jail."

"I know." He blew out a breath. "Just stay safe, okay?"

Now that was nice. I nodded, pleased with his turn of attitude. Finally.

He started to walk away, then said over his shoulder, ruining all of that goodwill, "And keep your nosy book club out of it too."

I forced myself not to respond and hustled over to my friends. I gave Dash a big hug. He looked worried and keyed up yet tired at the same time. "What the heck, Dash?" I heard a few swears from those standing around the stretcher holding the body but couldn't see anything or make out what had surprised them.

Dash groaned. "I can't go back inside because the police want to go through my house. Can we go somewhere and talk?"

"So you're not a suspect?" Cat asked.

"I'm very much a suspect," he growled. "I don't understand any of this, and I'd rather not hang out in my boxers on the street."

I hadn't realized those weren't shorts. The poor guy. "Want to head to my place?" I needed to get back to Cookie.

"Yeah. Wait for me." Dash left to talk to Roger.

"We're going home to grab our stuff. We'll be at your place in ten," Teri said and yanked Cat with her.

"More like fifteen, but we'll be there." Cat waved.

Dash returned with a small bag of what I assumed to be clothing.

"Roger let me grab some stuff, but he had to watch me do it." Dash looked freaked out. "And he told me not to leave town, that they'll be talking to me shortly at the station. I don't understand any of this."

I patted him on the back and walked away with him, conscious of Berg and several others having turned to watch us leave. "Was it Rachel Nevis?"

Dash nodded. "She was lying on one of my recliners in the back. She looked peaceful, actually."

"Like she'd had a heart attack?" I murmured.

"I have no idea. I only know she wasn't stabbed or shot. Or at least, I didn't see any blood. Hell, I was sound asleep, then I heard banging on the front door. I went out to see what it was and saw Roger Halston, of all people. I asked him what was going on, and he asked to come in."

"Did you let him inside?"

"Sure, why wouldn't I?"

This was so strange. We continued walking toward my house, and I could feel Dash's nervousness. "I'm so sorry this happened. I want to know why she was in your yard."

"I have no idea." He looked shocked. "Rachel and I dated a while ago. Then after the other night when she was drunk in the bar, we hung out after closing. But she was drunk. Nothing happened between us." He frowned. "We were supposed to meet up this weekend, actually, for dinner and a movie."

"And you previously dated Marilyn Freeman."

"What about Marilyn?"

I was seeing connections that wouldn't do Dash any favors. "You dated Marilyn too. And she's dead."

"Of a heart attack," he said, sounding defensive.

"But what if it wasn't?"

He paled. "Oh crap. Then I'm really screwed."

I nodded. "Right now, nobody believes Marilyn's death is involved. But Dash, I have a gut feeling it is."

"Two women I had relationships with are dead. One of them was found in my backyard."

We walked up the front steps to my house and entered to find Cookie dancing in place, excited to see her favorite people. Dash knelt and gave her a hug.

She stilled, no doubt sensing his shock. Cookie has always been good like that, able to calm those needing some peace.

Dash pulled back and patted her. "Thanks, Cookie, I needed that."

He didn't look any less freaked out, so I gave him a huge hug, holding tight, aware he held me just as tightly.

"Lexi, I'm scared."

"So am I." It seemed like someone was out to frame my friend, and we had no idea why. And poor Rachel. Why had she been targeted? Because of something she knew about Marilyn? Because of something she'd done? Or did it all circle back to Dash? A jealous ex, maybe?

I pulled back. "We'll figure this out, Dash. But in the meantime, you need to get a lawyer. And say nothing without your lawyer present."

"But doesn't that make me seem guilty?"

"Who cares? Innocent people go to jail all the time. And no matter what Berg says, I just know they're going to connect another dead woman you dated to the dead woman in your yard. Forewarned is forearmed."

"Yeah." He rubbed his head.

"Why don't you take a nice hot shower?"

"You don't mind?"

"Go ahead." Even if he left me nothing but cold water, the guy needed to get himself together. "I'm going to take Cookie out then feed her."

"Thanks, Lexi." Dash leaned forward.

Expecting a kiss on the forehead or cheek, I let him. So when he gave me a gentle kiss on the mouth, I was stunned.

He didn't seem to notice my surprise as he pulled away and closeted himself in my guest bathroom. But I'd felt heat to my toes.

I could only stare down at Cookie. "Did that just happen?" I paused. "Did it mean anything?" But how could it? My friend had just been accused of murder, and things were bound to get worse before they got better. I highly doubted Dash had romance on his mind.

I blushed, feeling like an idiot, and hurried into my own bathroom to take the fastest shower known to man. It was luke-warm, since I hadn't wanted to steal any hot water from Dash. After dressing in a pair of denim shorts and a cute pink top, I hurriedly dried my hair and put it in a ponytail, all business.

I hated to think it, but the time had come. I'd need to call in reinforcements to handle this situation with Dash, because I just knew the subject of Marilyn would come up with Rachel now also dead.

After letting Cookie out to take care of business, I let my friends inside and fed Cookie.

Cat and Teri fought over who would shower first while Dash exited wearing shorts and a T-shirt and slumped on my couch. Cookie decided to be his blanket, and while I made coffee and breakfast for everyone, my dog comforted Dash as best she knew how, with a lot of licking.

Dash chuckled. "Okay, Cookie. Enough, girl. I just showered, you know."

By the time Cat and Teri rejoined us, coffee, eggs, bacon, and toast had been made.

"Wow. You really did it up," Cat said, scoping out a jug of apple juice I'd forgotten to bring over. "Thanks."

"Eat up, guys. We have things to talk about."

We ate quietly for a good ten minutes before Dash broke the silence. "I didn't kill Rachel Nevis."

Teri's eyes widened dramatically. "Oh, good to hear. I wasn't sure." She slapped her brother in the back of the head.

"Ow." He glared at his sister.

"Don't be a bonehead," Teri snapped at him. "Of course you didn't kill Rachel." She nodded to Cat. "Tell us what you heard."

"Okay, so I only got to talk to Roger for a few seconds, but Rachel Nevis was dead on your chair out back, Dash."

"I knew that already." He sighed. "An anonymous caller dialed 911 and sent Roger out to my place for a closer look. Rachel Nevis. Dead, no question. I went out with him to see her lying there as if asleep."

"Roger told me there was a pool of blood underneath the lounger, right under her head."

I cringed. "Ew."

Dash paled. "I hadn't seen that."

"Yeah. Roger said it was pretty gross."

"Rachel looked to me like she was sleeping off a bender or something. She was dressed in jeans and a jacket. They couldn't tell me when she'd died. But I was at work last night until closing."

"What time would that be?" I asked.

"Midnight, and we hung around after for a drink."

"We?" Teri asked.

"Noah and me. Mike had to get back to Sherry, Lisa took off a few minutes after he did, and the others left not long after her. Noah and I shared a drink, played some darts, then went home. I got home around one thirty, I think."

"Did you go home alone or with Rachel?" Teri asked.

"I just said alone, Teri." Dash frowned. "Wait. Are you *interrogating* me?"

"We need details," I said before they could argue. "So you left the bar, came home, and . . . ?"

He shrugged. "I was tired. I locked up and went to bed."

Cat leaned in. "Did you go out back before you went to bed? Did you see anything out of place in the house or out back?"

Dash shook his head. "Nope. I did look out the back door to check that it was locked. I didn't see anyone outside, and if she'd been there then, I'd have seen her."

"So if Rachel had been killed in your yard, it would have to have been after you went to bed."

"Hold on," Teri interrupted. "How do you know she was killed? She might have just died like Marilyn did." She paused. "Except for the blood. Unless she was drunk and tripped and hit her head or something. Then she tried to sleep it off and died?"

"No," I said. "She was either poisoned or killed with something they'll find during an autopsy. They didn't do one of those on Marilyn because she didn't have a suspicious death. But Rachel certainly did."

"What if it was suicide?" Dash asked, then shook his head. "No. She'd just made a big sale and was ecstatic not to have to deal with Marilyn anymore." He pushed his plate away, his appetite not affected by death, I noted.

"We don't know what's going on, so we need to figure things out. And I know just who to call . . ."

Chapter Nine

After inviting the Macaroons to meet for an emergency "book club" on Thursday, giving me a little time to gather information and form theories, I spent the morning at work listening to talk about Rachel Nevis. Even the tourists had heard from someone who had heard from someone else about the dead woman.

By noon, word had spread throughout the downtown area. And I had someone important I needed to talk to. Because yeah, my uncles had been firebombing my phone all morning long.

"Hey, Cat. I need to hit the hardware store for some light bulbs. Can you take charge till I come back? Cookie will be coming with me." Hearing her name, my dog trotted to my side and cocked her head. "Want to go see Uncle Jimmy?"

Cookie left and returned moments later with her leash in her mouth. That was a yes, then.

"Sure, I can be in charge." Cat smiled. "Can you pick me up a milkshake from Eats 'n' Treats on your way back?"

"Not a smoothie from Sal's?"

"No, I need the extra sugar and fat from the ice cream."

"You need it, huh? Whatever, Ms. Muscles." No lie, Cat had really been trimming down lately, which I wouldn't have thought possible with all the yummy baked goods she'd been making for Roger and bringing into the bookshop.

"Ha ha. You know, you should take notes. Start eating my diet and working out with me and Roger. You'll be buff in no time."

"Eh. I'm good. What flavor shake?"

"Chocolate banana."

Hmm. Now I wanted a milkshake. "Will do. We should be back in an hour."

"Take your time. I'm enjoying all the talk about Rachel." She said in a lower voice, "But no one's mentioned Marilyn at all. Even mention of Selma's faded. All the attention is on Rachel's murder."

"Have the police officially called it a murder yet?" Heck, they'd only found Rachel six or so hours ago.

"Not yet, but it makes no sense. Really? Rachel died of a heart attack just like her boss did a week ago? Oh, and she happened to bleed all over the patio too? No way. It's fishy as all get-out."

"I agree." I opened the door for Cookie, and she jogged out. "See you soon."

"Later." Cat turned to help a customer reach a book on a top shelf.

Cookie waited long enough for me to clip the leash to her collar, foregoing the harness today. I'd forgotten it at home, not like I really needed it. Despite Cat making fun of me last night about breaking the rules, Cookie had to be the most law-abiding canine on the planet. She even looked both ways before crossing.

As I walked her toward my uncle's hardware store, I stopped to let Cookie take her afternoon constitutional and called in an order for two milkshakes and a chookie—a cheddar dog cookie—a new item Mel had added to the Eats 'n' Treats menu that had become super popular with our dog-loving community.

"There," I said. "Something snacky for Cat, me, *and* you, Cookie."

She finished and returned to me, gracing me with a regal nod while I cleaned up after her then sanitized my hand with a wipe, because *ew*.

I laughed under my breath at her cockiness and followed her toward Jones for the Job Hardware, located around the corner on Cinnamon Avenue, just a few stores down from the Ripe Raisin.

I wondered if Dash would go in to work tonight. How was he doing? I remembered how awful I'd felt when I'd been accused of killing Gil Cloutier. He'd been a grumpy old man not many in town had liked. Rachel, on the other hand, was a lovely young woman with a lot of friends. Would people automatically blame Dash? Would they steer clear of his business because of the accusations? I sure hoped not. Dash had poured his heart and soul into the bar, and he deserved for it to flourish.

I didn't want Dash to suffer what I knew would be coming his way.

Shoot. We needed to get started on solving this mysterious death. But for that to happen, we needed information. And by we, I meant the Macaroons Mystery Club. Stefanie insisted we call it the Macaroons Murder Club, but I thought that sounded a little presumptuous. What if something got stolen, or something odd happened in town? Did it have to be a murder to be investigation-worthy?

Alison had agreed with me, and we were keeping it the Macaroons Mystery Club for now. Although for those not members, we were simply the Macaroons, a book club.

One that had a mission.

Cookie and I found Uncle Jimmy talking it up with a bunch of regulars. Rodney, our mailman; Clint Ayers, a big property investor; Gary Conroy, a developer out of Bend who'd been trying to drum up business in Confection; and Foot, our mayor.

Why Foot, you ask? The mayor had played collegiate level soccer and refused to let anyone forget about it. Not a bad guy, but I preferred his wife, to be honest. Her smiles were less wide, her conversation more real and less "elect me when I next run for office."

My uncle looked up as we drew closer and smiled wide. "Ah, my favorite niece."

"Your only niece."

"A technicality. Oh, and Cookie. Hey, who needs a treat?" Jimmy reached into a glass jar by the register and pulled out a dog biscuit.

Cookie, suddenly the most attentive dog on the planet, sat and raised a paw for a shake. Then she gently took the treat from my uncle's callused fingers and crunched, licking up any lost crumbs.

"Now that's impressive," Foot said. "She's the cutest thing. And a town hero," he reminded the others.

Gary blinked. "How's that?"

Clint answered, "Not too long ago, Cookie helped take down Gil Cloutier's murderer."

"No kidding?" Gary looked impressed. "Wasn't there some scandal behind it all?"

Clint nodded. "Yeah." While the men discussed Gil's demise, I stepped away and motioned for my uncle to join me.

He did, and Cookie followed.

In a low voice, I asked, "What do you know about what happened this morning?"

"Probably about as much as you do," Jimmy whispered back. "Rachel Nevis was found dead in Dash's backyard. The fact that she was spotted in his bar two nights ago and had plans to go on a date with him this weekend doesn't look so good."

"How do you know about the date?"

"The police scrolled through her phone."

"Oh." Yeah, they'd have done that. "Did Rachel have family here?"

"Her sister and her sister's family. The rest of them live in Beaverton, I think. Pastor Nestor was in here earlier, and he shared a bit with me. Apparently, Rachel's brother-in-law has already been talking to Nestor. The family's really shaken up. They said Rachel was so happy lately, what with selling that development to Clint and making a ton on it."

"What property is that, exactly?" I kept my eye on Clint. He was a nice-looking guy in his early forties, I'd guess, worth a fortune thanks to savvy property investments. He had a perpetual tan and shrewd brown eyes, always looking for the next best deal. He and Marilyn had been good friends. I'd once seen the pair of them laughing, arm-in-arm, while walking downtown. That had been a few months ago.

Jimmy had a sour look on his face. "Remember those protests out by North Church Street? By the open field by that large pond?"

I gasped. "Oh man. Strawberry Fields?" Our town loved to keep things as green as possible, but developers had been nipping at our heels for decades, trying to build as much as they could despite our desire to keep the town small and picturesque.

The large pond on the northside of town bordered by lush grasses and thick oaks was like a heavenly oasis. It had two small docks on either side and was used by everyone. Only non-powerboats were allowed, and the pavilion nearby could be rented out, the funds used to preserve and keep the area clean.

I frowned. "How the heck could Rachel sell property that belongs to the town?" Oh boy. Heads were going to roll when the city announced the land had been sold.

"I don't know. But Gary has been pestering Clint because he wants the rights to build. That was something he and Marilyn had been working on before she died. I think she had a deal with Gary, or maybe with Clint. But she died, and Rachel managed the sale. But now Rachel's dead." Jimmy frowned. "I wonder if the sale will go through?"

"That's a good question." And bam. I had our first motive for Rachel's murder. Money and land.

"Is Dash okay? Has he told his parents?"

"I don't know. I would think if he hadn't told them, then Teri would have."

"Poor Inina and Ben. I'm going to call them."

"Thanks." I kissed him on the cheek, then whispered, "Thursday night at Sweet Fiction. We're having a 'book club' meeting. Find out as much as you can about Rachel and Marilyn before then."

Jimmy nodded. "Marilyn too, hmm?"

"Yeah."

"I'll be there." He paused. "But we'll need to have food."

"You and Uncle Elvis and your stomachs."

He grinned. "You know it."

"We'll do a potluck," I said, wanting to keep down expenses. "Bring something sweet."

"Oh, Elvis has been working on a new peach cobbler that's amazing. We'll bring that."

"Great. See you then." I grabbed Cookie's leash, waved at the others, and walked with her back toward Eats 'n' Treats.

Marilyn supposedly involved herself in suspect real estate deals, as well as other women's men. Seemed like maybe she had a habit of taking things—and people—that didn't belong to her. But rumor didn't equate to fact. I needed to talk to someone who had known both Rachel and Marilyn. Someone at her place of business.

I went to the back of Eats 'n' Treats to get my food from the takeout window with Cookie by my side, dogs allowed as evident by the many canines lying around in the grassy outdoor seating area. Oversized umbrellas shielded customers from the sun, while grand containers and pots decorated the scene with color, the scent of diner fare and sweet flowers a welcome combination.

I grabbed my order from the window and Mel, the owner and a good friend of my mom's, handed it over. "Hey there, Lexi. How're things?"

"Pretty good, I guess." I left that hanging, waiting for Mel to fill in the silence.

"Sad about Selma and now Rachel, isn't it?" She leaned forward, her dark hair frosted with gray cut short and stylish. A good choice considering how hot it could get in her kitchen. She handed me two milkshakes and a baggie with Cookie's treat. Cookie noticed and sat up straight.

"Really unexpected," I agreed.

"Marilyn too." Her eyes narrowed. "That's a lot of dead people all in a row."

"I know. But Selma's was expected. She was having some health issues, and her family's happy she's now at peace, joining her husband."

"Yeah. I loved that gal. But she really missed Herman. Used to talk about him all the time. They would come in on Wednesday nights and always order the special." Mel's eyes misted. "That closeness was so heartwarming. Makes me realize how much I need to appreciate Rick."

"Yeah." Not like I'd know. The one guy I'd almost married hadn't worked out, and that was over three years ago. Talk about being in a romantic rut. I forced a smile. "Love is a many splendored thing . . . which is why I bought my best friend her own treat." I shook the bag and watched Cookie's attention fixate. I swear she hadn't blinked since Mel had handed it over.

Mel laughed. "Enjoy. Oh, and tell Cat I need to talk to her about her muffins."

"Why? Is there something wrong with them?" Did Mel have tips for my friend's recipe? Because that would *not* go over well. Cat was pretty laidback, but not about her food.

"Wrong with them?" Mel snorted. "Honey, they're *amazing*. I'd like to carry her food in here, as a matter of fact." In a lower voice, Mel confessed, "She's twice the baker my niece is, but you didn't hear that from me."

"Gotcha." I smiled and left, glad for Cat. She worked hard and deserved more validation.

Which made me think of my parents, who had worked hard their whole lives and were now living the dream. And that reminded me that I had yet to talk to them. The morning had been so busy I hadn't had time to reach out. But considering how fast people seemed to be dying around here, I didn't have time to waste.

I returned and dropped off Cat's shake, giving her a heads up about Mel.

Cat flushed. "Oh man, oh man. What will I say? I can't bake for her. Can I?" Before I could answer, she answered herself and kept spazzing. "Yes, well, maybe. I'm not sure. How often will she want to order?"

"Hey, you mind watching the counter for another ten minutes? I have to call my Mom and Dad."

She nodded to the door, still talking to herself. "I mean, the muffins maybe. But my last batch of cookies was off. Wasn't it? But the scones, I don't know." She sucked hard on her straw and sighed. "Mmm. Chocolate . . ."

I fed Cookie her treat. "Seriously, only ten minutes and I'll be back in."

Lost in a haze of chocolate, banana, and stress, Cat waved me away.

I took my milkshake out front, sat on a nearby bench, and called my mom.

Before she could say anything besides, "Hello, honey, how are you?" I interrupted with, "I love and miss you. Everything's just fine. This time Dash is the one being accused of murder."

Needless to say, my conversation lasted well over ten minutes.

Chapter Ten

After convincing my parents that I was just fine—which took a good half hour—I tucked my phone away and spent the remainder of the afternoon with customers. We had plenty of people in the shop to actually buy books, in addition to talking about how lovely our town was despite a murder.

By closing, I'd gotten responses from all the Macaroons about meeting Thursday night. I'd also told them to bring a book of their own in case Berg saw them and got suspicious. Sure, we could have met elsewhere to discuss our newest case, but I felt a better vibe at Sweet Fiction.

Dash needed us, so we'd have to be at our best.

Cookie and I took the long way home, enjoying the cool evening breeze as the sun began to set. I never regretted my decision to move back home, though I was annoyed with myself for not working harder on my book. Fear of failure? Fear of success?

Either way, now I had a real reason to procrastinate finishing. I had to help Dash not get arrested for a murder—if it even was a murder—he hadn't committed. Maybe Rachel had gotten drunk and wandered into his yard by mistake. Maybe she'd shown up to convince Dash to indulge in some hot and heavy fun and had an aneurism, then conked herself in the head and miraculously fell into a lounge chair.

I sighed and continued with Cookie, who seemed content to trot beside me, not stopping until we'd reached home.

We found my neighbor, Abe, sitting on my front porch.

Upon seeing us, he stood right away. "Sorry for intruding, but I need to talk to you."

"Sure. Come on in." I unlocked the door, and Cookie and Abe followed. Once inside, I asked, "Want something to drink? I have some iced tea."

"Thanks. That'd be great."

Abe looked jittery, kind of excited yet nervous.

"What's up?" I handed him a drink and took one for myself.

"I overheard something really odd the other day."

"What day?"

"Monday, the last day anyone saw Rachel Nevis alive."

I sat at my table and nodded for him to do the same. "Spill it, Abe."

He sat and said, "Okay, so I was wiping up some tables outside the smoothie shop. Business has been really good lately, and we're always packed. So anyway, I'm outside, cleaning a few tables, when I see Cathy and Natalie arguing."

"Cathy Salter?" Of Salter Realty? "And which Natalie?"

"Yep. She and Natalie Childers, who works for SunSweet Realty. Cathy said something about a few illegal bids or something. Natalie acted surprised, but Cathy was pissed. She said, and I remember this part, 'You're just as big a liar as your coworkers. You're all going to pay, sooner or later.' It was just so dramatic and in-your-face. Natalie stood there, staring after her, when Cathy noticed me and stalked away. I swear I could almost see smoke coming from her ears."

"Wow. That's just . . . Rachel died sometime between yesterday and today. What Cathy said is pretty suspicious."

He nodded. "Yeah, especially after Marilyn died just a week ago."

"You need to tell Detective Berg."

Abe shifted uneasily. "I'm not real fond of the cops. They had the nerve to suspect me of being involved in Dad's death. And Officer Brown has always been kind of a bully. Granted, I got into some trouble when I was drinking, but he never lets me forget it."

"He's a jerk, for sure." And a good friend of my nemesis, Nadine. "But Detective Berg's not like that."

"Maybe not, but I'd feel better if someone else told him about Cathy and Natalie."

"You want me to." Obviously.

Abe nodded. "You and your friends solved my dad's murder, Lexi. I trust you." When Cookie nudged his knee, he smiled down at her. "And of course, I trust Cookie." He took a large swallow of tea.

"I'll tell him, but you know he'll probably want to talk to you about it."

"Sure, but at least you can break the news to him. I don't mind telling you, Detective Berg can be a little intimidating."

"Tell me about it." I mentally added the words *irritating* and *alarmingly, kind of attractive,* descriptions I'd keep to myself. "Look, I'll tell him." I wondered if Abe might want to join the Macaroons. He'd been helpful with information, and he had a great spot, located in Sal's Smoothies downtown, to keep an eye on people. That he had Cookie's approval worked in his favor. Something to consider when murder was off the table.

Abe stood. "That's all I wanted to say. Thanks for the tea." He smiled, looking a little uneasy, then left.

I stared at the front door and shrugged. "Guess he didn't want seconds." I glanced at my tea. "Of course, it's nowhere near as good as that pink lemonade he makes. But Cookie, that guy is going to be a good fit for the Macaroons. I can feel it."

She grunted and left, returning with her food bowl in her mouth. I didn't need the accusation in her dark brown eyes to know I had better feed her. Or else.

After Cookie ate and settled down, I took my laptop out onto the back porch and tried to find out who owned that piece of property Rachel had sold to Clint. But all I found were more links to real estate websites requiring me to register for information.

Frustrated, I grabbed my phone and called my expert on all things investigative. "Alison," I said when the Macaroon's number one researcher picked up the phone, "I need your help."

"I'm ready and able," she said, a smile in her voice. "What do you need?"

I told her what Abe had overheard and what I had learned that morning at Uncle Jimmy's store. "Who owns Strawberry Fields? And what ties did Marilyn have to the owner? She was due to sell then died. Then Rachel sold it to Clint. And Cathy is upset about some weird deals going on. I'm wondering if Strawberry Fields is one of them."

"And what young Natalie might know about it." Alison paused. "Making some notes, hold on."

I waited.

"Got it. Anything else?"

I wondered. "Do you think you and Stefanie could try to find out about Gary Conroy's connection to Clint Ayers? I wonder if they have anything questionable going on between them that might have contributed to Rachel's death."

"Will do. We're getting together Thursday night, right?"

"Yeah. I wanted some extra time for us all before we meet, to do some digging."

"Perfect. We'll have notes come Thursday. Oh, and I'm bringing a couscous salad. Stef's bringing a peanut butter pie. It's delicious."

"Can't wait." I'd have to chain Cookie to my side at the meeting.

"See you then!" She disconnected.

Knowing a retired librarian and retired teacher were on the case really helped. Alison knew gobs of secrets about the people in this town, and Stefanie watched everyone like a hawk. Between the pair of them, they'd suss out any intriguing information.

But that still left our other Macaroons. I wrote down a list of things to investigate and made calls.

Darcy would look into any odd bank transactions for Sun-Sweet and Salter Realty. I didn't know how she'd get the information or whether she might be crossing any legal/illegal lines and didn't want to know. But she didn't seem to mind, enthusiastic about getting what we needed and bringing a casserole Thursday night.

Alan had orders to sniff around Strawberry Fields, and his wife would take pictures of the area in question. Alan was keen to go undercover on a picnic there tomorrow while getting information from anyone he could about the area and ideas to preserve it. He'd bring crab rolls.

Still not completely giving up on a chamber of commerce tie-in, I tasked Kay with getting character descriptions of the noisiest of the chamber members, including Ed Mullins. I couldn't help recalling him and Pastor Nestor talking about Marilyn, and it continued to nag at me that Ed had been a past chair, and Marilyn a current chair, the pair often butting heads. I also told Kay to work with my uncles and looped them into the conversation. She couldn't wait and promised to bring a pasta salad.

Everyone seemed super excited about their assignments and pot luck items. Cat got to pepper her boyfriend, *carefully,* for details about the murder that the police would have firsthand. And Teri would see what she could find out at the DA's office, though I had a feeling it would be little since she was related to a chief suspect.

And me? I would deal with Detective Berg and Dash. Berg needed to know a few things I didn't think he was aware of, and Dash hadn't shared nearly enough about his relationships with Marilyn or Rachel. I would have asked Teri to talk to him, but no way would she want to know about his sexual history. Heck, *I* didn't want to know, but at least I wasn't his sister. I couldn't imagine asking my own brother to share his dating history and cringed just thinking about it.

So we all had our marching orders.

I went to bed early, intending to ease into a sleep I more than needed, having been up extra early that day. But my dreams became nightmares centered around dead women, Berg, Dash, and wine, for some reason.

* * *

The next morning, I woke semi-refreshed and even had plenty of time to take Cookie on a walk before hitting the shop. Since Cat usually arrived late on Mondays and Wednesdays, I had the shop to myself before opening.

I put on some music through overhead speakers and was jamming to some soul rock, the scent of coffee brewing as I swayed and tucked books away. The sudden banging on my front door nearly caused me to have a heart attack.

Eh, not the best exaggeration of surprise, not with what had happened to Marilyn.

Cookie lifted her head and promptly laid it back down, secure under the counter on her doggie bed with Mr. Leggy, her pink stuffed octopus, resting under her chin. I snapped a quick picture with my phone—*so adorable*—before turning to the front door.

I stared with suspicion at the tall, broody man waiting for me. Should I open it or not?

"I can see you," Berg growled.

With a sigh, I unlocked the door and let him in, then shut and locked it behind him. I had another half hour before the start of business and didn't want to tease anyone unnecessarily by looking open. "Good morning to you too."

He sniffed. "Do I smell coffee?"

His hopeful tone softened me. I'm a fellow java addict, so I appreciate coffee lovers.

"I take it you want a cup?"

He shot me a smile. "I'm a paying customer."

"But we're not open yet."

"Sorry, but I've been swamped lately. I came in to grab that book I asked you to hold for me last week."

"Oh, right." I grabbed him a large coffee without asking. "Room for cream?"

He snorted.

"So sorry. I'd forgotten you like your coffee dark and bitter, like the way you see life."

He tried to hide a grin but I saw it. "Just like I'm sure you like yours light and sweet, kind of the way you keep your head in the clouds, dreaming up fantasies to entertain the masses."

"You got that right."

A moment of coffee-loving solidarity had us clinking our paper cups together.

We drank, staring at each other.

Well, this is uncomfortable. I had intended to go in softly but instead blurted, "I have some things you need to hear."

Berg groaned. "Please, no. Not again."

"Look, I'm not trying to solve a murder or anything." I totally was. "But I've been hearing things you need to know."

"Fine. Shoot." He blinked. "Never literally. The thought of you and a gun makes me nervous."

I smiled through my teeth. "As it should."

Berg had the nerve to laugh, his eyes sparkling. "I only say that because I can totally envision you shooting at me. But go ahead and tell me what you need to." Slowly, deliberately, he set his coffee down on the register counter and took that hated notepad out of his back pocket. His smile was almost evil. "I'm ready."

"I hate that notepad."

"I know."

I had to laugh, and my amusement took me by surprise. Heck, maybe I'd been a little too tense lately and hadn't noticed it. In any case, I felt worlds better after my coffee and giggles. "Sorry."

"No, please, laugh while you can. Before you and the miscreant"—he nodded at Cookie, still snoozing on her bed—"break the law again."

I sighed. "And here I thought we were having a moment."

He cocked his head, seeming to look at me a little differently.

I suddenly felt nervous, which made me mad. So I coughed to clear my throat and dove head on into several suspicions sure to put Berg in an arresting frame of mind.

"Okay, first off, Dash didn't kill Rachel, and that's if Rachel was even murdered." Which I was 99 percent sure she had to be.

Berg's lips thinned.

"What? What do you know?"

"I can't tell you. But I can tell you Rachel definitely didn't take her own life."

"Poisoned. I knew it."

"No. Well, not exactly." He scribbled something.

"But then, you couldn't know yet, could you? Doesn't the M.E. need time to perform drug screens?"

"M.E., hmm?"

"Medical Examiner. I do research, you know."

He smirked. "I'm so glad you're keeping up on *Murder She Wrote* and *Quincy* reruns."

I flushed. "First of all, how old are you? Those shows are from the 1970s and 80s, and I only know that because *my mom* streams them." Ha. Nice to see him turning pink for a change. "And for your information, *Detective* Berg, you don't have to be in law enforcement to like shows or books about law enforcement." I paused, letting him feel the sting of my wrath. "I actually prefer *Snapped* and *Forensic Files*."

He frowned. "Isn't *Snapped* about women who are pushed over the edge and kill?"

I let my smile widen. "Why yes, it is."

He gave a grudging smile. "For someone so small you're a huge pain."

"I'm not small."

"You're not tall," he shot right back. "But I will grant you that *Forensic Files* is a pretty good show."

I nodded in agreement. "I watched that last night then saw an even better show. If you like great drama and profiling, you really should watch *Mindhunter* on Netflix. Supposedly, they're going to add more seasons, because it looked like they were stopping at just two."

"Really?"

I nodded, warming to the topic. "And if you like British procedurals, *Vera* stands out. *Inspector Lewis* too."

"I've watched all those. Have you seen *Midsomer Murders*? The ones with the original Barnaby, though, not his cousin."

"I know. When they let his cousin take over, it ruined it for me. But I love, *love* the first season of *Broadchurch*."

"Now on that I completely agree."

We smiled at each other, as only fans of murder mysteries can.

An odd pall of silence made us both realize we were enjoying the conversation. I reached for the book he'd asked me to put aside at the same time Berg cleared his throat, all business again.

He laid his little notepad on the counter to write. "Okay, so tell me what you've found out that's so important."

"A few things, actually." I paused. "First, my neighbor overheard Cathy Salter and Natalie Childers arguing." I told him about what Abe had heard, pleased to see Berg taking notes. "I also think it's odd that Rachel sold a property Marilyn was selling but died before she could close the deal."

"Who told you that?"

"Uncle Jimmy. He hears everything in that hardware store. Seriously."

"Hmm."

"So Rachel sells the property to Clint Ayers, and Gary Conroy is doing his best to be Clint's builder. But I can't figure out what property it is." I paused in thought. "Rumor has it the property in question might just be Strawberry Fields."

"Really?" Berg looked up. "I hadn't heard that."

"It's just a rumor so far." I rang up his book, and after he paid and I handed him the receipt, he slid it between the pages of his book. "Hey, wait a minute." I thought back to that note I'd seen on the ground a couple of days ago. "I saw something odd Monday. There were a ton of people around, and there was this typed note."

"Typed?" Berg frowned. "What did it say?"

"Something about a wine vintage." Crap. I couldn't remember what the note had said. "Wait. No. Initials. Don't forget. Something." Frustrated, I couldn't for the life of me recall the exact words. "I think it might be important."

"You think everything is important," he drawled, still scribbling in his notepad.

"Don't you think it's odd Marilyn had wine glasses out, ready for a date, but it took her housekeeper to find her the following day?"

"I did think that. But then I realized Marilyn liked to be circumspect about her many lovers, so it would make sense that whoever she was involved with wouldn't want his—or her—name known."

"Wait. Or *her?*" Oh man. That might add a whole mess of possible suspects if Marilyn's lovers weren't just men.

"I only meant we're keeping our minds open for any possibility, though I haven't heard of Marilyn being attracted to women. Have you?"

"No." Heck, she'd slept with so many people, according to many around town. "I do know she supposedly slept with Connie Oliver's husband, Tad."

"Of Taffy Toys next door?"

"Yeah. Teri overheard Connie snarking about Marilyn at the Ripe Raisin a few nights ago." I stared hard at Berg, willing him to take me seriously. "I know everyone thinks Marilyn died of a heart attack, but now Rachel's dead too. I think their deaths are connected."

"That could be one way to look at things," Berg said, his tone noncommittal. "But we'd need her next of kin to okay an autopsy, and he's not willing to do that."

"How do you know?"

"Because I asked." Berg snapped his notepad shut and put it in his back pocket.

"Wait. Who's Marilyn's next of kin?"

"Her sister, but she deferred to Marilyn's ex-husband." Berg frowned. "And he's been here in town since before she died." He looked at me with real focus. "Now Rachel's dead too, and we have no idea what to make of the real estate goings-on at Sun-Sweet. Huh."

I nodded. "See? It's way too weird to be a coincidence. Maybe whoever poisoned Rachel also poisoned Marilyn."

"Marilyn died of a heart attack. That I know. Even her doctor signed off on her cause of death. But Rachel . . . She wasn't poisoned. Or at least, it doesn't look as if poison did her in."

"Seriously? Then how did she die? Blood loss?"

After a pause, Berg put his hand on my forehead, and I froze. "Hmm, no fever. Yet you would have to be sick—because you're not stupid—to be *trying to interfere in an ongoing investigation*."

"Argh! Come on. We were vibing. Connecting. You know I'm onto something."

He glared.

I glared back.

"I will arrest you if I have to." He took his book and stepped back, and I noticed the worry on his face. "But I have other things more pressing. I sure hope you're around to give your boyfriend the support he needs."

"What?" Confused, I frowned. "I don't have a boyfriend."

"Oh? You looked pretty cozy with Dash Hagen yesterday."

"I'm friends with his sister, Detective Know-It-All." I shook my head, and then the import of his words hit. "Wait. What?"

"Thanks for the book. Be seeing you. Oh, and I might need your dog again next week." He left me standing there, my jaw hanging open, as he unlocked the door and walked out.

Before I could follow with more questions, a woman popped her head in.

"Hi there. It's nine. Are you open?"

I forced a smile and walked to the door to turn over the sign. "We sure are. How can I help you today?"

And how could I help Dash before they took him to the slammer? For murder!

Chapter Eleven

I called Dash, only to get his voicemail. Shoot. He might be sleeping or he might be getting into the back of a police car on the way to the station.

After helping a few customers and hustling back and forth to the coffee counter, lamenting our lack of baked goods today, I finally thinned the crowd enough that I could make a quick call to Teri.

"Yo, wazzup?" she asked, and I heard gum smacking as she chewed.

I lowered my voice, watching as Cookie made her rounds, sniffing at customers and receiving her expected *oohs* and *aren't you cutes*. "I think Dash is going to be arrested."

"He's going in for questioning, but I don't know anything about any arrests being made," Teri said quietly. "How do you know?"

"I don't, not for sure. But I had a talk with Mt. Bachelor this morning," I said, preferring to use Berg's new code name. "Rachel wasn't poisoned. Well, maybe she was, but it sounded as if she was killed some other way. I left a message for Dash, but he didn't answer."

"He worked last night. The police questioned him. But they let him go. They didn't say anything about Rachel's time of death, at least not to him."

"Okay, well, shoot, I have to go. Bye."

"Later."

I slid my phone into my pocket and returned to the counter to check out a customer. We chatted about the cooling temps and how cute Cookie was, helping people around the store.

My canine con artist had been looking for food since I hadn't brought her any treats today, the canister in the back kitchen unfortunately empty.

"She is a sweetie." I smiled at Cookie, who grunted and continued to circle the floor.

The lady gave her a last pat and left.

Cookie and I spent the rest of the morning cleaning up the store and chatting with customers, not too busy but busy enough I couldn't dart out for a muffin or egg sandwich, and I was extra hungry for some reason.

Perhaps because my brain kept zooming at a million miles a minute. I could almost feel a connection I hadn't yet explored, something between Rachel, Marilyn, that deed of land, and that typed note I couldn't quite recollect adding up to an important revelation.

Dang it. My stupid memory wasn't being agreeable today, and I had myself to blame. I should be investigating, not sitting on my butt while every other Macaroon had a real job.

I needed to talk to Dash. But more importantly, I needed to talk to Natalie Childers of SunSweet Realty, to see what she knew or didn't know about her coworkers and Cathy Salter.

I drew out my phone again. But before I could call my cousin, I answered a call from Cat. "Cat, I'm starving! When are you coming in?"

"Would it be okay if I missed today? I got to working on a new recipe for Mel and I want to run with it."

"Will I get to taste it before Mel does?"

"But of course."

"And will we get to sell it here too?"

"Um, maybe."

"*Maybe?*"

"But you totally get to try it first," Cat said, sounding worried.

I laughed. "I'm kidding, doofus. Sure. I've got it covered."

"Thanks. I'll call you later to come sample the goods."

She disconnected, and I called Collin. When my cousin answered, I couldn't help smiling. His voice sounded so deep, a lot like Jimmy's. For a nineteen-year-old, he was surprisingly mature and dependable. "Hello, my favorite cousin!"

He groaned. "What do you want, Lexi?"

"To tell you how much I love you."

"Oh man. I was looking forward to fishing with Dad later today." Dad meant Elvis. He called Jimmy Pops.

"He'll keep. Or heck, maybe he can come in and help out at Sweet Fiction today with you. I mean, if he's not getting enough Collin time, working together would be just the ticket." I ignored more groaning. "Collin, I wouldn't ask, but Cat's busy and it's just me today." I lowered my voice. "And I need to do some things."

I heard rustling.

"Would 'some things' involve investigating Rachel Nevis's murder?"

"Yes, and shh. We can't let anyone know." Though it seemed like everyone *did* know, even Berg. That throwaway comment the other day about not telling my book club. Did he realize the Macaroons were now on the case?

"Gotcha. When do you need me? Us?"

Great. That meant he'd rope in Elvis. "After lunch? One?"

"I'll be there." He muttered something under his breath I didn't try to decipher. "You owe me for this."

"I know. You're now my favorite cousin."

"Hey, I thought I was always your favorite cousin."

"Gotta go!" I hung up and turned to see Nadine Kim standing in front of my register, sipping from a coffee mug with her store's logo on it in bright letters, screaming Confection Coffee. Ugh. "And what do you want?"

Nadine smiled. Unfortunately, her outside did not reflect her annoying, obnoxious inside. She had perfect skin, a perfect figure, and shiny, straight, black, to-die-for hair. She was that woman you hated on principle because she acted like she could do no wrong. She'd taken exception to me in our high school days, and though I didn't know or care why our feud had started, I did enjoy fanning the flames of our dislike.

Nadine and I were at our best when sniping at each other, and she reminded me of the life I'd left behind in Seattle, which hadn't been all bad. I missed the hustle and bustle and quick-witted rivalry between competing publishing houses. But here in Confection, I settled for Nadine.

She sipped, slowly and loudly. "So, what can't you let anyone know?"

"What?"

"I heard you talking to your cousin."

"You have big ears."

She snorted. "And you have a big mouth. We all have our crosses to bear."

"You're mine." If leaping over the counter to smack her one wouldn't have landed me in jail, I might have taken my chances.

I might be a few inches shorter than Miss Priss, but I was scrappy. "What do you want, Nadine? I wasn't aware you could read."

"Ha ha." She sipped and looked around, only a few customers browsing in the sudden lull. "Don't you look busy?"

"Did anyone ever tell you the sound of your voice is like nails scraping down a chalkboard?"

Her lips twitched. Yeah, that had been a good one if I did say so myself.

"You're right, I shouldn't stay long. I mean, *I* have *customers* to see to. Customers are what we business types call paying clientele. Do you need me to explain what that means?"

"Oh my gosh, why are you *here?*"

Nadine snickered. "I crack myself up."

"Nadine."

"Lexi."

We stared at each other. Then Cookie had to ruin all our animosity by sauntering over to Nadine and whining for some scratches.

"Oh, hello there." She set her cup on my counter. I sighed. She ignored me and petted Cookie into a dithering mess of happy dog and wagging tail. "Who's the best girl? Who's so pretty and smart and living with a pathetic woman more into books than having a life?"

"Hey. We at Sweet Fiction love books."

"Whatever." Nadine straightened, no longer so jovial. "I heard they're talking to Dash Hagen again today."

"They?"

"The cops." Nadine frowned. "I liked Rachel. Heck, everyone who knew her did. Well, except for Marilyn the past few months. But I think that was because Rachel was younger and prettier and getting more popular in the office. Rachel had been selling a ton of homes."

"Really?"

Nadine nodded. "Sad that Marilyn passed, but she had a history of heart problems."

"How did you know?"

"Heck, everyone who ever went to a chamber meeting knew. She was on pills, statins, I think. I talked to her about it once. Anyway, she and Rachel used to get into some god-awful fights. And in front of people! It was entertaining." Nadine sighed. "Chamber meetings won't be the same. Especially now that Ed's stepping in." She grimaced.

"What?"

"Yeah, Ed's been smiling and laughing and acting like it's Christmas. Same with a few of the ones on his side."

"Like . . . ?"

She shrugged. "Connie Oliver, Cathy Salter, the mayor, and a bunch of others who didn't like the way Marilyn used to run things, I guess. Probably not Dr. Lee though."

"Dr. Lee?"

"Dr. Lee Ryan, duh. Isn't he Cookie's vet? Because he's got a picture of her up on his wall."

The vet. I flushed. "Oh, uh, yeah. But we always call him Dr. Ryan." He was a nice-looking Black man in his late thirties with a welcoming grin. Intelligent, funny without being obnoxious, and with a set of shoulders I liked to think about now and again. I thought I'd once gotten a vibe from him about possible romantic interest, but nothing had come of it. For one, he was nothing but professional with all his clients. Secondly, he was a bit older than me, like my ex had been. And thirdly, I had been recovering from a man-hating period at the time, and I think he might have sensed that.

I admit, it has taken me a long time to get my head straight about relationships and what they can and should mean. But I was stronger because of it. Though now I realized that if Dr. Ryan actually asked me on a date, I would totally say yes. I guess I had matured into a confident woman. Wouldn't my friends be pleased to hear that?

"Cookie loves Dr. *Ryan*," I emphasized. "In fact, I need to schedule an appointment. Someone is due for shots."

Cookie lowered her head and tail and slunk away, hiding behind a book tower.

Nadine grinned. "That's one smart dog." She looked at me. "I'm still not sure why you have her."

"I'm so sorry, Nadine."

"What?" She looked suspicious.

"You've exceeded the store's quota for jackasses today. I need to ask you to leave now," I ended in a super professional voice.

She snorted. "Well, I've exceeded my 'boost a loser' time for the day, so I'll be going." She paused. "But if you happen to see Dash, tell him I don't think he did anything wrong. And neither do a lot of people in this town. No matter what it might look like."

I watched her leave and sat with what she'd said for a while, now thinking about other motives for Rachel's murder that had nothing to do with Dash. Would someone murder just to remain in charge of a silly gathering like the chamber of commerce?

The answer might just be yes.

I groaned, not wanting to but now needing to see what exactly Nadine was talking about. I'd have to suck it up and attend a chamber of commerce meeting. One with Ed Mullins as the chair.

I mumbled a bunch of curses under my breath as I went to the laptop by the help desk and logged onto the chamber's website. And there, how lucky was I? They had a meeting scheduled for tonight. Looked like I had something to do with my evening after all.

* * *

Collin arrived with Uncle Elvis a little after one. We exchanged hugs, and I asked to leave Cookie with them. I'd taken her out for a walk during my lunch break, and I was starving. I grabbed my notebook, in which I'd jotted down suspects, ideas, and some to-do things prior to the Macaroons' meeting tomorrow night.

"Hey, Uncle Elvis, are you going to the chamber meeting tonight?"

"I hadn't planned to, why?"

"Because I'm going," I told him, "and I was hoping to have someone *not* Nadine Kim to sit next to."

Elvis grinned, and Collin, his mini-me, grinned as well. My cousin took after both his dads, in personality—a lot of Uncle Jimmy—and looks—an Uncle Elvis clone.

"It's Jimmy's turn tonight," Elvis said. "But I can switch with him if you'd prefer someone who keeps the peace."

I thought about it. "No, actually. I think I want to see some muck stirred up, if you don't mind. Time to see if we can figure out a new motive for murder."

Elvis and Collin raised their eyebrows at me, and I laughed.

"What?" Collin asked as he petted Cookie.

"You look just like your dad."

"That's why all the girls keep calling," Elvis said with a sigh. "He hasn't yet learned how to make small talk. Instead, he keeps mimicking Jimmy with a lot of embarrassed bluster." To me, Elvis said, "Jimmy's a sweetie, but he's not great at flirting. At all."

Collin turned bright red. "Geez, Dad." He glared. "I'm right here. I can hear you, you know."

"Hey, Collin," a young woman with bright blue eyes said from the front of the store. "What's up?" She smiled.

He stammered, "Oh, h-hey Belinda. I'm, uh, it's all good. How are you today?"

Elvis caught my wince and murmured, "See what I mean?"

"Sadly, I do."

While Collin hid behind the counter and made awkward conversation with the pretty Belinda, I said my goodbyes to Elvis and Cookie. "I'll be back in a few hours to close."

"Take your time." Elvis pulled me close for a kiss on the cheek. "We need to help Dash. It's not looking good for him."

"What happened?"

Elvis walked me out the front door, looked around and, spying no one close by, shared, "I heard from a friend that they think Rachel was killed by a blow to the head. Whoever did it cleaned up the bloody mess they made."

"I heard blood had pooled under the lounger from her head wound."

"Oh. That's weird." He paused, looking serious. "Because they found a bloody towel in Dash's house."

"*What?*" I said loudly.

"Shh." Elvis frowned. "I don't know any more, but I wouldn't be surprised if Dash doesn't come home after his questioning today. He's still at the station, according to Nicholson."

"Officer Nicholson?" I asked in a hushed voice.

"Yeah. I finished his man-shed yesterday, and he filled me in on the case. But you can't tell anyone."

"Who will I tell? Everyone who needs to know will find out by tomorrow night's meeting."

"Right." Elvis nodded. "Now get out of here and find something to prove Dash's innocence."

I left, heading for home. I needed my car today. I had several stops to make.

The first was SunSweet Realty.

Chapter Twelve

I parked in the SunSweet Realty lot filled with several other vehicles. The leading real estate business in Confection, Sun-Sweet regularly feuded with Salter Realty and a few smaller agencies vying for smaller pieces of the real estate pie in town. Marilyn Freeman had been a big seller, attracting million-dollar buyers. From what I knew, Rachel Nevis had been another big seller in the company, but after Rachel, I didn't know the pecking order.

Pushing through the front door of a charming Craftsman that listed itself as the Robert Lee Smith Home, 1912, I looked around and saw a half dozen people flittering about, everyone busy busy busy.

Several couples sat with agents at desks, while an older woman waited on a plush chair in the seating area, reading a *People* magazine.

I approached the administrative assistant at the front desk with a wide smile. "Hello. I was hoping to talk to Natalie Childers."

"Do you have an appointment?" the assistant asked, her manicured nails, cropped bob, and trim suit both stylish and business-like. "Natalie's been swamped due to . . . She's really busy."

"I know, and I'm so sorry." I leaned in and added in a low voice, "I'm here to talk to her about Marilyn. It's important I talk to Natalie about her."

The assistant's eyes opened wide. "Oh, well, please, have a seat. I'll let Natalie know you're here right away."

"Thank you." I tried to look sad and must have nailed it because the assistant gave me a kind smile and called Natalie as promised.

A few minutes later, Natalie came out of a back office and held out a hand as I rose. "Hi. I'm Natalie Childers." A white woman about my age, she had kind brown eyes, freckles, and pretty features. She also appeared super stressed.

"Lexi," I said and clasped her hand. "I'm so sorry about Marilyn."

Natalie looked away. "We miss her. Please, come with me."

I followed her back to her office and sat when she gestured to a chair across from a massive desk filled with stacks of papers.

"Would you like something to drink?"

"Oh, thank you. Anything cold would be wonderful."

Natalie pressed a button on her phone, asking someone to bring two lemonades.

In seconds, a young man dropped them off.

"Josh, please make sure we're not disturbed, okay?"

"Sure thing, Natalie." He closed the door behind him.

Natalie's grief dried up as if it had never been. "Okay, Lexi. What exactly do you have to tell me about my *wonderful* dead boss?" Whoa. Talk about sarcasm.

Well, that was unexpected. "Marilyn Freeman and Rachel Nevis. Tell me about them."

"Why? Who are you?"

"I'm Lexi Jones," I said, not bothering to lie. "My good friend, Dash Hagen, is being questioned concerning Rachel Nevis's death. He didn't do it."

"Dash?" Natalie blinked. "Dash would never kill Rachel."

"I know." I started to relax, realizing Natalie seemed to know and like Dash. "But the police found Rachel's body in his backyard. I have a feeling Marilyn's death might be related to whatever happened to Rachel."

Natalie looked fascinated. "Really? Why?"

"I don't know."

Natalie stared at me. "Hold on. Aren't you the woman who nearly got killed by her neighbor? Gil something, right?"

Gil had been killed, not the killer. "Not exactly, but you're close enough." I wondered if that connection would ever fade, though to be fair, it had only been two months since his death. "I can tell something doesn't fit with Rachel's death, and I need your help getting the police to look at someone other than Dash. I swear, I won't mention you told me anything at all. I just need to get some idea of where to look other than at my friend."

"Wow. I knew they found Rachel dead, but I hadn't heard it was at Dash's house." She sat back in her chair, looking frazzled, and guzzled her lemonade.

"Let's start at the beginning. How did you know Dash?"

"I saw him a few times at the Ripe Raisin. But I met him when he was dating Marilyn. He'd come by SunSweet every now and then to pick her up. He was always a sweetheart." Natalie sighed. "He could have done so much better than Marilyn. I was glad when they broke up. Not that it was serious. Marilyn never did serious. But still. Dash was so nice. Not like her other hookups."

"From what I've heard, she had a lot of them. Not judging, just saying what I heard."

"No, judge away." Natalie sounded bitter. "I didn't like Marilyn, but she was a decent boss. Until she wasn't. Truthfully though, she didn't sleep with half the men she was accused of boffing. But she flirted a lot, and men seemed to be attracted to her. Old, young, the richer the better. They loved her. Unfortunately, the men she did sleep with often had significant others that talked badly about her. Personally, I think she thrived on her notoriety."

"Were she and Rachel friends?"

"At first. Marilyn took Rachel and me under her wing. I'm licensed and acted as her assistant, and we always have work to do. I mean, she's dead but the piles of paperwork keep growing. Rachel was a real estate agent, a licensed broker who made her own fair share of deals even before joining SunSweet. She was pretty and fun and didn't like the way Marilyn used people."

"You mean men?"

"I mean people." Natalie sighed. "You've heard we're under investigation, right?"

I nodded, despite having no clue what she was talking about.

"Well, from what I've heard, Marilyn had a bad habit of snowing her clients. She'd take multiple bids, acting as both seller and buyer's agent, and only let the client know about bids she got a piece of. And you know, she didn't need to do that. As the principal broker, she took in twenty percent of all our sales. SunSweet is bursting at the seams with clients, despite the market being a little tight right now for buyers."

"You're okay telling me this?" That didn't make sense. "Not that I plan on sharing this with anyone, but it seems a little like sensitive information."

"I know Marilyn was guilty of both fraud and breach of contract. But I can't prove any of it. And I was her assistant, worked on all her paperwork. But the special deals went around me." Natalie frowned. "When I told her some numbers weren't adding up, she told me not to worry about it. Because if I did, I might take the blame for any perceived negligence. That was a month ago when it all came to a head. I threatened to quit, and she threatened to report *me* to the Better Business Bureau and the Oregon Real Estate Agency."

"Oh, wow."

"Yeah, she was a real piece of work." Natalie glared at the stacks of paper in front of her. "I was crying after that meeting, and Rachel found me. We talked, and Rachel told me she'd take care of it."

"Really?"

"Rachel was a good person. She cared, and she didn't screw others at her own office out of contracts, the way Marilyn sometimes would. Rachel was making a real name for herself."

"I heard she settled the Strawberry Fields sale."

Natalie smiled. "Marilyn had it all ready to go then died before it could be signed. I was mad, because I wanted her to do real jail time. Rachel did too. But then we figured karma had taken care of Marilyn in the end. Her family has a history of heart disease, you know."

"I had no idea. It was common knowledge?"

"With us in the office, sure. And with her friends. She shouldn't have been drinking with all the pills she had to take, but she was famous for wine parties. We had some really fun times here. Despite Marilyn's nonsense, we're a real family at SunSweet." Natalie wiped her eyes, and I realized she cared about the people in the office. Not Marilyn so much, but she seemed to miss Rachel. "Between you and me, I wondered if maybe Rachel did something to Marilyn. She was thrilled when Marilyn died but tried not to show it."

Apparently, Natalie didn't know about Rachel's drunken "the witch is dead" rant at the Ripe Raisin.

"Then sadly, Rachel died too." More tears followed, and I reached for a box of tissues on Natalie's desk to hand one to her. "Thanks." She blew her nose. "Sorry. The office is now a mess. Rachel's work, on top of Marilyn's work, is too much to handle."

"Who's next in line to take over?" They might have motive.

"Marilyn's ex-husband, can you believe it?"

"No, I can't."

"They parted on good terms ten years ago and still shared a lot of business dealings on both coasts. Hank Stillwater, that's his name, he'd just come to town to talk to her about a new venture—not sure what it was—when she passed. He's been inconsolable. He still loved her."

"That's so sad." And so suspicious! He happened to be in town when his ex-wife died? And he inherited her business?

"A few of the other agents here are working their tails off to finalize paperwork and keep deals in place. Hank's actually been a huge help keeping us afloat, though I know we've lost some business to Cathy Salter. You can't rest on your butt around here when it comes to buying and selling property. Even though it's the end of the summer, we're still jumping."

"Wow. I hadn't realized any of that."

"I don't know if it will help get Dash out of the hot seat, but I can tell you Marilyn was seeing someone else when she died."

"Who?"

"I don't know, but she was different this time. This relationship seemed more real." Natalie frowned. "I want to say I heard her arguing with Hank about it, but they never stayed mad at each other for long." Natalie blushed. "I overheard a lot of her phone calls."

"Oh. Were they more than friendly exes?" Lovers maybe?

"I don't think so. No." Natalie shook her head. "Hank's always been a sweetheart, but his life is in Maine. His business with Marilyn brought him by a few times a year, at least it has as long as I've been working here. Three years this October." Natalie sighed. "I want to become a full-time agent on my own, not just an assistant. I think I can do that if Hank takes over. Rachel would have been perfect to run this office. Now I guess he'll probably hand management over to Louise. She's super nice and deserves it. After Marilyn and Rachel, she was probably the third best agent in the company."

"What about Cathy Salter?" I asked. "How did she deal with Marilyn?"

Natalie leaned closer, her eyes bright. "They hated each other. Marilyn would call Cathy an old hag and a has-been, and Cathy would tell Marilyn that she'd passed her prime and was reflecting her own insecurities. The chamber meetings were the worst." Natalie paused. "She and Rachel used to fight a lot too."

"Cathy and Rachel?"

"No, Marilyn and Rachel, but I think it was mostly for show. Marilyn liked to be the center of attention." Natalie looked sad. "I'm talking bad about her. She could be a real pain, but she could also be sweet. She helped me earn a commission on my first sale right before she threatened to implicate me in her messes. She even sold me my house. Heck, she would get all kinds of deals for her friends."

A memory stood out. "I heard Mike Todesco, the bartender at the Ripe Raisin, say Marilyn helped him and his girlfriend get a house."

"She could be like that. Sweet and kind, then a real jerk. Competitive but caring. It was weird, but her ability to charm people and work her magic with that smile really did make her a star in the business." Natalie tapped her glass with a pink, manicured nail. "I don't know if I have it in me to be like that, so intense and fake-happy. But I'm going to try."

I didn't have much more to ask, I didn't think. "Natalie, you've been a big help."

"Do you think any of that will help Dash?"

"Maybe." I stood. "Can you think of anyone who might want to kill Marilyn or Rachel?"

"Sure. Anyone trying to sell a home in Confection," Natalie said wryly. "Between you and me, if Marilyn didn't die of a heart attack, my money's on Rachel. As to who would kill Rachel, well, I have no idea. Because she was genuinely nice."

"Thanks again." I paused. "Um, if anyone does come to talk to you about Rachel or Marilyn, like say, the police, can you forget I was ever here? I wouldn't want them to think I was interfering in an investigation or anything."

Natalie winked. "Who are you again?"

I smiled. "Hey, anytime you want a free coffee or muffin, stop by Sweet Fiction. It's on the house."

"Oh, thanks." Natalie walked me out, and I left having more questions than answers.

I got into my car and rolled down the windows, sitting for a moment.

Marilyn had been under investigation for possible fraud. She had a ton of money and regularly shafted her own people. She slept around, but not too much, and had a new boyfriend who was different than the others. Her ex-husband was in town before she died, the executor of her estate, maybe, and he still loved her. Although, Natalie thought Rachel had maybe murdered her boss. But if Rachel had killed Marilyn, who had killed Rachel?

I started the car and decided to tackle Salter Realty, only to learn that Cathy was out of town but would be back the following day. I made an appointment to talk to her Thursday morning at ten thirty. And I felt like an idiot for not asking Natalie about Cathy's threat. But hey, I'd ask Cathy about it when she got back. If I didn't like her answer, I could always go back to Natalie.

After driving home, I parked and debated returning to work right away. Instead, I made some notes, then did what I'd been dreading and opened my novel on my laptop.

I had no working title, but the book's first draft was close to done. It needed revisions and definite retooling before I had to fight for the courage to query a publishing house. One of my friends in Seattle might be impartial with edits if I didn't tell them I'd written it.

But who to get to help?

While I pondered, I made some notes on the murder, needing to see what the Macaroons knew as a collective.

My cell phone rang, and I picked it up. "Hello?"

"Hi, Lexi. Sorry to call you so soon. It's Natalie."

"Hi, Natalie."

"It was after you left that I realized I had forgotten to mention something I found odd."

My heart raced and I prepared to type whatever she told me directly into my computer. "Oh?"

"Yeah. What first made me suspicious about Marilyn's side deals. I found some paperwork about Lot 49–71: Strawberry Fields. Herman Livingston owned it, and when he died, it went to his widow, Selma. But she could only either pass it down to her kids or will it to the city, which is what Herman wanted her to do. We'd been in the process of making that happen a while ago when I saw paperwork on the field's sale. And that made no sense, but Marilyn told me she'd spoken with Selma and it was a done deal."

That sounded very wrong. "Interesting."

"Yeah, isn't it? I forgot about it, to tell you the truth. Then Marilyn died, and we still had paperwork needing to be signed. So Rachel signed off on it. Selma died, and it's all been a big blur, you know?"

"I get it." My Scooby-sense was barking, gathering so many clues. I typed like a madwoman, writing it all down, and hit save. "Thanks, Natalie."

"Yeah, well, not sure what good it will do you. Clint Ayers and Hank Stillwell are now the proud owners of the field. I think. Heck, I'm not sure what's what anymore."

"This is why I'm glad to work in a bookstore. It's easier."

We both shared a laugh.

"Anyway, now you know," Natalie said.

"Did I say a free coffee and muffin? Let's add a cookie too when you come in."

"Deal. I—oh, I need to go. Bye."

I disconnected and stared at what I'd typed. Whoa boy, we had a lot to talk about tomorrow night. Because I had a whole new host of suspects and a lot I needed to figure out. Like how to share any of this with Berg and not be thrown in jail.

The phone rang again, and I saw Teri's name on the caller ID. "What's up, buttercup?"

"Oh, Lexi. It's awful."

"What's wrong?"

"They've arrested Dash for murder."

Chapter Thirteen

I met Teri at her apartment after picking up Cookie from the bookstore. Elvis and Collin were happy to close for me after I'd told them what Teri had said about Dash being arrested.

"Go help your friends," Uncle Elvis had said after giving me a hug. "They need you."

Collin shooed me away. "We Jones men got this. See you."

Sitting in my friends' two-bedroom place at Pixie Apartments, just down the road from Dash's house, Cookie and I watched Teri pacing a hole through the rug as she talked to her mom on the phone.

I leaned closer to Cat, who sat at the kitchen counter. "Fill me in."

Cat sighed and ran a hand through her hair, making it stick up in a clump of red curls. "Dash went in for more questioning today while the cops used a search warrant to go more thoroughly through his house. Apparently, the first time they went through they found a bloody towel in his closet."

That I already knew.

"They matched the blood to Rachel. And then when they went through again, they found a a pair of Rachel's panties in his hamper."

"Seriously?" That was very, very *bad*.

"When they asked Dash about it, he said nothing and asked for a lawyer."

"Praise the Raisin, he listened." I ignored her raised brow and asked, "Who's his attorney?"

"You might know him. Cody Redston."

"Wait. The attorney I used when I had to talk to the police was Amy Redston."

"Yeah, this is her husband. He's a criminal attorney and supposedly pretty good. Mr. and Mrs. Hagen hired him for Dash."

"How are the Hagens holding up?" I asked, watching Teri march back and forth, her expression fierce.

"They're angry and scared." Cat sounded subdued. "Mrs. Hagen cried, and she had Teri crying. Mr. Hagen was ranting about heads rolling. We all know what happened."

"What?"

"Someone is framing Dash for Rachel's murder. There's no way he did it, and he wasn't seeing her, so why would her underwear be in his house? And a bloody towel? Why?"

"Yeah, why?"

"Supposedly, he used it to make it look like she died peacefully and not from a bash against the back of her head. But that's stupid. Of course the coroner would see the broken skull and bruises under her hair, not to mention all the blood on the patio under the body."

"It's clearly murder." I frowned. "They'll do a tox screen too." I wanted badly for them to find something to lead back to Marilyn. "I found out a heck of a lot today that points to real estate shenanigans as the reason behind the murders. But why frame Dash, is my question."

Teri slipped her phone onto the counter and turned to us with tears in her eyes. After a big group hug and many loving licks from Cookie, Teri gave a big *ugh,* went to the bathroom to wipe her face, and returned looking much better.

"Sorry, guys. This is stressing me out."

"No kidding." I patted her knee.

Cookie consoled her by lying by her feet and licked her toes now and then, causing Teri to smile. "Goofy dog." She stroked Cookie behind her ears. "So Cat told you about Dash getting arrested. Cody Redston is working on getting him bail. He doesn't seem like much of a lawyer, but we kind of grabbed him off a golf vacation. He showed up in a Hawaiian shirt and long shorts."

"Nah, that's how he and his wife roll." I told them about Amy, a sarcastic woman with curly hair dyed purple and the fashion sense of a stoner. But the woman had a more than agile mind. "If Cody is anything like his wife, Dash is in great hands."

"Well, the Redston reputation is pretty darn good," Teri said. "My mom liked him."

"And your mom hates everyone."

Teri flashed me a look then sighed. "Yeah, she does."

"Dash will be okay. Look, all the Macaroons are meeting tomorrow night at Sweet Fiction to share. I learned a ton today." I told them everything I could remember about what I'd heard.

"Wow. That's some good stuff." Teri seemed excited now, not so sad. "There's a lot to unpack. Was Marilyn killed or did she die of natural causes? Who killed Rachel? Why blame Dash? Was it related to Rachel's land deal or to something else?"

Cat nodded. "Yeah, that connection to Selma Livingston is too much of a coincidence."

"But we know Selma died in her sleep," I argued.

"Do we?"

Teri looked from me to Cat. "I'm sensing we need to talk to Selma's relatives."

I nodded.

"Let my mom do it," Teri said. "She's friendly with Selma's daughter. And honestly, I know the family. They aren't greedy people. They genuinely loved Selma, so I doubt they had anything to do with her death. But Mom will find out."

"How does your mom know Selma?" I asked, needing to connect the dots.

"They fix pancake breakfast together at church sometimes." Teri pointed to both me and Cat. "I expect to see you two at church this Sunday."

"I'd planned on it." I nodded. "I'll be watching the grieving folks while they listen to Pastor Nestor ramble on."

"You're going to hell for that," Cat muttered.

"You are," Teri agreed with a grin. "He does ramble, though, doesn't he?"

"Totally."

Teri would know. Her mom routinely guilts her into attending Sunday service. Cat never goes unless it's Christmas.

Pastor Nestor would be remembering Marilyn on Sunday, and he'd probably talk about Selma and Rachel too. I needed to be there, though I didn't look forward to attending. Pastor Nestor was part of the CGC mafia, after all. He'd once accused a church member of murder over award-winning potatoes. No, Nestor didn't mess around when it came to growing things. His wife was just as bad, a judgmental older woman who didn't like me much.

Oh yeah. I couldn't *wait* to go.

Trying to ignore my dread, I asked Teri, "Have you learned anything from work?"

She sighed. "No. My boss is keen on keeping me from the murders. It's the smart thing to do, to negate any appearance of impropriety, but it's hard not knowing what's going on." She looked at Cat. "What about you?"

Cat flushed. "Roger's being pretty tightlipped. He's afraid I'll tell you guys."

"Which you will, because you're a great friend," Teri said.

"Yeah. But I swear I'll get something out of him."

"I'm going to hit Berg up again," I told them. "He needs to investigate SunSweet and Hank Stillwater. The ex-husband seems awfully suspect. And this connection to Selma is weird. I just need to find the right way to tell him."

We all looked at one another and said as one, "Anonymous note."

Yep, we certainly shared the same brain.

"Hey, guys, another thing, I—" My phone rang. "Hold on." I answered it. "Hello?"

"Niece, it's me." Uncle Jimmy. "I heard we're going to the chamber meeting together."

"We are."

"Well, it got postponed to Friday evening. Be ready for a nightmare of a time. Ed Mullins is leading things. This should be fun. And by fun, I mean like having a root canal without pain meds." He snorted. "Okay, I'll see you tomorrow night at Sweet Fiction. Be safe." He disconnected.

I turned to my friends. "I'm going to a chamber of commerce meeting Friday night instead of tonight, apparently. Meeting got postponed."

"Did I hear the name Ed Mullins?" Teri asked. Girl has ears like a bat.

"You did."

"Oh boy. I heard stories from my dad about what the chamber was like when Ed helmed it. Kind of like a crazy ringmaster running his own three-ring circus."

"I can just see that." I paused, considering. "I think I might bring Cookie Friday night."

Cat and Teri looked at each other and grinned.

"I might show up," Cat said. "I mean, if I open my own baking business, I should join the chamber to make contacts, right?"

Teri poked her. "Is this more of your pretending, or are you really going to make this work? You know both of us are behind you."

I nodded. "I've been telling you since I got back to Confection that you have real skills. I know you can make it happen if you want to. But you have to want it. We can't want it for you."

"I do want it. But I'm scared." Cat flushed. "Mel was super complimentary, but what if she was just being nice?"

Teri snorted. "Seriously? Mel's a businesswoman. I've heard her order her husband and grown sons around like a general at war with celery."

"Weird image, but okay." I agreed. "Mel isn't nice, Cat. She's honest and kind, but she'd never do anything to possibly screw up her business. What reason does she have to tell you she loves your food and invite you to provide it? No reason except to make more money."

Teri nodded. "Just think. If this works, you branch out to other coffee shops." She ignored my groan. "Confection Coffee, Sal's Smoothies, a few of the small foodie places north and south of town. Maybe the grocery stores. How cool would that be?"

"You'll need branding and marketing, but we can help with that," I said, excited for her. Cat always worked so hard and she'd been such a help at the bookshop. "Before you know it, you won't have time for books. It'll be all baking, all the time."

Teri smiled, but I saw a shadow in her eyes. "And you'll need a bigger kitchen."

"Maybe one she shares with a certain police officer?" Whoops. I'd pushed too far.

Panic made Cat's face super red, and she rushed away and slammed herself in the bathroom.

"Sorry," I said when Teri glared at me.

"I'm sorry too. But I can see her future clear as day."

"Me too. She's got skills. She just needs us to help nudge her there."

"Maybe a little more slowly and gently though," Teri said.

I sighed. Cookie whined at the door, which opened and closed after letting her into the bathroom.

A few minutes later, Cat exited, her face no longer so pink, her eyes shiny. "I can do this."

"Right. At your own pace," I said firmly. "Sorry. We got a little too excited for you."

"And what about you?" Cat asked. "How's the book coming?"

"It's not right now. I slowed down with my broken wrist. But the first draft is pretty done. Um, Gil's death kind of helped me nail a few things down. And right after all that happened, I wrote a lot that made more sense. Now once we get Dash out of jail, I'll work on my revisions. I'm actually thinking more about my future too." I paused. "I had a thought the other day that if Dr. Ryan asked me out, I'd totally date him."

"Oh my gosh, I would in heartbeat." Teri nodded.

Cat agreed. "He's hot. Older man hotness."

"He's only ten years older, I think," Teri argued. "Not that old."

"It's old enough. Trust me, my ex was ten years older, and it didn't work out." I shrugged. "Not all because of the age difference."

Cat snorted. "Because he was a tool."

"Pretentious." Teri sneered. "What a jerk."

"He was, wasn't he?" My mood restored, I watched Cookie out of the corner of my eye tiptoe toward a plate of cookies Cat had left out on the kitchen table. "If you do it, there will be consequences," I said to the sneaky dog.

"What are you talking about? Dating Dr. Ryan would be a thrill," Teri said, "And we were talking about *you* dating him, not me."

"I was talking to Cookie." I nodded as she delicately gripped the end of one cookie in her mouth and slowly backed away.

Cat bounded up. "You drop that right now, you little thief!"

Cookie took a nibble but hadn't devoured the whole thing.

"Just tell me there isn't any chocolate in there," I said, realizing how bad that would be.

"No, just peanut butter with a hint of cinnamon."

"Oh, I gotta get one." Teri rose, started toward the plate, then darted at my dog. "Ha! You're surrounded now."

Cookie chomped down on the cookie, then made a mad dash for the hallway. Seconds later, a door closed behind her.

Cat blinked. "Did she just shut herself in a room?"

"Sounded like."

Teri gaped. "That dog is possessed."

"Tell me about it." I rose and grabbed a cookie myself. I ate it in three bites. "But you have to admit she has excellent taste.

Cat smiled. "Not bad, eh? Time to try the strawberry rhubarb pie I made for Mel."

I narrowed my eyes at the pie. "I'm getting the first sample taste, right?" It was very important that Cat trusted *me*, not Teri, Roger, or Mel with it. Silly, but with all the changes coming soon to my friend's life, I needed to know I mattered enough to judge her food.

She nodded, solemn. "You're first. You have the best taste buds—and most honest feedback—of anyone I know." She paused. "Well, with the exception of Mrs. Hagen. But she's not nice when she doesn't like something. You're a little more diplomatic."

"Yeah. And I know better than to ever tell you something isn't *moist* enough."

"Let it go, woman." Cat growled, still sensitive about her past dry muffins.

I grabbed a fork and plate and accepted a slice of pie. I couldn't comment until I'd eaten the whole thing. "I need another slice to be sure."

Cat was dancing with impatience.

I grinned. "A winner! It's delicate, light, and delicious. And geezy-peasy, if you don't give me any more I might die."

"Give me some," Teri insisted.

So we ate pie, released Cookie from the bedroom and scolded her for stealing food, then told each other funny stories about the people in our lives. We conspicuously avoided any mention of Dash or murder.

Reality could keep for one night. But real friendship couldn't.

Chapter Fourteen

Thursday morning at ten thirty on the dot, I sat in front of Cathy Salter's desk, intrigued by the differences between Salter Realty and SunSweet Realty.

Marilyn's agency had been quaint, with understated wealth and a busy but not frantic feel. Fabrics had been in bolder and darker shades, accented by the historic home's original woodwork.

Salter Realty felt fresher and more modern. Unlike Sun-Sweet realty, that maybe had a dozen people working there, Salter Realty had twice as many people, and a frenetic sense of urgency seemed to fill the cheerful faces of those working in the open office. Cathy had a large, airy office filled with plants and beach scenes. The decor of the place was bright and fun, filled with possibilities.

Oddly enough, though I loved the old house SunSweet worked out of, I preferred the atmosphere in Salter Realty. It just felt . . . open.

"So you're asking questions about Marilyn, huh?" Cathy kicked back and grinned. She was a white woman in her early forties, I'd say, with long blond hair and tired eyes. Tall and thin, she had an organized feel about her, from her desk to the file folders, each with their own place. Even the stacks of paper on the table in the corner looked even and level. A photo on the wall near her credentials showed a handsome family of five at Disneyland. And it looked recent.

"My friend, Dash, is being accused of Rachel Nevis's murder. Since Rachel worked for Marilyn, and they had plenty of tension between them, I figure Marilyn might be involved in Rachel's death somehow. I know it sounds odd, but I've learned some disturbing facts that might help my friend."

Cathy swallowed down a Diet Coke and nodded. "Well, we all know Marilyn died before Rachel did, so you know she didn't kill her. But let me save you the trouble of asking. No, I didn't kill Rachel either." At my raised brow, she huffed. "Or Marilyn."

"I heard you two argued a lot, especially at chamber meetings."

"God, did we." Cathy sighed. "Look, I'm all-in with my business. It's put my husband through grad school, bought us a big house with land, and given my kids plenty of private lessons and ski passes. Salter Realty means the world to me. And I'll be damned if I'll let some underhanded whore sleep her way to millions when she should be working hard like the rest of us, not spreading her legs for a commission."

"Ouch."

Cathy shrugged. "That's what I'd tell *you*. I told the police yeah, I disliked her, but not enough to hate her. Marilyn made women real estate agents look bad. We don't all sleep with clients. In fact, most of us are by-the-book professionals. My company has lost quite a few bids due to some immoral client tampering. Nothing illegal, but it's something upright agencies don't do to each other. And then there were the fraud and breach of contract allegations. I know for a fact she never let her client in on a few of our bids. But we couldn't prove it."

"And what about Lot 49–71?"

Cathy's smile turned from a frown into a wide grin. "Ah, Strawberry Fields. Now that was a case of karma biting her in the butt. Selma Livingston, bless her, made a provision in her will to leave that land to the city. She, like her husband, never intended it to be sold or developed. They were a true Confection family. Her kids and grandkids all feel the same way. We were working with her and a lawyer to untangle whatever Marilyn and Clint Ayers did to steal it away. They had—have—no legal right to the property."

"No kidding."

"No kidding." Cathy drank more soda. "But in case you're wondering about Selma, she died peacefully in her sleep surrounded by family and friends. I was there. And I promised her that we'd make sure the land went to the city. I've tried, but I can't seem to connect with Hank Stillwater, Marilyn's silent partner, to clarify matters. From what I hear, he might be taking over the company. But then, I'm not privy to Marilyn's will. Maybe she left her assets to someone else."

"What do you know about her relationship with Hank?"

"They were friends. He's actually a pretty nice guy, just got tired of always standing in Marilyn's shadow. That's why we argued so much, you know. She constantly tried to tell everyone what to do at chamber meetings, and the idea of being chair is to delegate and spread the wealth to help everyone, not just yourself."

"What about her and Rachel?"

Cathy laughed. "Those two would screech and harp on each other, but the minute you tried to take sides, they'd come together as one and tell you to mind your own business. Marilyn had an odd way of treating her people. Nice yet not so nice. She wasn't all that great to her assistant, sadly, because I think Natalie has a lot of potential. But then, that's my humble opinion. You ask my assistant, she'll tell you I'm a monster."

A woman knocked and entered, dropped a stack of papers on the side table, and nodded. "She's *such* a monster. Ingram's papers are here, Cathy."

"Thanks, Barb." After Barb left, Cathy added, "I would never, ever undercut anyone at Salter Realty to make myself more money. As the principal broker, you provide services that your agents pay for with a slight commission. I'm not hurting for money, and I can always look at myself in the mirror after selling a house. I'm out for my clients, number one. My agency and myself, number two."

I liked everything about Cathy, even that hard gleam of determination in her eyes.

"What about a nasty argument overheard outside the smoothie shop between you and Natalie?"

Cathy didn't look perturbed at the mention. She waved it away. "Oh that. Just me blowing off some steam. No biggie."

"Um, this might be a delicate question, but did Marilyn ever make any moves on your staff? Your husband? Did you know who she was dating recently?"

Cathy lost her humor. "Yes, she did hit on my husband. Several times, but he and I talk and I have utter faith in him. I know they never slept together, not for lack of her trying. She wasn't a huge floozy or anything, but she could wrap a man around her fingers with ease. I know a lot of women didn't like her for that. The last person I know who had a real beef with her about a philandering husband was Connie Oliver."

"So was Marilyn dating Tad, then?"

"No. I think they fooled around a while ago, but Marilyn liked to bring it up now and then in front of Connie because Connie went with us instead of SunSweet on a new house for her folks. And Connie's folks have money."

"Ah, business gone bad."

"I understand frustration, but you can't screw people over when they've made their choice. Instead of Connie being open to working with Marilyn in the future, Marilyn burned that bridge pretty badly. Of course, she's dead now, so it's a moot point. But still, you see what I'm saying."

"I do." Hmm. "Why are you being so frank with me?"

"I have nothing to hide, Lexi. Plus, I like your mom and dad." Cathy smiled. "They bought from me years ago when they could have gone with Marilyn. And I think it's sad what happened to Rachel. It makes no sense. I like Dash Hagen. He's personable and savvy about business. I just can't see him killing Rachel for no reason."

"People are saying he was seeing her."

"Really? Because the last time I saw Rachel, she was complaining about the lack of good men in this town. I think she'd recently broken up with someone. An accountant out of Bend, I think."

"I hope the police are learning all this. Dash is in jail for something he didn't do, and it makes no sense."

"I feel ya." Her phone rang. "I'm sorry, but I'm expecting this call. If you have any other questions, just let me know." Cathy picked up the phone and put it to her shoulder. "And if you ever want to sell that house of yours, call me." She leaned across the desk to hand me a card. "It's so charming, and your grandma took great care of it."

"Thanks."

She nodded and said into the phone, "Cathy Salter here. How can I help you?"

I smiled as I left, passing a cluster of happy home buyers and real estate agents making deals and arguing terms.

Once outside, I stopped and considered what I now knew.

The lead with Selma Livingston and Strawberry Fields didn't seem to have legs. Unless Rachel had been killed because she objected to the sale of a lot that shouldn't have been sold. Yet she was on cloud nine having supposedly made a ton on the illegal property.

Hmm. I wondered if I could get an audience with Hank Stillwater, Marilyn's ex. I bet he could tell me a few things no one else knew. But would he? And what might his connection to Rachel have been? Secret lover? New boss? Nothing at all?

I felt like I had fewer answers than before, but at least I could put a line through Cathy Salter as Rachel's killer. It just didn't feel right, and yes, I admit, I liked her. Hmm. I should have brought Cookie. My canine sleuth had a nose for bad guys.

I'd keep that in mind when, and if, I got a chance to talk to Marilyn's ex-husband.

* * *

That evening, as the Macaroons gathered to share food and information, I prepped the large whiteboard and arranged markers while everyone grabbed plates and filled them with so much home-cooked goodness. Not to be outdone, I'd made a batch of pink lemonade that was the best thing I'd ever tasted. It had taken a lot of lemons, watermelon, sugar, and trial and error, but I'd balanced the tart-to-sweet ratio and could give Country Time a run for its money.

Cookie had on a leash, wrapped to a doorknob in the back, and I'd given her a ton of warnings to behave. I'd let her go free once we'd finished our first round of eats. Stefanie had a definite eye on my dog, though Cookie did her best to pretend she hadn't noticed all the glaring directed her way. To keep her occupied, I'd given her a brand-new beef bone she was slobbering over on the doggie bed I'd brought in as well.

"Talk about a heck of a spread," Elvis boomed. "I can't believe it's taken me this long to join book club."

"Technically, you joined two months ago," Alan said with a grin.

"Yeah, but now I feel like a real member. I made cobbler, and Jimmy contributed the pot pie."

"Yeah, hope you like it," Jimmy said, eyeballing the food table.

Fortunately, Elvis hadn't made a strawberry rhubarb or peanut butter pie. Instead, he'd fixed a fruity dessert while Jimmy brought along a savory dish, Jimmy having taken the recipe from something he'd seen on the Great British Baking Show, a program my uncles could watch over and over.

I'd seen it once and thought it was okay, but I was partial to crime shows. Like Chad Berg.

Did he believe Dash to be guilty? Going over the evidence, it didn't make much sense. Dash was too smart to leave a victim's DNA in his house, right outside where he'd leave her dead body. Dash was a lot of things; stupid wasn't one of them.

I pushed aside thoughts of murder and enjoyed the food. We all discussed the cooling temperatures, loving our mountain air, and were pleased to see a lot of the tourists leaving since school would soon be starting.

Stefanie plunked her plate in the trash, took a big gulp of lemonade, and stood in the center of our circle. All our folding chairs faced inward and looped around the standing whiteboard. It was the size of a large chalkboard and could be flipped to use the other side as well, set on casters. I'd bought it from the elementary school for a steal back when I'd first started working for Sweet Fiction.

"Okay, folks," she barked, and Cookie jumped. "Before Lexi calls us all to order, I just want to remind you that we have real work to do. Teri's brother is accused of murder. This is serious stuff. Not like last time."

I stood in shock. "Hold on. *I* was accused of murder last time! That was pretty serious to me."

Stefanie waved away my concern. "Bah. That was a loose charge. The one on Dash has evidence framing him. You just had a journal stolen, and you never did admit to killing Gil, now did you?"

I sputtered for a moment before admitting, "No, I never did."

"There. Now, the floor is yours."

Thanks so much, Stefanie. I cleared my throat and waited for her to take a seat next to Alison. "First of all, thanks for coming." I picked up the black dry-erase marker and wrote SUSPECTS on the left-hand side of the board. "I've learned an awful lot since calling this meeting, and I bet you guys have too. But before we start, I think we need to list our suspects."

"Good idea," Alan said.

I started writing. "Dash."

Teri crossed her arms over her chest and glared at the board.

"Sorry, Teri, but we have to," Cat said.

"Rachel—suspected of killing Marilyn."

Alison whistled.

"Shh," Stefanie said.

Kay nodded. "Keep going."

I added, "Chamber members who argued with her a lot, like Ed Mullins, Cathy Salter, Connie Oliver, Tad Oliver—"

"He didn't argue with her," Elvis interrupted. "He just slept with her."

"That counts," Darcy said.

"Right." I continued to write. "We have Clint Ayers, Gary Conroy, Natalie Childers, Hank Stillwater. Did I leave anyone out?"

"A lot of women didn't like her," Darcy said.

"True, but any in particular?"

"Besides Connie and Peggy Donahue?"

"The pastor's wife?" Alan goggled.

"Yep." Kay nodded. "She talked a lot about Marilyn right after she died."

Elvis frowned. "Hold on. Rachel never slept with Tad. I thought this was about who killed Rachel, not who killed Marilyn."

Great. Now I was getting confused. "Wait. My mistake. You're right. We have to assume Marilyn had a heart attack. Let's stick with who might have killed Rachel." But as I stared at the board, I realized everyone we'd listed had motive to kill Marilyn, not Rachel.

Cat held up a hand. "How about we talk about motive instead of suspects? That might help get us started."

"Good idea." Stefanie harrumphed.

"And this is where I come in," Darcy said proudly.

"What?"

"I never told you this, because I can't possibly know it." She looked around at us all. "Right?"

"Oh, sure, right. You never said it." I nodded. Darcy must have erred on the illegal side of information gathering, I was assuming, from her banker husband.

"Did you know that Rachel Nevis had applied and been denied twice for a loan to start her own company?"

Zing. We'd hit paydirt. I could feel it. A glance at Cookie showed her looking intently at Darcy. Yep. That nailed it.

Stefanie looked confused. "But I thought she was going to make a lot of money on the sale of Strawberry Fields?"

I shook my head, but before I could speak, Alan did. "Nope. I learned yesterday on my undercover picnic that Lot 49–71, what we all call Strawberry Fields, in addition to our lovely public pond, belongs to Selma Livingston, who willed it to the city after her husband willed it to her. There's no way Rachel would see a penny of the sale of that land, and she had to know it."

"Dun dun dun," Cat added, and Cookie grunted.

I walked over to Cookie and freed her from her leash. She gave Stefanie a look and hurried to sit between Elvis and Jimmy.

"That, right there, is going to free my brother." Teri gave the board a sharp nod, and I returned to it to write down *Rachel— illegal lot sale.*

"Unfortunately, that doesn't explain how her DNA got in Dash's house," Elvis said.

"Now hold on, we're jumping ahead." I tapped the marker against my lip. "Think about it. We know all about Marilyn being not so nice, but everyone seemed to love Rachel. Why murder her?"

"Because of something she knew? Something she saw that had to do with Marilyn?" Teri leaned closer to the board. "Or maybe because someone didn't want her taking clients away from SunSweet when she left."

Now we were getting somewhere.

"But Marilyn had already died before Rachel did, so maybe she had no idea Rachel was going to leave," Kay said.

"Marilyn had a silent partner," I told them. "Hank Stillwater. The man might or might not have had motive. If she died and he inherited, his motive would be money."

"It's not," Alison said.

We all turned to her.

"How do you know that?" Jimmy asked.

"Because he told me so when I asked."

Chapter Fifteen

"When Hank comes to town, he stays at my B&B." Alison owned A Sweet Retreat, a lovely Victorian bed-and-breakfast on Mocha Drive, a street over from mine. "He's a lovely man, and we occasionally enjoy dinners together when he's in town."

"She's biased," Stefanie grumbled.

Alison flushed. "I am not." She deliberately turned her chair away from Stefanie, and I had to bite back a grin. "I've known Hank for years. He's not perfect, but he's very aboveboard in his business dealings. That's one reason why he and Marilyn sometimes fought, because their ideas about the future of their business kept growing further apart. They were in the midst of breaking up their partnership on this visit. Everything split between them amicably. Hank told me he probably wouldn't be back to Confection for a while, because he's expanding his business in his home state, using the money from his and Marilyn's shared split to finance his new Airbnb venture."

"And he doesn't inherit with her dead?" Teri asked.

"No. From what he told me, Marilyn has a sister with children who will inherit when she passes. He gets nothing since they divorced, and it's been ten years."

"Huh. Well, maybe we can strike Hank off our list." I chewed my lip, thinking. "Any reason he might be upset if Rachel had her own business?" Odd that Natalie had seemed to think Hank would be taking over.

"Not that I can think of," Alison said.

"What about the idea that he still loved Marilyn?"

"As a friend, sure. But there was nothing romantic between them. Hank's been engaged to a nice woman for some time. I met her a year ago, when he brought her with him. She lives in Maine with him, and apparently they're doing very well, financially." She cleared her throat. "Not one to just take someone's word for it"—she speared Stefanie with a glare—"I researched and corroborated what he told me."

"Okay," Stefanie muttered. "So he's not an ax murderer. Still doesn't mean he's a glowing pillar of his community."

"Oh hush, you old bag," Alison snapped.

A bunch of us laughed, and the tension melted away. "Right," I said. "Well, before we keep going, I think maybe we should go around the room and tell everyone what we've learned. I'll go first."

I filled in the group on the illegal sale of Strawberry Fields, on what Natalie had told me about Marilyn's and Rachel's respective characters, and what Cathy had said. As a group, we struck Natalie and Cathy off our suspect list.

Cat then told us what she knew about the evidence against Dash.

"Hold on," Darcy cut in. "So the police think Dash Hagen is stupid enough to not only leave his victim's body out in plain sight in his backyard, but to also hide how she died, *then* leave evidence of how she died in his house?"

"Yeah. Makes no sense," Teri grumbled.

"I'll say." Darcy paused. "Are they sure it's Rachel's blood on the towel?"

Cat nodded. "And the underwear had been worn, but there was, um, no evidence of a sexual encounter."

"Which jibes with what Dash said about seeing her when we did at the Ripe Raisin, where she was drunk and happy about Marilyn being dead." I explained the encounter to the group. "Hold on. Cat, were those panties hers, as in, her body wasn't wearing any?"

"Huh? Oh, no." Cat blushed. "She was wearing underwear under her jeans when they found her. The panties had to have come from her house or from when she and Dash allegedly spent time together at his place before she died."

I frowned. "They had a brief past relationship, but he hadn't been around her since then. And that was months ago. Dash apparently planned to go out with her this weekend." Shoot. I really needed to talk to him. At the police station, I assumed.

"Were they serious before?" Kay asked Teri.

She shrugged. "I don't know. I do know he dated Marilyn over a year ago. So there is a connection between Dash and both women. But he had no reason to kill Marilyn. Not for money or romance or anything."

"Yeah, there's no motive," Cat agreed. "Also, a source told me they didn't find any of Rachel's fingerprints in the house or on the recliner she was lying on, which was really weird. And Dash's prints aren't on the bloody towel or Rachel's underwear. So they're saying he must have worn gloves to handle those items, but they can't find the gloves. None of it makes sense."

"None of it," Teri repeated, her expression grim.

Cat hurried to say, "Anyhow, Teri, what did you learn?"

"Not much." She sighed. "I talked to the DA about all this, and she agreed the evidence of Dash's guilt doesn't make a lot of sense. Everyone knows Dash, and a ton of people knew Rachel. Plus, no one but us thinks Marilyn died of anything but a heart attack. So they're not connecting her at all."

"That's a problem," I said. "Because even though I feel in my bones she was murdered, there's no proof."

"None," Alan said.

Teri nodded to him. "Your turn, Alan. I'm done. Nothing to add except it's killing me that Dash is being accused of murder." Her eyes looked glassy.

Cat patted her back, and Cookie ambled over to put her chin on Teri's knee in support.

"Aw." Alan smiled at Cookie before retelling what he'd learned about Selma's lot. "You know, the more I think about it, the more I think the illegal sale of Strawberry Fields is just a coincidence. Selma did die of natural causes by all accounts."

"Yeah," Darcy agreed. "Strawberry Fields sheds light on some illegal happenings at SunSweet Realty, though. And if you take Dash out of the equation, then you have SunSweet Realty connecting both women who died, not counting Selma. Although technically you could count her too, because it was her lot. But you know what I mean."

Alan cocked his head. "It just makes no sense to kill Rachel. Well, anyway, on to Kay."

Kay sat straighter, excited to share her part. "Well, I, along with Elvis—"

"And Jimmy," Uncle Elvis said, to whom Jimmy gave a wide smile.

"Sorry, Jimmy," Kay apologized. "*And* Jimmy, looked into several members of the chamber of commerce. Ed Mullins is at the top of our list, because he didn't like Marilyn or Rachel. He thought Marilyn was way too full of herself and didn't like Rachel always arguing when they should have focused more on chamber issues. I don't know that Ed would kill over it, though. Now, if you messed with his roses, maybe. But the chamber? He already did his time as chair. He's always been grumpy, but I don't see him killing Rachel over the chamber of commerce."

"I agree." Elvis nodded. "Connie and Tad Oliver, however, are a different story. Connie talked a lot of smack about Marilyn. She hated her, and the feeling was mutual. A few times, Rachel did stand up for her boss and made some slights against Tad for his wandering eye. That didn't go over well with either Tad or Connie. Especially with Marilyn acting all smug."

Jimmy took over. "Then you have Cathy Salter, who frequently disagreed with anything Marilyn proposed, usually just to mess with Marilyn. Let's see. Mimi Van Hosen had an argument with Rachel that got super heated because Rachel had a problem making a festival dog-friendly. Again, nothing to be murdered for, I wouldn't think."

Kay offered, "And don't forget a bunch of the ladies that didn't like Marilyn on principle. Mostly because rumors circulated that she'd sleep with your husband or boyfriend. Sadly, I think there are too many to count."

"That doesn't help." I felt frustrated, mostly because I sensed we were missing something.

"I know." Kay sighed. "Our best angry chamber members are Ed Mullins, Cathy Salter, and Connie Oliver."

"Jimmy and I tried, but we couldn't come up with anyone else," Elvis said by way of apology.

"Hmm." I had nowhere else to go with Kay's group, so I turned to Stefanie and Alison. "What did you guys come up with? Anything interesting with Clint Ayers and Gary Conroy?"

"The moneyman and the builder," Stefanie said with satisfaction. "As a matter of fact, yes."

"Oh?" I asked.

"Gary's out of Bend, where it's super competitive lately with contractors. And Gary's had some not-so-great reviews on Yelp, Angie's List, and with the Better Business Bureau."

"Yeah?" Maybe Gary was what we'd missed.

Stefanie grunted. "Man's a hack. His company does some projects well while leaving others half-assed."

"Stefanie, language," Alison murmured.

"Well, it's the truth. Gary's been trying to do better, by his most recent reviews, but his finances, if we can trust his accountant, aren't the best." Stefanie's eyes twinkled. "I made a call using a burner phone to pretend I worked for him. Yeah, a burner phone." She looked poised to chortle, extremely pleased with herself.

Heaven help us. The Macaroons were using burner phones.

Stefanie kept talking, and I saw out of the corner of my eye my dog making a subtle move toward the food table. I glanced from Elvis to Cookie and saw him try to hide a grin as he rose to make it look like he intended to grab more food. "So my money on Gary being a loser is strong, but not so much that he killed Marilyn or Rachel. Now he and Clint definitely have something going on, because Clint knows this town, and I can't see him using Gary when he could use a better quality of builder."

Alison frowned. "That concerns me too. We all know—"

"I don't know," Cat interrupted. "Who is Clint exactly?"

"Oh, sorry." Alison took a sip of lemonade before continuing. "Clint Ayers is a property investor who owns a lot of real estate in this town. Apparently, he and Marilyn had worked quite a few deals in the past. Clint is part owner in the new boutique hotel on Mint Lane. He owns part of the movie theater and the strip mall on the north side of town."

"That tacky bunch of shops? Meh. They're just chain stores." Stefanie scowled.

"That bring in money," Elvis said. "Not everyone shops downtown at our local places all the time. Some people have a hankering for Jamba Juice and Taco Bell, Stefanie."

"Disgusting."

I happened to know she had a real thing for a particular chain restaurant, so she shouldn't be throwing stones. I shouldn't either, because Stefanie and I had bonded over our love of all-you-can-eat biscuits, chicken fried steak, and those annoying but addicting tabletop peg games, not to mention the vintage candy and knickknacks in the store at the front of our local Cracker Barrel. We really had no room to judge.

"Well, I still don't buy it," Stefanie said. "Rachel used Marilyn's deal to make herself and Clint some real money. Why would he kill her?"

"Because he knows the deal is illegal and she changed her mind about it, maybe?" Teri said.

I shook my head. "That's jumping to conclusions."

"All this is jumping to conclusions." She pointed to the whiteboard, where I'd been taking notes.

Right now, the only suspects we really had were a lot of annoyed women, Ed Mullins, and maybe Clint. Frustrated, I opened my mouth to say, I don't know what but something, when I heard familiar crunching.

I turned around to see Elvis and Cookie sharing crackers and a slice of Stefanie's peanut butter pie. Uh oh.

"You gave her my pie?" Stefanie thundered. "That's for people!"

"But it's delicious," Elvis mumbled, his mouth full as he and my dog chowed down. Cookie looked extremely pleased with herself and her enabler. My uncle tried but couldn't help laughing at Stefanie, who looked ready to combust.

"There, there." Alison put an arm around her. "It's a compliment, really. Cookie loves your food."

"She should. It's delicious." Stefanie glared at the food thieves, and we raided the table once more, our stomachs hungry since our brains were starving for clues.

We broke up shortly afterward, and Cookie did her best to keep me between her and Stefanie.

Jimmy gave me a kiss goodbye, planning to meet Collin for a late-night soda at the local arcade. Of course, he didn't stop with me, giving Teri and Cat hugs as well, saving a special smooch for his husband.

Elvis decided to walk the rest of us home, and we parted ways with Teri and Cat at Peppermint Way. "Great meeting," he said.

"I don't know. I feel like we know less now than we did before."

"Not true. We learned an awful lot. We just have to keep going at it."

"I was going to attend the chamber meeting tomorrow night, but now I'm not sure if it's worth it."

"Go, if for no other reason than to see the dynamic there. Something might come to you." He stopped me in front of my house and put his hands on my shoulders. "Lexi, saving Dash isn't your burden. You're a good friend for trying though."

I felt silly for tearing up. "No, I'm selfish. I just like solving mysteries." I sniffed. "But it feels so much more important this time.

"More important than last time, when you had to clear your own name?"

"Yeah. I don't know why, but I feel like we can't fail or Dash is going to suffer."

Uncle Elvis gave me a hug, and Cookie whined, shoving her furry face between us to be included. "Don't worry. Dash is a strong guy. He'll hold his own until the truth comes out. Believe in that."

"I will." I kissed my uncle on the cheek and stepped back. "I'm tired."

"It's been a long day." Elvis sighed. "Get some sleep."

"Thanks. And thanks for watching the shop for me."

"Anytime." He smiled, waved, and walked away.

"Come on, Cookie. We need a break."

She gave a soft woof. So we went inside, watched TV, then fell asleep.

But the next morning, I had one major thing on my agenda.

A meeting with Dash in jail.

Chapter Sixteen

I had to leave Cookie with Cat at the bookshop and explain, *several times,* to my pouting pooch that she couldn't accompany me. "No, they don't allow dogs in jail. I'm not kidding," I told her, because the dog refused to believe me. She whined. "I know you miss Dash. We'll get him out soon." Or maybe he'd get out at his bail hearing, which his attorney had pushed for him to get, since he was currently being held without bail. I had no idea how these things worked.

Cookie glared at me before stomping away, all the while grumbling under her breath.

"Wow, she holds grudges," Cat said with wide eyes.

"Only until I leave. She'll be happy to see me when I get back." Because Cookie was a dog, and dogs enjoyed life to the fullest, always living in the moment. Bad moods never lasted, because life was too great to waste. I needed to be more like my dog.

She shot me another look before darting under the front register to curl in her dog bed with Mr. Leggy.

Huh. There was a thought. I should find my own Mr. Leggy.

For some reason the thought of Mt. Bachelor and his long legs came to mind. Envisioning him all in pink made me laugh.

"Um, you okay?" Cat handed me a tall coffee. "Here. You look like you need this."

"I really do. Thanks." I took a large sip and sighed. "Now that's good." I glanced at the small glass bakery display case filled with muffins, scones, and cookies and smiled. "That looks amazing." I looked right at her. "They just look so . . . moist."

She smacked me on the arm. "Idiot."

I snickered, in a much better mood than I'd been last night, despite my intended destination. I carried my phone and a small notebook and pen. I had my license—for identification purposes—and a credit card in the back pocket of my shorts.

I left through the back of the store and made my way to Court Street by way of Cinnamon Avenue. But instead of turning south, toward my home, I went north, toward the courthouse, which was attached to our police station.

We're a small town, so we only have a dozen or so members in law enforcement, and the ones we're used to seeing are our community service/parking enforcement officer and Roger, who did a lot of community outreach while patrolling town. I tended to ignore his partner, the obnoxious Officer Brown, when I saw him. But Roger, now dating Cat, had always been more than friendly.

And then there was Berg, our lone detective. Transferred from Portland, he'd supposedly come to town to be near family, since his aunt and his cousin, Noah—Dash's partner at the Ripe Raisin—lived here.

I didn't know if I'd run into Berg at the station or not, but I'd mentally prepared myself. I had every right to see Dash, a friend, and to talk to him. I wasn't interfering in any kind of investigation by supporting my innocent pal. Nope. Not at all.

I took deep breaths to calm myself as I reached the courthouse and smiled at the guard by the front desk.

"Hi there." The older man wore a security guard uniform and had a wide smile. "Courthouse or police station?"

"Um, I'm here to visit a friend in the jail?" The last time I'd been to the station, Berg had driven me and taken me through the east side door. But coming on my own, I decided to use the main entrance at the front.

"Ah, station it is." He nodded to the small basket near a conveyor belt that led to one of those scanner things they had at the airport. "Please put any metal or electronic devices in here, in addition to anything you're carrying."

I put my stuff in and waited.

"Now walk through there."

The metal detector looked pretty shiny. "Wow, is that new?"

The older man grinned. "Sure is. It'll see if you have any weapons, which we can't allow. It's not an X-ray machine or anything, so don't worry."

"Right." I stepped through. After a minute, the basket containing my things came out as well, and I picked up my phone.

"Turn right at the wall, and follow the arrow."

"Thank you." I followed the arrow, pleased at clear directions. Before I knew it, I was standing at the main counter of the police station. Beyond the clerk in front of me, I saw a few administrative folks and a few officers. But no detective.

I wasn't sure if I felt relieved or disappointed.

Like the guard, the clerk had a nice smile as he asked what he could do to help.

"Um, I need to visit my friend, Dash Hagen. I think he's here in jail."

The clerk didn't lose his smile. "No problem. I'll have an officer take you to him."

The guy didn't need to look through files or search out the exact cell, which told me our town wasn't reeling from a crime wave.

"Is he the only person in jail?"

"Nope. We have a disorderly and a flasher, but that's about it. He's in his own cell, though."

"A flasher?" Huh, I hadn't read about that one in the paper.

The clerk leaned closer. "Actually, it was a drunk who was caught peeing in the bushes. But the elderly lady who saw him wanted him charged since she nearly fainted at the sight of him." He grinned. "The drunk guy had just turned twenty-one and is supposedly grounded for life, according to his mom. But he'll likely be let off with a warning after he sobers up."

"Wow. Bummer of a birthday."

"No kidding. So, can I see your ID, please?"

I gave him my license, waited for him to write it down in a log, then took it back.

"Thank you. Hold on a second." He picked up his phone and called someone, and I was relieved to not hear Officer Brown's name mentioned. "Officer Nicholson will take you back."

"Thank you."

"You're welcome."

"Hey, is it okay for me to take all this with me when I see him?"

"Officer Nicholson will likely take the phone and the pen."

"Bummer. But okay."

The peppy clerk and cheery attitude made me feel better for some reason. No one here seemed out to put folks in jail or ruin lives. They were doing their jobs and keeping the town safe.

So different from life in a big city. The police there wanted the same, but so many people to deal with made everything impersonal. The one time I'd helped a friend who'd had her purse stolen, the experience had been cold and sad, dealing with a tired cop and frustrated friend who never did recoup her losses.

"Lexi Jones?" The officer looked to be around my uncles' age, with honest eyes and a professional bearing. He wore his dark blue uniform well, in shape and light in step.

"Yes, that's me."

"You're Elvis's niece."

"You know Uncle Elvis?"

The man smiled. "He's a character, all right."

I realized this was the police officer who'd given Elvis a few details about the search on Dash's house I wasn't supposed to know about. I liked him for that alone. "He sure is. He just joined Sweet Fiction's book club and is having us read comics as his choice for reading material."

Officer Nicholson laughed. "Sounds like fun."

We made small talk as we wound around a few corners and ended up in the back of the building. We passed a small office in the middle of the wide corridor. It had glass windows and was currently unoccupied. Past that, we came to a T junction and made a right.

"How many jail cells are there?" I asked, more than curious. The building had been converted from a homestead seventy years ago.

"Five on the men's side, and two on the women's over there." He pointed behind us, at the other end of the T. "Here, we have three solitary cells and two large ones for those who commit the typical misdemeanor."

"Typical?"

"Assaults, usually from bar fights. Public drunkenness. The occasional bike theft. Your garden variety crime."

"Ah, got it."

We walked past a large cell that had two people, one a young man snoring on a bench. The drunk guy, I'd bet. The other an older man lying on the ground, staring at the ceiling. Then three empty cells until we came to the final cell, where the hallway ended at a barred window that had been opened to allow a breeze. The window was too high on the wall and way too small to allow anyone to pass through. But that it was there at all made me feel better.

"Wow, low crime."

He cringed. "Please don't. You'll jinx us."

"Oh, sorry."

"Nah. We typically fill up on the weekends. What with the festival season over, we're thinning out, as we always do. Well, here's your guy. I'll be in the office you passed. If you need anything, just press the intercom and I'll be here." He motioned me to the intercom on the wall. "I'm sorry, but I need to take your things with me."

"Here you go." There went my note-taking. I'd have to commit Dash's answers to memory.

Officer Nicholson turned and left, and I finally looked at the person sitting on his bunk, leafing through a magazine. Dash looked just fine. Annoyed but clean, his hair combed, wearing shorts and a T-shirt. The bunk had a mattress, a blanket, and a pillow. A stainless toilet sat at the far corner of the cell, in addition to a pedestal sink but no mirror.

The pale blue walls behind him in addition to the sunlight streaming through a small square window next to me, the window ajar to let in a fresh breeze through the bars, made the area feel less oppressive.

"Huh. A window right next to your cell."

"That's to tempt you with what you can't have," Dash said, his voice gravelly. He smiled at me. "Nice to see you."

"I thought, you know, since it's Friday and all, I'd go slumming."

He laughed.

"You seem better than I'd thought you'd be."

He stood and stretched. "Because I know this nightmare will end with me free and clear and the criminals framing me behind bars."

"Well, good. Because I have a few questions for you."

"Oh boy."

"Yeah. Well, we've been doing some digging." I looked around, and seeing no one, sat cross-legged in front of the bars. Dash sat as well, and I lowered my voice, filling him in on everything we knew.

"You guys have been busy." He seemed to approve. "Now what can I tell you?"

"First, I need to know about you and Marilyn. Your relationship. Not too many details." I blushed. "But a feel for her would help. Same with Rachel."

"Shoot. Fine. Whatever." He ran a hand over his jaw, and I noticed the stubble that made him look even more attractive. Dash noticed me noticing and frowned. "What? I'm in jail. No shaving for a while."

"Right." I cleared my throat. "So, how did you meet Marilyn? Start there."

"Marilyn used to come into the Ripe Raisin quite a bit. Sometimes with clients, other times with dates."

"I thought she was taking medicine for her heart." And wasn't alcohol contraindicated for heart medication?

"I think she was. I don't remember her ever getting sloppy drunk. She might have ordered nonalcoholic drinks.

I don't know. I do know we shared wine now and again. But never much."

"Okay."

"The relationship, such as it was, was over pretty quick. She came in, flirted, we hooked up." He shrugged. "I liked her a lot. But we both knew it wasn't going anywhere. She always had work to do. I get it, I mean, running the Ripe Raisin is a full-time job, even having Noah as a partner. But I love it."

"You're good at it."

"Thanks." He smiled. "Anyway, I don't know what else to tell you."

"Did you know Hank Stillwater?"

"Her ex?" He shrugged. "I knew of him from what she'd said. They still worked together on a number of projects. She thought he was smart and dedicated but naive. I got the feeling Marilyn didn't always color in the lines when it came to the letter of the law, if you know what I mean."

"I'm coming to understand that. So, um, this might be kind of personal"—I talked over his groan—"But was everything you guys did in bed, um, normal?"

"Huh?"

My cheeks felt hot, but I needed to know. "Did she have any weird fetishes that might have been dangerous? Like, maybe a lover hurt her accidentally and caused her to have a heart attack?"

"Nah. Marilyn was fun and a little naughty. Nothing dangerous about her . . . proclivities."

"I'm more surprised you know a big word like 'proclivities' than that you're sharing details with me."

"Details?" He chuckled. "That's nothing. Now if you want details, I can tell you—"

"How did you get involved with Rachel?" I interrupted, not letting him get started on that track.

"Ah, now Rachel was a real sweetheart. After Marilyn and I stopped dating, Rachel came into the bar one night and asked me out. She's—she *was*—beautiful and sweet. We hit it off. But like Marilyn, she was super competitive. I kind of wondered if she slept with me to get back at Marilyn in some way."

"Did she?"

"I don't know. I didn't trust the feeling I had, so we called it off. She didn't mind, and it didn't bother me either. We parted as friends. And before you ask, no, she didn't have any weird fantasies she wanted to play out in bed either." He paused. "Wow, your face is really red right now."

"Shut up."

He chuckled. "I hadn't hung out with Rachel in close to a year. Then she got drunk the other night, and we got to talking. If the world hadn't turned inside-out, I'd be going on a date with her tomorrow night, not wondering if I should attend her funeral." He gripped the bars in front of him. "Damn, Lexi. People think I murdered her."

"People who know you don't think that." I put my fingers over his, and the contact seemed to settle him. "Now think, Dash. Tell me about going home the night Rachel died. This past Monday night."

He sat back and rubbed his face. "Okay, Monday night. We had a steady crowd. Mike was once again arguing with Sherry on the phone, so I had to remind him to keep his private life private."

"Business as usual." I shook my head, annoyed with Mike all over again.

"Yeah. We had plenty of regulars mixed with tourists. Every-thing seemed pretty normal. I closed up with Noah, we shared a drink, then I went home. I did look out at the backyard on my way to bed and thought it was a pretty night, the moon shining down before the clouds covered it. I could see the backyard, and Rachel wasn't there when I went to bed. I swear."

"I believe you." He'd told me all this before, and his story remained the same.

"I woke up the next morning to Roger pounding on my door, and I was confused as hell. He went through the house, straight through to the backyard. I followed and had the shock of my life to see Rachel there. When he took her pulse and said Rachel was dead, I was floored. Lexi, she looked like she was sleeping." Dash swallowed. "She was gone. And she was so young. It's terrible."

I saw his eyes shine, knew he felt awful, and commiserated. "Her sister and brother-in-law are going to have her buried next week. I'm not sure about a viewing."

"They won't want me there. That's if I can get out on bail. I'm being charged with *murder*."

"How did they find that evidence in your house?"

"I have no idea." He scowled. "Why kill her and leave her in my backyard to be found? I have no motive for killing her. And how did I murder her but leave none of her DNA in my house? None of *my* DNA on the bloody towel? Why make her look like she was sleeping when she was dead? None of it makes sense."

"Unless she was killed elsewhere and dumped in your yard. Then someone planted evidence while you were sleeping."

"I don't know." He paused. "But if they knew about my hide-a-key, under that fake rock . . . No. Hardly anyone knows it's there."

"Who knows?"

"Teri, Cat, you. Noah. My parents. Your uncle." At my look, he explained, "I had Elvis do some work for me a few months ago. But that's it."

"Oh. Could someone have overheard you talking about your hide-a-key?" I wondered.

"I guess. I don't know." He sounded tired. "And then the other thing. The roses."

"What about roses?"

"When Berg was questioning me, he kept asking me about the rose petals on Rachel. And the dark compost on her shoes. But Lexi, I don't have roses in my back or front yard, certainly no compost. I don't have time for gardening. Heck, I haven't even bought flowers for a woman since I gave them to my mom for Mother's Day."

Now that was a new clue. And something about it stirred a connection I was close to making. "Roses, huh?"

"Rose petals." Dash looked confused. "They also say she was bashed in the back of the head, the same blood that dripped through the recliner to the ground. Yet no blood on her clothes or the front of her head. Obviously wiped away. Which is just stupid. If I killed her, why wipe away any evidence of blood from her body?"

"That doesn't make any sense, no," said Detective Berg from behind me, and I gave a little shriek in surprise. "Sorry to cut your visit short, but Lexi, can I talk to you?"

Uh-oh. His expression might be blank, but Berg's clenched fist told another story.

"Stay strong, Dash. We'll get you out of here soon."

"Thanks." He put his hand through the bars to squeeze mine, then moved back to sit on his bunk again.

I followed Berg out to the office Officer Nicholson had been using but had now vacated.

Berg shut the door behind him and leaned back against the wall, his arms crossed over his chest in what I termed his aggressive pose.

We watched each other in silence, the tension building.

Then he growled, "What did I tell you?"

"Give me a break! My friend is in jail because someone is setting him up, and what are you doing about it?"

"Gathering evidence," he said through his teeth.

Well so am I! would be a stupid thing to say so close to a jail cell and a seething detective. "I'm not interfering in anything. Asking my friend questions to help figure out who might be setting him up is not hurting your investigation, is it?"

"Well?"

"Well what?" I snapped back and narrowed my eyes on the sudden curl of his lips. "Are you laughing at me?"

"What? No." He stood up straighter and cleared his throat. "Do you know of anyone with a grudge against Dash?"

"No. I don't. Unlike Marilyn, Dash doesn't sleep with other guys' girlfriends or wives. He's a standup guy. And he's *not* my boyfriend," I said before Berg could somehow insert an intimate connection into our dialogue. "He's Teri's brother, and she's my best friend. Dash is therefore also my friend." I studied Berg, wondering at his sudden lack of hostility. "You know he's not guilty," I blurted, realizing the truth. "You know he's been set up."

Oh my gosh. Berg might just turn out to be an ally. And didn't that just beat all?

Chapter Seventeen

"I'm not stupid. Of course I know that," Berg shocked me with his admission. "But I can't prove it. Not yet. Hagen is an annoying, entitled scion of Confection. His parents are beloved, his sister's got a glowing reputation with the DA's office, and everyone in town spends evenings at the Ripe Raisin. I can't find anyone who *doesn't* like the guy, especially many of the ladies in town." He eyeballed me, his focus a little unnerving. "So why put a dead body in his yard? Why blame him for her death?"

"That's a great question. I considered that Dash might be the one person connecting the murders."

"Murder, singular," Berg insisted. "Get it out of your head that Marilyn Freeman was killed. She had a heart attack."

"So you think." I was sticking to my guns. "We've got shady real estate dealings, a troubled chamber of commerce, and angry women all over the place. Everyone and their mother had a reason to want Marilyn dead. But who might want Rachel dead?" Before Berg could ask any questions, I plowed on. "And what's this about rose petals being found on her body? And dirt on her shoes?"

"That's confidential information."

"Oh, give it a rest! Dash already told me. And you know what? If I had a few brain cells, I might put them together and think that Rachel had been killed somewhere else. Near roses and loose dirt. And then she was dragged to Dash's yard and put there. Where someone who knew where he kept his hide-a-key used it to enter his house and plant false evidence. You have none of his DNA on the bloody towel or her underwear. None of his DNA anywhere on her body either. Does that make sense?" My voice had risen.

So when I stopped speaking, the office grew oppressively quiet.

He just stared at me. "You're a real firecracker, you know that?"

I growled at him.

He grinned at me. "You remind me of Cookie."

"I swear, if I was a dog, at this moment I'd bite you."

He had the nerve to laugh. A startled Office Nicholson stood outside the door to the office and stared at us. He opened the door. "Uh, Detective?"

"What's up, Nicholson?"

"We got the M.E.'s report on Rachel Nevis." He glanced from Berg to me.

Berg looked at me and sighed, long and loud. "Go ahead. Tell me."

"Well, seems as though she was poisoned. It wasn't the bashed head that did her in after all. It was an overdose."

Berg and I both straightened and stared at Nicholson.

"An overdose of what?" I asked.

"Ketamine," Officer Nicholson said. "Enough to put down a horse."

Berg frowned. "We had problems with Special K in Portland, but I'm not aware of any major pushers in Confection and the surrounding areas. Not that you can't have those problems on a smaller scale."

"What?" I was confused.

"Special K is a known recreational drug, common to partiers and those wanting to get high. Damn. Nicholson, tell the lieutenant we need an autopsy on Marilyn Freeman."

I wanted to pump my fist in victory but didn't think that appropriate just now.

"Why's that, Detective?" Nicholson asked. "I'll tell the LT, but I'm curious."

"Because ketamine can cause an increase in blood pressure, leading to heart problems."

Nicholson nodded, his eyes widening, and took off.

Berg and I stared at each other.

"Marilyn's been dead for a week," I said. "Do you think the ketamine will still be in her system?"

"Probably not, but we need to check. And we'll run tox screens for anything else that might have been used to kill her, because yeah, I think she might have been the first."

"I told you."

He pinched the bridge of his nose. "This might surprise you, but I have thoughts about things I don't always share with others. *Especially* civilians."

My blood was pumping. "This is the link, right? Marilyn and Rachel. Dash. SunSweet Realty." I could feel it just beyond my reach. "And the roses. Why roses?"

I squeaked as Berg lifted me off my feet to look into my eyes. *Man,* was he strong.

"Okay, Lexi Jones. This is where we have a come-back-to-reality moment."

I just hung there, off my toes, blinking at him in shock.

He gently set me down but kept his hands on my shoulders. "I truly appreciate all your effort to help your friend. You know I want nothing but the truth. We—the police—have been doing our own investigating. Into SunSweet Realty, into Salter Realty, into the men Marilyn had affairs with. All of it. No, I don't think Hagen is guilty, but now I have evidence to point me in another direction. Hopefully not back in *his* direction," he muttered, still staring at me. "Let me do my job," he said more gently and gripped my shoulders before letting go. Then he shocked me by tucking a finger under my chin to close my mouth. "You're cute when you're speechless." He opened the door and nudged me through. "Doesn't happen often, does it?"

"I . . . you . . . I just . . ." I had a tough time getting my thoughts together while he chuckled, walking behind me and herding me toward the exit. A lot like the way Cookie herded me toward her favorite dog treats when she wanted a snack.

After Berg dumped my belongings in my hands, he ignored my resistance and gently shoved me out the back door of the station. "Now, go back to work or go home. Somewhere that's not here."

I stopped him from closing the door. "That note I found."

"What about it?"

"I . . . don't know. But I think it means something."

"When you find out, let me know."

My second huge shock of the day. Berg wasn't treating me like I knew nothing, but actively encouraging me to share information. Not knowing what to do with my weird feelings, I left, walking back to work and trying to plan what to do with what I'd learned.

But I couldn't stop thinking about how nice it had felt to be held by those huge hands.

Off the frigging ground!

* * *

Naturally, as soon as I got a spare moment to share what had happened with Berg, I told Cat. Cookie listened as well, enrapt under the counter while she gnawed on the bone I'd gotten her for the Macaroons meeting.

Cat's eyes grew huge. "Are you kidding me?"

"Shh."

A few customers stared at us before going back to browsing.

"Poisoned by ketamine?" Cat whispered. "What the heck is ketamine?"

"A drug. I need to look it up."

Cat waved at the laptop. "I'll wait."

I returned with interesting information. "Apparently, it's used in medical settings as an analgesic, to dull pain, and as an illegal recreational drug. Berg called it Special K. It's also known as Vitamin K, purple, jet, and horse tranquilizer. And a few other names too."

"Weird. So people take it to get loopy? Maybe Marilyn or Rachel was on it to get high."

I hadn't thought of that. "So what? Rachel got high and overdosed? And whoever she was with then bashed her head in to make it look like she died of a murder? Then dumped her at Dash's after wiping her head clean?"

"Well, when you put it like that, you just sound stupid."

I glared at her.

"What? You did."

"But Cat, I learned something else."

"What?"

"That ketamine doesn't stay in your system that long, and finding it would depend on how much she weighed and how large a dose was used. Marilyn's dead, so I'm not sure if they'll be able to trace it, but at least they know what to look for." I was holding out hope that Berg would continue to play nice and actually let me know if they found anything.

"You know what else is super weird?" Cat asked.

"The rose petals? The dirt?"

"That Berg let the officer tell him about the ketamine in front of you." Cat's eyes narrowed. "And tell me again about him holding you up. Off your feet?" At my nod, she grinned. "That's impressive. How much does he deadlift? Do you know?"

"Oh my gosh. Get your head out of the gym for a minute." I popped her in the back of the head.

She laughed.

I wanted to say more but had a customer, so I left her to wait on the man with a book about Ancient Rome.

The pace picked up, and I didn't get a chance to talk to Cat about Dash or the case again because we got super busy and had to take alternating lunches. But I didn't mind. I had yet to wrap my mind around Chad Berg, and those rose petals bothered the heck out of me. What did it all mean?

My phone pinged, and I glanced down at Uncle Jimmy's text: *Will swing by 2 get u after u close. CoC mtg at 630.* Goofy face emoji. *C u then.*

I guess I had work to do tonight, studying the many faces of the chamber of commerce—the CoC.

Uncle Elvis had agreed to watch Cookie for me because Ed Mullins would never allow my dog to come to a meeting. As I wasn't officially a member of the CoC to begin with, I didn't want to push my luck. But as an interested potential member, he'd likely let me stay—at least, my uncle thought so.

Elvis appeared at a little before closing to get Cookie, who didn't give me a backward glance as she danced over to my uncle and licked wherever she could reach until he not-so-subtly got her to remain still with a jerky treat. He told her to grab any toys she wanted to bring. Cookie walked right by me, grabbed Mr. Leggy, and rose up on her hind legs to lick my hand before leaving.

Elvis fixed the leash to her collar, blew me a kiss, and took her away.

Traitors, the both of them.

I rode on the back of Uncle Jimmy's Harley, hugging his waist as we drove north along Church Street. The chamber used to regularly meet twice a month in the library basement, which had been converted into a large meeting space. But since Marilyn had been in charge, they'd been holding it at a fancy meeting hall in an upscale development out past my parents' house. Marilyn owned a percentage of the property and always made sure it was catered with delicious food.

Apparently, Ed had no designs to change up a good thing. But who would be paying for the party—I mean, meeting—with Marilyn dead?

I asked my uncle, who after parking his hog, told me, "Oh, Marilyn had funds set up for the year. It's not her money paying for it, but membership fees and donations from members forking the bill. Though we do get the place rent-free because she's part owner."

"Wow. They have a nice pool." Being used by many older people, I noticed. I didn't see many children. Make that, *any* children.

"It's an age-up alternative living environment." Jimmy huffed. "Marilyn had fancy names for 'privileged rich old people community.'"

One such older patron frowned at Jimmy.

My uncle ignored him, looking like a tough guy in a leather vest, white tee, and jeans with biker boots. The tattoos on his forearms and biceps also made a statement. *Mess with me at your peril.*

"You weren't really in a biker gang when you were in your early twenties, were you?" I asked him, familiar with my dad's stories.

Uncle Jimmy grinned. "Your dad was afraid of me."

"Really? Because he likes to tell the story of when he kicked your butt in front of your gang and they invited him to join up. But my mom wouldn't let him."

Jimmy laughed and laughed, which wasn't exactly an answer.

We entered the clubroom and saw a lot of familiar faces.

"A lot more people tonight than we usually have. Probably here to see what's up with Marilyn and Rachel dead."

"Probably," I agreed.

I saw the Danverses, one of the couples in the CGC mafia I actually liked, who owned the flower store down the street from Sweet Fiction. Pastor Nestor and his wife, Ed Mullins—holding court like a king—Connie and Tad Oliver, Cathy Salter, Nadine (ugh), Mimi of the golden doodle, Noah, Didi, who owned a B&B in town, Mel, and a bunch of other people.

As I studied the group, I noticed members congregating in groups according to their businesses. Foodies with foodies, clothiers to the left, entertainment businesses to the right. While Uncle Jimmy left me to grab some food off a side table and chatted up the owner of Filler Up, our local independent gas station,

I spotted Noah, Dash's partner, standing by a tray of cupcakes and joined him.

"Hey, Noah."

Noah, who had been concentrating on the cupcakes, started when I spoke, then smiled down at me and gave me a hug. "Hey, short stuff."

"Not you too."

He laughed. "How are you doing?"

"I'm okay. How are you?"

His smile faded. "Stressed, to be honest." He added in a low voice, "We all know Dash didn't kill anyone. But I can't say it's hurt sales. We've been busier than ever since he got arrested, which is just weird."

"Heard anything strange that might help his case?"

"No, but I did notice something that bugged me. I—"

"We're calling this meeting to order," Ed boomed. "There'll be time to chat after we're done. Now please, take your seats."

Freaking Ed! I nodded to Noah. "Hold that thought. Don't leave before I talk to you."

"Will do." He saw his mom waving to him and joined her and Nadine, who glared my way.

I glared back, then sat next to Uncle Jimmy and Mel. At a glance, I'd say there had to be close to fifty people in attendance. My uncle had once told me that the CoC was a terrific place to talk about fishing with his friends, and oh yeah, to give back to the town and help businesses prosper. Tonight, all anyone could talk about was Marilyn, Rachel, and what to do with the chamber.

Ed invoked a moment of silence for the past chairperson and fellow member.

I thought that was a nice thing to do.

Then he ended it with a reading of William Butler Yeats's poem "The Rose Tree":

'O words are lightly spoken,'
Said Pearse to Connolly,
'Maybe a breath of politic words
Has withered our Rose Tree;
Or maybe but a wind that blows
Across the bitter sea.'

'It needs to be but watered,'
James Connolly replied,
'To make the green come out again
And spread on every side,
And shake the blossom from the bud
To be the garden's pride.'

'But where can we draw water,'
Said Pearse to Connolly,
'When all the wells are parched away?
O plain as plain can be
There's nothing but our own red blood
Can make a right Rose Tree.'

After a pregnant pause, Ed said, "I wanted something nice for Marilyn and Rachel. They loved roses, and that's my true love, after all. Nothing but our hard work and dedication to their memory and service can make right what happened to them. I think we should hold them in our hearts."

I stared in awe at Ed "Grumpmaster" Mullins, never having expected that kind of depth from the man who had literally yelled at me to get off his lawn.

But he'd mentioned roses. How interesting.

The meeting continued, dragging on as they made plans to elect a new chairperson. The secretary read minutes from their last meeting. The treasurer read her report. And blah blah blah, they finally got to the meat of the meeting, the annual Confection Owl Hoot that would come just in time for Halloween.

I loved the Owl Hoot. We had a festival—surprise—to celebrate the spooky season, with a hay maze, pumpkin decorating, pony rides, a pumpkin pie contest, and food and craft booths. Since Halloween was my favorite holiday, I listened with rapt attention to the details.

And found out why Jimmy and Elvis sometimes found the CoC meeting so entertaining.

Dr. Ryan and Dr. Thomas, a handsome older medical doctor, wanted to dedicate the festival to Marilyn. Cathy, Connie, and Ed immediately poo-poo'd that idea, calling it insensitive.

"How is that insensitive?" Dr. Thomas looked down his nose at everyone, despite being just a few inches taller than me. "The woman was an important part of the community and the heart of—"

"Oh my God, do not say the heart of Confection," Cathy said with a lot of tone. "She might have been close to *some* members." She gave him a dismissive once-over that had him scowling. "Like half the men in this room, but she was no better or worse than the rest of us. I don't hear you wanting to dedicate the festival to Rachel."

Dr. Thomas blustered, "Well, maybe we should. Rachel was well-liked." The look he shot Cathy told me that clearly, in his opinion, *she* wasn't.

"Nope." Ed shook his head. "This festival is for the town of Confection. Not any one of us."

Mimi Van Hoven, dog mom to Cookie's good buddy, Sherman the golden doodle, huffed. "You can bet your bottom that if anyone from the CGC had died, Ed would be wanting to name a rose and town festival after *them*."

So, not an Ed fan.

Ed responded, "You know, Mimi, maybe if you spent more time with people and less with animals, you'd see we're trying to grow the town with goodwill. Stepping through dog crap while eating pumpkin pie won't help."

"Dog crap?" Mimi stood in a rage, her eyes shooting daggers through her funky glasses. "My dog doesn't crap in the street! He's a pure breed."

Okay, now *I* took offense to that. Cookie had a mixed heritage that had turned out the perfect dog. Well, not perfect, but nearly there.

"He's a mutt," Ed shouted back. "And he nearly dug up the Confection Rose two days ago!"

Taco Ted, one of my favorite entrepreneurs who made the absolute best fish tacos, chimed in with, "Actually, Ed, I think that was the mayor's pooch." He turned to Foot and shrugged. "Sorry, my man, but the truth will out."

Mayor Anthony "Foot" Russel stood. "Slander!"

"You mean libel?" Noah's mom asked. She owned Honey Threads, the cute clothing boutique on Main. "I always get those confused."

Paul Abbott, a lawyer and a friend of a friend of Alison's, shook his head. "No, libel is when you defame someone in writing. Slander is when you defame them through oral communication."

Noah's mom scratched her cheek. "You sure about that, Paul? Isn't your area of expertise estate law?"

"Yes, but I once defended a friend in a defamation suit. He had no money and I was the best he could do." Paul shrugged.

"I'll sue you for slander!" Foot tried again, pointing at Taco Ted. "Muffy is not a killer!"

I blinked. "Wait. Your dog's name is Muffy?"

Foot flushed. "Maddie named him." His wife.

"She's a Doberman named *Muffy?*" I couldn't help laughing. "Then why do you call her Duke?"

Several people around us laughed.

"That's why," Foot muttered and sat back down.

Mimi sniffed. "Vindication."

Paul grinned. "Truth is the best defense."

"See?" Jimmy murmured and wolfed down gourmet popcorn, watching everything. "Isn't this fun?"

Chapter Eighteen

Finally, the meeting seemed to be winding down. Ed asked for any new business at the end, which no one—*thank God*—had. Though the meeting ended, people made no move to leave; instead, they grouped up again as they laughed and argued and laughed some more.

Hmm. Maybe I should start attending these things. This was a lot more interesting than I'd thought it might be.

I wandered closer to Connie, deep in conversation with Cathy, Peggy, and Nadine. I heard a few mentions of *that witch* and *that whore* and steered clear, not wanting to get in Peggy or Nadine's way. Apart, I could handle them. Together, I wasn't sure.

To the left of them, Dr. Ryan and Dr. Thomas were talking with Tad and Noah, so I couldn't ask about what Noah had left unsaid, which was *killing me* with curiosity. What had Noah seen that had bugged him? Something that might help Dash?

Jimmy rejoined me, this time eating from a small plate of mini quiches, crab puffs, and deviled eggs. "What?" he asked, seeing my attention. "I'm a growing boy."

I snorted. "Is it always like this?"

"Nope. It's usually a lot quieter, but with the murders and Ed getting bossy, it's livened up quite a bit. Helps that more folks showed tonight." He nodded to the group of men I was studying. "Interesting gathering there. I'd bet you ten to one they all slept with Marilyn and/or Rachel."

"What? Really?" I tried to look like I wasn't staring. "Even Dr. Ryan?"

"I know. Sad." Jimmy sighed. "All those looks and brains and he went for a vindictive blond and her sidekick."

I turned to Uncle Jimmy. "*And* her sidekick? You mean he slept with Marilyn *and* Rachel?"

"Yep. His brief fling with Marilyn was no secret, but I saw Rachel and him kissing early one morning outside her house. Oh, probably back in November last year. Elvis had done some work there and needed me to drop off some supplies. Caught an eyeful, I can tell you."

"Interesting." I studied the men, bummed about Dr. Ryan, because, well, it made me like him a little less. Was he into casual affairs or something more serious? And why did I care? "What do you know about Dr. Thomas?"

"That he's very much married, and his wife very much loathed Marilyn."

"Ah."

"He totally would have divorced his wife for Marilyn. In a heartbeat. But Marilyn only had boy*toys*, not boy*friends*."

"Not what I heard."

"I can't think who she might have been serious with." We continued to surreptitiously watch the group of Marilyn-lovers when Jimmy said, "Tad was just bumping uglies with her to annoy Connie. She was getting clingy and then had the nerve to invite her mother to stay with them last summer. He was beyond angry. He hates her mom."

"He told you this?"

Uncle Jimmy nodded. "You hear all sorts of stuff at the hardware store. It's better than a barber shop."

"I'll take your word for it."

He grinned. "Not as good as a bar though." He nodded at Noah. "Now Noah and Marilyn, I'm thinking not. But he did have a brief relationship with Rachel."

"He did? Why didn't you mention that at our meeting?"

"We never did go into all of Rachel's exes, did we?" He shrugged his thick shoulders. "Not like I kept my nose in Rachel's business or anything. I just know what I saw one night at the Ripe Raisin—the pair of them giving each other mouth to mouth before darting down the hallway of the bar." He watched me and quirked a grin. "They disappeared into a closet and didn't come out for a good ten minutes. I know that because Elvis bet they'd be gone longer. I won."

I just stared at him. "No way."

"Yep. Confection's got a seamy side to it. Shocking, eh?" He laughed. "I love this town."

Trust Jimmy to be enamored with sex and gossip. And trust me to love that he was. "I need to talk to Noah."

Just then, my phone vibrated. I glanced down and read a message from a number I didn't recognize: *Gotta run to Raisin. Emergency. Meet there 2 talk.*

I glanced up and saw Noah racing out the door. "Shoot. Well, Uncle Jimmy, it's been a hoot."

"Ha. The Owl Hoot. I see what you did there." He nodded to me. "Nicely worded."

"Thanks. But I need to get to the Ripe Raisin to talk to Noah."

"Sure thing, niece. Just let me finish up some appetizers and we'll head back." He wandered back to the food table and started chatting with the Danverses and Pastor Nestor.

I glanced around, needing to keep my distance from the pastor's wife, who hated me. And Nadine, who didn't like me. And well, there was Cathy raising a toast to me. She didn't hate me, I didn't think. But Connie spotted me and narrowed her eyes, said something to Nadine, and smiled.

It was as if someone had just walked over my grave . . .

"So, you're Lexi Jones."

I turned to see Noah's mom staring down at me. Like Noah, she had height and good looks. And as I stared, I saw a slight resemblance to her nephew, Chad Berg. Cropped dark hair framed lovely features, with dark eyes and a smirk I often saw on her nephew's face. She studied me as if I was a curiosity.

To be dissected.

"Um, hello. I'm Lexi Jones, yes. I run Sweet Fiction just down the street from Honey Threads. I love your store."

The woman's stern look eased into a pretty smile. "I'm Jillian Nichols. Nice to meet you."

We shook hands.

"You might know my nephew, Detective Chad Berg."

"I know him."

She laughed, and I wondered if she heard any attitude in my simple phrasing, because I'd tried really hard not to sound judgmental or scornful. Really.

"Chad's a good kid. A little more straightlaced than my son, but—Where did he go?"

"The Ripe Raisin. He said he had an emergency."

She sighed. "No doubt. Leaving that place in Josie's or Mike's hands was a mistake."

"Oh?"

"They're nice people, don't get me wrong. But Mike's not all that trustworthy. Thinks too much below the belt, if you get my drift."

I flushed. "Yeah, I've heard."

"I just don't understand that kind of relationship. Why would you want to be with a man who's sleeping around?"

"No idea. Not my style, for sure."

She nodded. "That's because you've got a sense of self. I'd say your parents raised you right, but your self-worth has more to do with you than genetics."

"Right." Odd lecture from a woman I just met, but okay.

"Chad, now, he'd never cheat on a woman. Not Noah either. Or Dash." She looked at me, and her expression softened. "I'm really sorry about Dash."

"Me too."

"Noah's told me what a friend he is to you and Cat, and of course, Teri's got to be hurting. We all know Dash didn't do it. But heck if I can think of who would want to blame him for something like that. Everyone loves Dash. He and Noah are like brothers."

"Yeah. I just hope the cops solve the case before Dash ends up going to jail for it."

"They will." She patted my shoulder. "Don't you worry. My Chad won't let an innocent man suffer. That's why he left the Portland PD, you know."

"Oh?" Fascinated, I waited for her to expand on that.

"Great meeting you, Lexi. It's getting late, and I have a date."

Disappointed, though I tried to mask it, I said, "Good luck. Enjoy your evening."

She smiled and left.

As I looked for my uncle, I spotted him at another table with a new plate of food.

Nadine stepped in front of me and asked with a sneer, "So who let you in?"

Crap on a cracker. Would this night never end?

*　*　*

Half an hour later, Jimmy dropped me off at the bar. "You're still mad at me?"

I glared. "Did you really need all those empty calories? I thought you and Elvis were on diets."

"Nah. We decided to accept ourselves and just work on being happy and fit." Jimmy made an impressive muscle. Then he looked at my arms. "You know, if you ever want to work out . . ."

"Oh my gosh!"

He chuckled.

I kissed him on the cheek. "Go home to your husband and thank him for watching Cookie for me. I'll come by tomorrow to get her."

"No problem." He waited.

"And thanks for taking me," I grudgingly added, knowing he'd helped. "It was a real experience."

He guffawed. "You got that right." Then he groaned. "Oh man, my stomach hurts. Gotta go."

Served him right. If I'd eaten as much as he had, I'd be stuck in the bathroom for a week straight. With a grin, I sent my Uncle Elvis a text message: *Jimmy coming home. Good luck. He ate enough for 8 people. Now his stomach hurts.*

My uncle sent me the little sick-faced emoji, and I laughed.

Entering the Ripe Raisin, I noticed the crowd right off. And a few overturned tables. And Officer Nicholson and another officer I didn't recognize talking to some disheveled men and women.

Seeing my stare, Josie Letford swaggered over. "Hey, Lexi. You missed a glorious fight. Some tourist told Mel's husband that Eats 'n' Treats served terrible meatloaf. Then Rick and his sons insulted them back, and the obnoxious tourists tossed beer at them. Got ugly fast."

"Wow." The town was going nutty. Had to be some planet in retrograde making the cosmos wonky.

Josie darted away to deliver her order. I saw two other staff members usually called in on short days, but no Mike. Noah worked steadily behind the bar, whipping orders at customers with a smile and his trademark charm.

Noah and Rachel?

I shook my head, wondering why I was constantly surprised about the secrets I learned.

Before I could dart over to question the busy man, pondering if I should offer to help out, I spotted Mike and Sherry arguing in the hallway leading to the restrooms, positioned between the men's and ladies' room.

I passed by them, nodding, and entered the ladies' room, then stood by the door and cracked it to overhear.

"No. I'm sick of them looking down on me." Mike sounded annoyed.

"My parents don't look down on you. They don't like you cheating on me, though," Sherry snapped.

"Bull. They have money and expected you to find someone just like them."

"Yeah, and instead of going to law school, I got a job as a vet tech because I love it." She paused, and I swore I heard a smooch. "And I love *you*."

"Then why did we have to buy the house, Sherry?" he growled. "We were happy in our apartment. Now we have a mortgage payment each month that's more than we can afford."

"My parents will—"

"*No.* I don't want their money."

"Well, maybe if you weren't so busy messing around all the time, you wouldn't worry about your job so much."

"Funny coming from you," he said. "Then again, I'm not shacking up with my boss to get overtime."

"You bastard!" Sherry cried and the sound of flesh striking flesh sounded super loud despite the bar noise behind them. "I never slept with Dr. Ryan. Is that what you tell yourself every time you're slumming with those trollops? Marilyn, Rachel, Josie, Lexi. The list goes on and on, doesn't it?"

Wait. *What?*

"What the hell are you even talking about? I'm yours, but you never believe me, too busy blaming me for everything. So what if I flirt? It gets me better tips. And we need the money."

Yikes. Even I didn't buy his gaslighting.

"Is that all it is? Just flirting?"

I cringed at her hopeful tone. *Come on, Sherry. Think.*

"Aw, baby," Mike said in a deep, cajoling voice. "We fight and break up and make up. And I always come back to you, don't I?"

"You do," she said, sounding pleased. "*My* Mike. Now honey, don't worry about the mortgage, okay? You let me handle my parents. They really do love you, no matter what my dad says.

Remember, I'm an only child and I've always been a daddy's girl. You know how overprotective he is."

"I know."

More kissing sounds. Some groaning.

I hustled away to a stall and made use of it, trying to clear my mind. After washing up, I left and found the hall empty. I searched for Noah and saw the Ripe Raisin once again in order, the masses taken care of.

Mike had returned to helping Noah behind the bar. Noah saw me and nodded for me to join him at the end. He fixed me a coke with a cherry. "On the house."

"Oh, thanks." I guzzled it, parched.

"Sorry for bailing on you. We had a fight break out, and Josie freaked and called me." He glanced at Mike but said nothing. "Anyway, what was I telling you?"

I wanted to punch him. "Noah, you said something at the bar bugged you, remember? Something that was weird, around the time Rachel died?"

"Not Rachel. No, it was before that. Before Marilyn died, actually."

"What?"

Josie interrupted. "I'm so sorry, but Noah, the couple at table six want to talk to you. But it's all good. They're part of a big video tour group with a ton of followers on YouTube. And they want to feature us! It's a big deal."

"Oh." Noah looked at me.

I sighed. "I'll wait here. Go, get good publicity."

He smiled and darted for table six.

Josie took his place behind the bar and started flirting with Mike, who flirted right back. Sherry must have left, because I didn't see her glaring or trying to rip Josie's hair out.

They caught a break, and I swear I saw Mike pat Josie's butt then lean in for a quick kiss on her cheek before heading back to the end of the bar to work.

Josie saw me watching and came over to me to refill my coke. "Don't tell." She winked.

"No way. I'm not getting between any of you. But Josie, Sherry's marrying him. And she's mean. Didn't you two get into a fight this past weekend?" Honestly, did no one around here respect the sanctity of marriage or relationships? Our town was turning into Peyton Place!

Josie sorted. "That woman has issues. But she can do all the damage she wants. My sister iced me up no problem. She's a nurse. Can you believe Sherry smacked me in the face?" Josie pointed to slight bruise on her cheek, masked by makeup I could see up close. "I shoved her on her ass, yeah, but only after she called me every name in the book. And then she got up and hit me."

"Are you going to press charges?" I gaped.

"No way. And let her think she beat me?" Josie laughed. "Besides, I'll have my revenge when Mike's sneaking out of my bed later."

"I don't understand you people."

"It's called drama. And it can be fun." Josie shrugged. "But don't worry. I'm not into boyfriends or married guys like Marilyn was. I'm only messing with Mike to get to Sherry. I can't stand her and her snotty, rich parents." A customer took her attention, and I nursed my drink as I waited for Noah to return.

Josie was the second person to mention Sherry's parents' wealth.

Noah finally returned. "Okay, before we're interrupted again, this is what bugged me. I remember a special reserve we'd ordered, an expensive bottle for one of our regulars, go missing. And that never happens. Our people may be screw-ups"—he glanced down the bar at Mike—"but they don't steal. I still haven't found it. And it was a terrific vintage too."

At that moment, I remembered *exactly* what had been typed on the piece of a paper that dropped from between the pages of the craft beer book. "Noah, quick! I need a pen." He took one from his pocket and watched as I wrote what I recalled on a napkin.

"What's that?"

"Do you have any idea where your cousin is right now?"

"Chad?" Noah blinked. "Um, I think he's off tonight, actually. He's been working nonstop all week."

"I need his address."

Noah gave me a wide smile. "Why, you sly dog. Using me to get to my cousin. Go, Lexi."

"Noah, gimme!"

He took the napkin and wrote an address down on the other side. "Good luck. But don't worry about working too hard. You're totally his type." Noah winked.

Chapter Nineteen

I didn't even want to know what Noah meant by "totally his type." I raced out the door and back home to get my car. I plugged the destination into Google maps on my phone.

I had a feeling I knew where the area was, though I didn't often get out to the north part of town, the swing 'n' bling notwithstanding.

Maple Circle Park's swing 'n' bling is a Confection bastion of kiddy friendliness, a children's park that's bright, always clean, and always filled with kids who want to run, climb, and play. Unfortunately, not long after Berg transferred to Confection, he'd been walking at the park and spotted my dog. Mistakenly under the notion Cookie was attacking small children, he'd dived in to save the two kids. In doing so, he'd scared the one little boy half to death. The kids had been playing lick-off-my-ketchup with Cookie. Oh, and the boy happened to be the son of a member of the prestigious town council.

That had not gone over well.

But the swing 'n' bling remained an awesome place to play and had been since I'd been young.

Berg lived near it, which surprised me. I had a tough time envisioning the stern giant being comfortable around small, goofy children.

I followed Darth Vader's directions (who needs Siri when Darth can tell you where to go?) and parked in front of a well-tended, dark-red cottage off Second Avenue a few blocks from Maple Circle Park. Yep, Berg lived in a family neighborhood as opposed to the bowels of hell. How about that?

I saw lights on in the house and left the car. And froze. What if he wasn't alone? What if he had a woman in there with him? Or a man? Heck, I didn't really know Chad Berg. Who knew how he liked to relax and entertain?

But I'd come this far, and I had to share this or explode. I walked to his front porch and rang the bell. Inside, I thought I heard music that shut off suddenly.

Nothing. Should I leave? No, I had information to share that might help exonerate Dash.

I rang the bell again. "Come on, Berg. I know you're in there," I muttered, now flushing at the thought of him having to put on clothes to come to the door. Man, it was getting hot out in the dark with my imagination soaring.

The door opened, and Chad Berg stood wearing shorts and nothing else.

I couldn't help staring. Holy moly, I'd been right!

"Sorry, I was working out."

I noticed the towel around his neck he used to wipe his face.

Then he noticed me, and his attitude changed. From pleasant to annoyed. "What are *you* doing here?" He looked over my head and around me. "How did you get my address? What do you want?"

Typical Berg. His rudeness made me feel much better, though I still found it difficult to look past that glorious wall of muscle in front of me.

I made myself swallow. "Why, hello, Detective Berg. Yes, it is a lovely night. What? You want me to come in? Sure. Okay. And yes, I'll take a lemonade, iced tea, or water. It's hot out, so I appreciate it."

He made a show of rolling his eyes before he stepped back and waved me inside.

The door shut behind me, and I jumped.

I swear I heard a small laugh, but when I darted my gaze to his face, I saw nothing but Iceberg in the expression.

"Your pick. Lemonade or water?"

"Homemade lemonade?"

He stared at me. "Is that a real question?"

"Yes, it is."

"Ah, it's from a mix." He opened a cabinet to show his shelves organized to the nth degree. Someone needed to loosen up a little. Geez. "Country Time."

"I like that kind. Sure. I'll have a cup. With ice."

He bowed. "Yes, my lady."

I sniffed. "This is how you should *always* address me." *And feel free not to put on a shirt.* No. I did not just think that.

He handed me a glass, with ice, and I sipped, concentrating on my lemonade. I could feel his gaze on mine and pretended he wasn't making me nervous, standing there half-dressed in his kitchen. Then he crossed his arms, and his biceps bulged. Oh, mama!

"Okay, what do you bench?"

"Sorry?"

"How much weight can you bench? Cat wants to know."

"She does, huh?" Well, he no longer looked annoyed. Now he seemed amused.

I preferred annoyed.

"You can tell her I typically bench 315, sometimes 350 if I'm feeling it. My max is 405, but I haven't been working out like I used to, so I haven't hit that in a while."

"Right." I looked him over. Heck, I couldn't help it. I'm only human. "315 is good, right?"

He flexed on purpose. "What do you think?"

I think I need to check myself for drool. I forced myself to look less than impressed. "I guess it's okay." I sipped more lemonade to cool my temperature.

Berg laughed at me and poured himself a large drink of water. "Okay, not that this isn't a ton of fun, having you here in my house, but why are you here on a Friday night? And how did you get my address?"

I didn't trust the look on his face because I couldn't tell what it meant.

I finished off my glass and set it on the counter, pleased when he poured me another. "I know what the note said."

"Note?"

"The typed, ripped note that was on the ground in the bookstore. I think I know what's going on." Maybe. "Your cousin gave me your address."

"Noah?"

"You have more than one cousin?"

"No."

"I was at the Ripe Raisin because Noah left the chamber of commerce meeting before I could talk to him."

"You went to one of those? I went once when I first got here. Boring."

"Well, this one wasn't. People were fighting, my uncle was eating enough to explode, and a lot of members do not want to remember Marilyn or Rachel at the Owl Hoot."

"The what?"

"None of that matters." I shook my head. "Because Noah told me he remembered something strange that happened at the bar before Marilyn died."

Now Berg looked interested.

"But I had to chase him down to the Ripe Raisin to find out, and I heard more fascinating stuff." I paused. "Aren't you going to ask me what I found fascinating?"

"Will you please get to the point?"

"Why the rush? Got a hot date?" I asked, snarky, and forgetting who I was talking to.

"What if I do?"

We both stared at each other.

"Do you?" I asked.

He flushed. "No. I'm rushing you because I'm hungry."

"It's past nine. You mean you haven't eaten yet?" No wonder he was all muscle and no fat. He needed to eat more.

"Would you please get on with your story?"

"I will if you cook yourself dinner. I don't want to hold you up." My stomach chose that moment to grumble.

He sighed and took color-coded containers from his refrigerator. He opened them to reveal cooked rice, chicken, and what looked like chopped fresh vegetables. I watched as he started tossing things together in a pan with olive oil.

The smell made me so hungry.

He waved a spatula at me. "What did you find fascinating?"

"My lady. 'What did you find fascinating, *my lady*?'"

He growled. "Don't push it."

I couldn't help laughing.

I heard a sizzle, and he swore and motioned for me to join him. "Here, come hold this."

I did as asked, confused until he came back wearing a shirt. "Ah, oil hit you in the chest, eh?"

"Yep." He took over for me, and this time our hands touched. It was way weird, because I kind of liked it.

So I took a seat far from him at a modern-style table in the corner of the kitchen and continued to sip my lemonade. "Right. So at the bar, I learned from Noah that a bottle of expensive wine went missing before Marilyn died. Not right before or anything, but before her death, at least." I drew out my crumpled napkin from my pocket. "The note I saw on the ground read, *Saw the wine. Nice vintage. Late to be out. CR 2am. Don't forget or el.* It had been torn, but it's obvious the last word was *else.*"

"Or else what?"

"I don't know. Implied repercussions. But I didn't put it all together until Noah mentioned the wine and Mimi mentioned Ed's roses."

"Now I'm confused." He added soy sauce to the pan and kept stirring, then added two eggs.

"Wow. That smells pretty good."

He mumbled something under his breath.

"What?"

"Nothing. What else?"

"Don't you get it?" I was loopy with delight. I understood the note. "This is blackmail. Don't forget or else."

"Hold on." He turned off the stove and grabbed two plates, I was pleased to see. He slid large portions onto them, then set one in front of me and another in front of the chair next to me.

He refilled his glass with lemonade and grabbed napkins and utensils from the drawer.

Then he proceeded to fold my napkin into a triangle before setting the table nice and neat.

I just watched.

He gave the table a critical look, nodded, then sat. "Now you can eat."

I took a bite. Then I took another. And another. It had to be a good five minutes before either of us spoke. I hadn't realized how hungry I was, but then I'd only nibbled at the CoC meeting, unlike my uncle, who had sampled every dish.

"This is really good," I complimented the chef.

"Don't look so surprised," he said wryly. "I'm a bachelor. It's expensive to eat out all the time if you don't know how to cook."

He had that right, but I couldn't resist saying, "A bachelor? You mean Mt. Bachelor, don't you, big guy?" I laughed so hard at the consternation on his face. "I'm sorry Rachel's gone, but that was pretty funny, her calling you that."

"You would think so." He shoveled more food into his mouth, eating slowly, with precision. He felt me watching him, because he said, "What now?"

"You ever do time?" He ate like a prisoner, and I knew because I'd seen a ton of documentaries on the prison system, prisoners, and law enforcement while writing my book.

"Nope. Military. Same thing," he joked.

"That explains a lot."

He sighed. "Are you going to tell me what your note means or do I have to—"

"So I figure if this is blackmail, then we're talking about something that could, potentially, involve murder. The 2AM is a meeting time. The reference to a nice vintage, wine that was stolen from the Ripe Raisin, maybe? And the CR . . . That had me baffled until Mimi mentioned roses and the CGC."

"I'm still not understanding your reference."

"CR—Confection Rose. Didn't Rachel have rose petals on her body?"

His eyes narrowed on my napkin, and he dragged it closer. "She did."

"And dirt. You could test and see if the petals are the same ones from the Confection rosebush."

"We already did. There are a lot of flower lovers in this town, and my lieutenant's wife is a botanist. She confirmed that the petals on Rachel are from the Confection Rose."

"Oh wow." I was right! "So think about this. Rachel writes a note to someone and hides it in a book. She's blackmailing someone—"

"Or someone's blackmailing her. She's dead, maybe the situation got out of hand when she went to pay."

"Or someone's blackmailing her," I agreed, "but we'll stick with my version for simplicity's sake. So she's blackmailing them about seeing them with that stolen bottle of wine. They have to meet her at 2:00 AM at the Confection Rose, or she'll tell."

"Then she winds up dead the next day." Berg looked at me. "Are you sure you saw that note before she died?"

"Yeah, on Monday. I remember because Kay's son felt bad about knocking over a stack of books. He said someone pushed him. And when I went to help, I looked back over and saw the note was missing." I paused. "Or someone saw me pick up the note not meant for me and created a distraction. Then they took the note back."

"Or the person who the note was meant for found it and took it. Then met Rachel and killed her later that night. Can you remember seeing anyone out of the ordinary that day?"

"No, I'm sorry. We've been so busy lately. And we don't have a camera installed. I mean, we're a small bookshop. We trust people."

"More fool you," he murmured, stroking the napkin. "This is good. It makes sense. Especially because we found higher traces of ketamine in Marilyn. Nothing conclusive, but it might just be what killed her, or led to her heart attack. She had two wine glasses sitting out but no wine bottle. No odd marks on her body or residue in her nose, so the supposition is she drank the ketamine."

"Marilyn's date brought the wine and left with it to avoid suspicion."

"Which works if you add that Rachel saw him leave with it. But how do we know Rachel wasn't the one being blackmailed?"

I thought about it. "She could have been, but it makes more sense that she was the blackmailer. She needed money to start a new business, and she hadn't been successful with her bank loans."

Berg scowled. "How do you know . . . No. I don't want to know." He swore under his breath. "I like the motive, but it's pretty thin. Nothing we can prove."

"Not yet."

He looked up at me. "What do you mean?"

"Nothing. I'm just saying, there's a lot going on that's not fitting yet. Not that I'm investigating or anything," I said quickly. "Because I'm not. I'm just observing life in our lovely town and seeing things that don't make much sense." I scooped up more food. "This is delicious."

He tugged my plate away. "Nope. We're not doing this."

"Huh?"

He moved my chair and his so that we were facing each other. "No more games."

"I'm not playing games."

"Let's stop pretending you always listen to me and I never tell you what to do."

"Now I'm confused."

"Join the club." He ran a hand over his head in frustration, his eyes like ice. "All of it. I want to know what you know. I promise I won't be mad."

"Or put me in jail for anything."

He frowned.

"I didn't do anything illegal. I'm a people watcher and listener. That's it."

"Fine. No jail, no threats of jail. Just share what you know." He left the table and returned with a pad of paper and a pencil. Old school. "I mean, share what you and your *book club* know."

"I have no idea what you're talking about. *But,*" I emphasized, "I have been hearing a lot that should make sense but doesn't. Where should I start?"

He downed his lemonade and sighed. "Where else? The beginning."

Chapter Twenty

I told Berg everything I could think of, from first learning about Marilyn to visiting Natalie Childers to learning about Lot 49-71—Strawberry Fields—and Selma's partnership with Cathy Salter to get it back from the people who stole it. I ended with my visit to the Ripe Raisin, including Noah's past relationship with Rachel as well as learning that Sherry's family had serious money.

"Why should I care about Sherry Resnick?" he asked.

"I'm not discounting anything that strikes me as odd. Sherry's family having money means she could be blackmailed. Especially if Mike slept with Marilyn." But that wasn't grabbing me either. Mike regularly slept around, and Sherry knew it. Plus, Marilyn had helped them both buy a house, so why kill her? Why kill Rachel?

I stared at Berg's notes and turned the paper to face me. The guy had clearly legible, impeccably neat handwriting. Nothing like what I regularly wrote in my unicorns-stabbing-ogres themed notebook.

Yeah, it's weird, but I like to think of my odd writer supplies as artistic.

"Look," I told him, "we know Rachel and Marilyn had relationships with Dash in the past. Maybe they both had relationships with another guy as well. Someone with a hate-on for Dash." It was almost there. I had it, yet I didn't.

"Noah slept with Rachel." Berg mulled that one over. What was his relationship with his cousin like? "Maybe he slept with Marilyn too."

"But if we go with who wanted to kill Rachel, and we think Rachel was the blackmailer, then who was Rachel blackmailing? Not Noah. He's not rich, is he?"

"No. The Ripe Raisin is doing well, but the money he and Hagen make goes back into the business. Let's see, what rich people might want to kill Rachel? Cathy Salter comes to mind. Not only a competitor, but a rich competitor."

I thought about it. "What if Cathy's husband was having an affair with Marilyn and Rachel saw? She could blackmail him for the money, and Cathy hated her."

"True." He wrote Cathy's name in block letters and circled it. "Then there's Dr. Ken Thomas, whose wife hated Marilyn. Thomas has money and motive. He didn't want his wife to know."

"She already hated Marilyn. She knew."

"Yes, but Dr. Thomas's wife would have taken him for everything he had if he ever tried to divorce her. Maybe Marilyn pushed him for more? Rachel found out, tried to blackmail the doctor, he killed her?"

"I don't know." I frowned. "He was pretty open about his devotion to Marilyn at the meeting last night. I really don't think he'd kill her."

"Maybe the wife." Berg jotted down her name.

I thought about everyone I'd talked to tonight. "What about Josie Letford?"

"What about her?"

"She works with Dash and would have access to ketamine through her sister, who's a nurse."

"But Josie has no money. She's working at my cousin's bar."

"Yeah, but do we really know she has no money? Sherry Resnick works as a vet tech, and her parents have money."

"Good point. I'll check out Josie." He scowled. "Hell, I'll need to look into a lot more people than I thought. Salter, Ed Mullins, Pastor Nestor, Dr. Ken Thomas. The list just keeps getting longer, and they all connect to your buddy, Dash. Everyone heads into the Ripe Raisin at one time or another."

"But Dash shouldn't be on the list."

"Unfortunately, until we can find a way to prove otherwise, he's stuck." Berg sighed. "Well, this is something more to work on. For me and my people," he said firmly.

I raised my hands in surrender. "Sure, sure."

"Lexi . . . Thanks."

I just stared.

He frowned.

I kept staring.

He flushed. "What now?"

"Are you really Chad Berg? Because, I don't now, but you just thanked me. And that is *totally* out of character for you."

"You barely know me."

"Huh." I glanced around. "You're a perfectionist. You like law and order." I smirked.

He let out a loud sigh. "That joke is *so* old."

"You work out, your drawers are way too organized for a person under ninety, and you look at everyone as if they're out to murder you."

"Not bad, except about my adherence to order. Nothing wrong with being neat, and that has nothing to do with age."

I shook my head. "You live alone."

"So do you."

"Yes, but I have Cookie."

"Wait right there." He left and returned with two balls of fluff.

I stared, enthralled with two black-and-white kittens.

"Meet Angel and Butter, short for Butterman."

"From *Hot Fuzz?*"

Berg's eyes widened. "You know that movie?"

"With Simon Pegg and Nick Frost? It's a classic."

"Wow. I might have to rethink my opinion of you." One of the fluffballs meowed pitifully, and the question I'd planned to ask got lost in my adoration for the tiny kittens. "Where did you get them?"

"I found them all alone off North Church Street when I was checking out Strawberry Fields. I called the vet, but no one is missing kittens. I think someone dumped them or they're strays. I waited around, but the mom never came back."

"You rescued kittens?"

"I'm a cop. I regularly rescue those who need help." He looked me over. "Case in point."

I snapped. "I don't need any help."

"Oh please. You can't even reach the autobiography shelf in Sweet Fiction without a ladder." He laughed at my pique.

"I'm surprised you took time out of your busy day to help these little guys. Or were they jaywalking or digging near rosebushes?"

"They're tiny kittens! I'm not a monster." Now he acted offended.

"I think that was super, super sweet of you." I couldn't stop looking from them to him, seeing a hero underneath all the attitude and muscle.

He turned bright red. "I'm just fostering them until we can find them a good home."

"We?"

"I mean me. Like, the proverbial 'we' . . . my lady."

I laughed. "Can I hold one?"

"Sure." He handed me the more black of the two, and I fell in instant love. They were like feline versions of my dog. "They remind me of Cookie, but not."

"Right? Same coloring. If they start herding you, beware."

Somehow, I spent the next hour cuddling kittens with Detective Chad Berg while we laughed and continued to speculate on who might have murdered Rachel and why.

Yes, hell had surely frozen over.

* * *

I took Saturday off, determined to forget how my night at Berg's had ended.

God, how embarrassing. And infuriating. And so, so filled with sexual tension I could melt, even now as I bathed in luke-warm water while reading a new book.

Cookie kept coming in, sniffing at me, giving me dirty looks, and leaving.

She did it again.

"Oh my gosh, Cookie! Give me a break. They were cute kittens! I'm not getting a cat."

She grumbled under her breath and kept nosing at my discarded T-shirt from yesterday.

Thoughts of Berg without his shirt continued to reappear in my mind's eye for no reason, so I buried my nose back in the detective serial I couldn't get enough of.

When I'd turned too pruney, I left the tub, dressed, and did some light chores, choosing to spend the majority of my day lazing around my house and enjoying the cooling temps, thanks to passing clouds shielding the sun. Out of nowhere, the temperature had dropped several degrees and had been predicted to stay cool.

My favorite time of year was nearing, when I could be comfortable in sweatshirts and shorts or T-shirts and jeans. I loved the falling leaves, autumnal colors, and the sweet taste of warm apple cider and pumpkin everything. Hello, September.

Unfortunately, my love of fall kept competing with ruminations over everything Chad—no longer just *Berg*—and I had unpacked last night. Unable to let it go, I called Kay for help.

She answered on a laugh. "Hey, Lexi. What's up?"

"Hi, Kay. Sorry to bother you on a Saturday."

"Oh please. I was just losing a tickle fight, so I can use the break."

I smiled, imagining Kay and her kids and husband playing around. A small pang hit me, and I hoped to have what she had in a few more years. Not any time soon, of course, but I'd like to have a kid someday, a mini reader like me. Now that made me smile.

"Lexi?"

"I think maybe Rachel was blackmailing someone."

"No kidding." Kay stepped away from the noise behind her. "Seriously?"

"Yeah. Remember when LJ said someone pushed him in Sweet Fiction, causing that stack of books to fall over?"

"I do."

"Well, before that, I'd seen a note stuck inside a book. I had picked it up and was reading it when that stack fell, stealing my attention. When I went back to look for the note again, it was gone. So my question to you is, do you remember seeing any of our suspects in the shop that day? Cathy, Ed, Dr. Ryan? Anyone?"

"Hold on." I heard her call for LJ, then they talked a bit. Kay came back. "Okay, so the people I remember seeing at the store that day, and this isn't everyone, but I remember Ed Mullins arguing with Bill Sanchez about gardening when we entered the store. They didn't move, so we had to go around them. I saw Sherry and Mike looking at bridal magazines, Pastor Nestor with an older couple I didn't recognize. I didn't see Dr. Ryan, but I did see one of his techs talking to Sherry, I think. Hmm. Not Cathy, but her husband was there with one of their teenagers. And hey, I saw Rachel." Kay's voice trembled with excitement. "Oh my gosh. She was there next to me and LJ. Then the books fell, and I didn't see her again."

"You're sure?"

"Yes, I am. Wow. I bet Rachel was there to meet with the person she was blackmailing. Oh, this is getting good!"

"Mom, what's blackmail?" LJ asked.

Time to let Kay get back to her family. "Go back to the kids, Kay. And keep this just between us Macaroons."

"Got it. Bye now."

I set my phone down, curious about the names she'd given me. All of them had connections to Marilyn and Rachel through real estate. But then, Kay didn't know everyone in town. What if the couple with Pastor Nestor that Kay hadn't recognized was Dr. Thomas and his wife?

I needed a photo for her to compare.

But that would have to wait. Mr. Peabody had returned with a few friends in the backyard, and Cookie was losing it.

My doorbell rang.

"Cookie, hush," I yelled.

It was nearly four. Who the heck could be visiting?

My uncles? Abe for a deadheading and weeding party? Cat and Teri were busy with their boyfriends. Dash was in jail. Oh, maybe Nadine had come calling to egg my house or toilet paper my yard.

The idea made me laugh.

I hadn't counted on seeing Chad Berg again so soon. I could see his head through the glass in my door-lites.

He stared at me through the glass. "Lexi, open up."

I swung the door open. "Got a warrant?"

He snorted and strode past me, pretty as you please. Cookie dashed back inside and came to a standstill seeing Berg with a pet carrier.

"Hey, Cookie." He crouched, and she sniffed him before bypassing his hand to lick his face. He laughed and shot me a sly glance. "Like dog, like owner, eh?"

My cheeks felt so hot, it was a wonder my face didn't melt off.

No. I refused to discuss last night with him.

But as he kept smirking at me, I lost my resolve.

He straightened, and I poked him in the chest. "First of all, I didn't try to kiss you. I tripped."

"And your lips fell right into mine. Okay."

"Oh, you've got the biggest ego! I did trip over your big feet, in fact. And I didn't want to smush the kittens. It was an accident. Maybe if you hadn't been so handsy trying to 'catch' me you wouldn't have gotten an accidental kiss. And come on, if you consider that a kiss, you need to get out more," I tacked on, being petty.

He didn't take the bait, still smiling at me. I swear, I'd been smiled at by Iceberg more in the past twenty-four hours than I had in the past six months of knowing the guy.

"Well, we'll have to agree to disagree."

"Disagree this," I muttered and mentally shot him the finger.

He loomed over me. "What was that?"

"Nothing." I huffed and petted my dog, who showed remarkably more sense than the XY chromosome bearer invading my personal space. "Did you have a reason for coming by, unannounced and uninvited to my house? Or are you just here to annoy me?"

"Has anyone ever told you how adorable you are when you're mad?"

"Patronizing jackhole."

He chuckled. "Okay, I deserved that."

"Why do you keep smiling at me? I find it disturbing." On several levels, because last night I'd started to really like the guy. That is, before I'd tripped and accidentally mushed mouths with him. Then argued about who had instigated the kiss that wasn't even a real kiss.

"Really? Because I find *you* disturbing. Great. We're even." He crouched and watched Cookie. "Cookie, I need you to watch my little buddies for me while I work today. Would you mind doing that? No eating the kittens. They're very small." He took one out.

"She won't eat them," I told them, secretly enthralled with the idea of kitten sitting. "What do I get if I watch your kids?"

The tips of his ears turned red. "They're cats, not kids. And I'm just fostering."

"A cat person. Figures."

He scowled. "I like dogs too."

Cookie looked from him to me and stepped forward. She sniffed the kitten, which put a paw on Cookie's nose and mewed, its eyes a bright blue. Cookie blinked, cocked her head, then licked its tiny ear.

"Great. That's a yes." Berg withdrew the other furball and let both kittens sit on the floor while they got their bearings.

We watched Cookie walk around the house with them, herding them away from anything she might consider dangerous. Like Mr. Leggy.

But she let them drink from her water bowl without a fuss and laid down to watch while they took wobbly steps and sniffed.

I shared a grin with Chad, like proud parents, and then did my best not to laugh after we simultaneously frowned at each other.

"So, uh, you watch the cats, and I'll make you another dinner."

"What, like a date?"

He stared at me.

"What?" I asked.

"I'm thinking."

"Don't strain yourself."

He barked a laugh. "Sure, we'll call it a date. And I promise not to get mad at you when you're snooping around the church tomorrow watching everyone at Marilyn's memorial service."

"You can't get mad at me for going to church."

He said nothing.

"I guess you could get mad, but going to church isn't illegal. Besides, I'll tell you what I see if I notice anything. Mostly I'll be there with Cat and Teri, supporting Teri's parents since they won't be sitting with their son." And keeping my distance from Mrs. Hagen because I didn't want to add to her already frazzled state of mind.

He nodded. "Okay. I'll be there watching as well. We can compare notes."

I had to know. "What is this? You're letting me help now?" Was he setting me up to take down later?

"That's a problem?"

"No, but you never let me help before."

"Before you were a murder suspect. I could have gotten in serious trouble for letting you interfere in our investigation. And you nearly died. Now you're just a nosy witness. I can work with that, so long as you stay out of everyone's way. No more questioning people. Just tell me what you hear."

I heard "more questioning people" and "tell me." I nodded but had to correct him. "I am not nosy."

He raised a brow.

"But I did talk to Kay earlier today. And guess what? She saw Rachel on Monday at the store, when I found the blackmail note."

His eyes brightened. "Oh yeah? Interesting. Who else was in there?" I told him, and he said, "I can get her a picture of Dr. and Mrs. Thomas. I'll bring it tomorrow to church."

"I don't know if she'll be at church."

He snorted. "Lexi, all your Macaroons are as nosy as you are. She'll be there."

"We're a book club, Chad. Not Scooby and the gang."

"Good. Keep it that way." Then he kneeled to pet each kitten and Cookie before walking to my door. "Lock up after me. Oh, and there's kitten chow in the compartment on top of the carrier. Bye."

No word of when he'd be back to pick them up. No thanks. No . . .

"Cookie, aren't they adorable?" We sat and played with the kittens for a while before I realized Chad hadn't left a litter box with them, so I took them outside into some dirt Cookie had been playing in and prayed they'd do their business.

And wondered when Berg had become Chad, and why I found our arguments no longer so much annoying as exciting.

Chapter
Twenty-One

S unday morning, I tugged at my neckline as I sat listening to Pastor Nestor talk about forgiveness and the beyond, annoyed I'd let myself wear my sleeveless blue sundress because of its flattering shape, when I should have worn my strappy, yellow sundress that was more cute than sophisticated yet comfier.

None of my fashion decisions had anything to do with impressing Chad Berg. Nope. It was all for Inina Hagen. I sat on the end of the pew next to Cat, who sat next to Teri, who sat next to her parents. I had a two-person buffer, which I hoped would be enough to protect me from Teri's mom.

Her parents, Inina and Ben, loved their children very much. So when I'd innocently convinced Teri to try a punk hairstyle back in the eleventh grade, and it had turned out more like a mullet, Mrs. Hagen hadn't been pleased.

She refused to let the incident go, though her husband had always been super nice to me. Of the two of them, he played good cop to Inina's bad cop. But right now, the pair looked tired and dejected. I really felt for them.

I reached across Cat to Teri and squeezed her hand on her lap. "We're getting close," I whispered.

She looked at me with surprise, then gave a sad smile.

I noticed a good-looking man sitting in the pew behind her with his family and nodded. Randy Craig, Teri's beau, nodded back. Yesterday's date must have gone well. Randy and his family were sitting close and providing support. Nice.

A few people had given Teri and her family space, folks who normally would have been chatty before the service. I'm sure Teri's mom made a note of those people. They had no idea what they were in for.

Pastor Nestor droned on, and I glanced around, having spotted Chad earlier. He sat in the very back, and when I turned to look, I spotted him staring at me. I frowned and nodded at the crowd. *Don't look at me. Look at them.*

He shrugged and shook his head, pretending he didn't understand me. Oh, he understood.

Fine. I'll do your job for you. I continued to scout around, spotting familiar faces and seeing a lot of bored people fidgeting in their seats. On the rare occasions I attended service, I sat in the way back, doing my best not to snore. But Cat had dragged me with her to sit with the Hagens, just a short distance from the front. An awful place to be, but at least I was on the end, so I had more latitude to look around than someone right in front of the pulpit.

Uncle Jimmy, Uncle Elvis, and Collin sat on the left side in the back, a primo spot. Collin saw me and made a face. Jimmy subtly smacked him in the back of the head, and Collin slouched in his seat, smirking at me.

I held back a laugh.

Kay sat a few rows in front of them, leaning close to a small, dark-haired head to scold, no doubt. Nearby, Alison sat with her boyfriend, and next to them sat Stefanie. Stefanie caught my eye and mouthed, "After."

She wanted to talk, apparently. I nodded.

The other Macaroons were in attendance, as were Noah and his mother, the Salters, Natalie Childers, Mike and Sherry, Dr. Thomas and his wife, Ed, a few CGC mafia heavies, and many other two-timers—those of us who came twice a year, on Christmas and Easter. But they were all here today.

"And so we thank God that our sisters are with Him now, *in peace,*" Nestor shouted and startled half the congregation into jerking in their seats.

"What the heck?" I muttered as I stopped myself from falling out of the pew.

Cat snickered but quickly stopped when Mrs. Hagen glared at us.

Teri's dad coughed to hide a laugh, especially when his wife turned back to him.

"Dearest Marilyn." Pastor Nestor clenched his fist and shook it high. "For whom the sun is brightest and the sweet smell of the afterlife beckons, may you rest with the Lord. Amen."

"Amen," we all said.

Geesh. What had lit a fire under Pastor Nestor? I glanced at his snooty wife and saw Peggy mouthing something, then making a motion for him to continue. Ah, the loving interference of the missus.

In a loud voice more suited to a pro wrestling announcer, he added, "And our sister Rachel, and our sister Selma, we pray for you."

His voice droned on, about how wonderful life was and not to take it for granted. Then something about Roman. No, Romans 8:35. I continued to watch people's reactions.

Most people stared straight ahead. Sherry and Mike appeared to be arguing. Big surprise. Cathy's husband had an arm around her shoulders, and her teens sat, looking bored but behaving. Alison left her seat and walked back toward the exit, likely for a bathroom break. Officer Roger Halston, in nice clothes, no uniform, slid next to Chad but looked around for Cat. Spotting her, he relaxed.

Pastor Nestor raised his voice again, and this time I was prepared. I didn't jump, though my heart thundered. "'. . . *For I am convinced* that neither death, nor life, nor angels, nor rulers, nor things present, nor things to come, nor powers, nor height, nor depth, nor anything else in all creation, will be able to separate us from the love of God in Christ Jesus our Lord.'"

"I wish he'd quit yelling," an older woman muttered from a pew in front of us.

A little boy started crying. "He's making my ears hurt." His mom rushed him to the children's room in the back, and I saw Peggy shaking her head.

Man, I wished my mom were here to pick me up and carry me away.

Had Marilyn even been a Christian? Though to be fair, her faith didn't matter. Pastor Nestor ran a nondenominational church. For all that he could be a pain about gardening and tight-around-the-collar snooty, he accepted everyone into his church, regardless of gender, race, sexuality, or belief. So though he annoyed me on a CGC level, I liked that he wanted to bring comfort to the masses. But exactly how much comfort had he and Marilyn shared?

I remembered him telling Ed what a large contributor she'd been. Just monetarily or emotionally? Sexually? I felt sick at the thought, though I wouldn't have minded if Peggy Donahue had committed the murder out of a sense of jealousy. Watching her carted off to jail in cuffs would be like a dream come true.

The service wrapped up, *finally*, and the congregation spilled out of the church, some to pancake breakfast, others to get away from all the preaching and yelling.

I turned to Cat. "I'll meet you outside. I need to stretch my legs."

She nodded.

"Roger's heading your way."

She brightened. "Cool."

I exited into the sun warming up our cool morning, promising a gorgeous day in the low eighties.

I remembered the last time I'd come, back in June, when I'd been looking into Gil's death. Dash had met me outside by my car, where Cookie and Teri had joined us. We'd laughed and talked, then headed for a pancake breakfast that had been delicious.

My eyes watered. Missing Dash. Great. Now I felt bad. I wiped my cheek.

"I like it." Stefanie harrumphed from my right. "The waterworks look legit, letting you blend in. A bunch of people are fake crying, but your sadness looks real."

I blinked to clear my eyes and looked around, spotting a few tears from several couples, Rachel's family, Natalie, and a lot of downtrodden men.

"What did you want to talk to me about?" I asked Stefanie before she could insult anyone nearby.

"I heard from Alison, who heard from Didi, about the chamber of commerce meeting last night. I think Dr. Thomas might be a suspect."

"I know. I was there. I filled in Detective Berg."

Stefanie stared at me. "What's that?"

I forced myself not to blush. "I told Berg. The cops are aware."

"Now hold on, sister. I thought *we* were investigating this?" She moved closer, keeping her voice down. "The cops need us to get into the places they can't."

"Like?" I didn't trust the look on her face. Just what had Stefanie been up to?

"Well, you see, I was buying some toys for my grandson at Taffy Toys on Friday, and while I was talking to Connie, Alison took Tad aside for a tough talk."

"What?"

Stefanie gave me a satisfied smile. "That's right. Connie and I commiserated on what a low-down lowlife Marilyn was. I told her the cops even had the nerve to ask me where I was when Marilyn died, because someone said she was killed—which we suspect."

"She was. Detective Berg found out Rachel died of ketamine poisoning and not from some gash in her head." I realized I needed to tell the rest of our crew about what we'd found. "We need another meeting."

Stefanie nodded, her eyes wide. "We sure as shootin' do. Tomorrow night at Sweet Fiction? I'll put the word out." She left before I could respond. So I had no idea what she'd found out from Tad and Connie. Oh well. Guess I'd learn tomorrow.

Roger and Cat were standing together talking near her car. Teri and Randy stood nearby with Teri's dad. But I didn't see Teri's mom.

Because she had stalked and snuck behind me. "You. Come here."

Time for a few prayers.

Mrs. Hagen motioned me over into the shade under a large oak tree back behind the church. The church had a large grassy lot behind it and an extra, smaller chapel behind that. To the left and right were parking lots, and farther down, adjoined to the left parking lot, sat the annex, where the church hosted pancake breakfasts, Sunday school, and other community events.

"Teri tells me you're working to free my son." Mrs. Hagen's dark eyes focused on my face. Although she was a few inches shorter, she made me very aware of her powerful presence.

"Um, not working, exactly. Just asking questions."

"I saw Dash yesterday. He was in good spirits. He told me not to worry." She took my hand in hers, and I readied myself for sharp nails or a tight grip. But Mrs. Hagen's eyes filled, and she squeezed my hand gently. "Thank you for helping him. And for helping Teri find purpose."

"Oh, heck. Teri's my best friend. Dash is my friend too. Of course I'd help them."

My second shock of the day. I felt her hands—not around my neck but around my back. She was hugging me. I stared over her shoulder at Teri and her dad smiling and nodding at me. I patted Mrs. Hagen's shoulder. "Sure thing, Mrs. Hagen. Before you know it, Dash will be back at work and telling Noah and everyone else what to do."

She pulled back, took a tissue from her purse, and dabbed her eyes. I couldn't even tell she'd been crying. Her makeup hadn't smudged one bit, and she still looked like a runway model in her late thirties, as opposed to a grown woman in her fifties with a grudge against happiness.

"Maybe I'll forgive you for my baby girl's hair." *From over a decade ago.* She sniffed and pointed a finger at me that froze me in place. "But if you ever tell her to cut it short, or to mess with Dash's style, *ever*, I'll get you."

I nodded. "Right. Never ever, and amen." She walked away, and I felt one step closer to not dying.

A large shadow covered me. "She scares me," Chad said in a low voice.

"Get in line."

He looked around at the crowd, which hadn't dispersed just yet. Like at Friday night's chamber of commerce meeting, people wanted to get together to discuss Marilyn and Rachel.

"Hey, move away."

"What?" He looked down at me, clad in a pair of tan trousers, loafers, and a pale green, short sleeve polo. Like a young professional with enough muscles to wrestle buffaloes.

"You're making me look like a friend of the po-po."

He sighed.

"Scoot." I subtly tried to shoo him away, but he remained standing as if rooted in place.

"Too many suspects here. But one good thing, Kay confirmed Dr. Thomas and his wife are the people she saw with Ed Mullins at the bookshop that day."

Oh, wow. "What do we do now?"

"Now *I* go eat pancakes, listen to people without looking like I'm listening, then go back and foster kittens." He paused. "I think they miss Cookie."

I glanced up to see him waiting patiently, an inquisitive expression on his face.

"Oh, heck no. You didn't see how mad she was when I came back from your place. She kept sniffing my shirt and growling."

Unfortunately, Cat and Teri happened to overhear that as they approached. My friends stared, slack-jawed, from Chad to me.

He flexed at Cat. "Three fifteen, sometimes three fifty." He lowered his arm. "Now quit distracting me, Ms. Jones. I have things to do." He turned and left without looking back, joining Roger as they walked together toward the annex.

Cat whistled. "I totally get why he has those guns now. Makes sense why Roger's so impressed." She looked at me.

Teri looked at me.

"What?"

"At his place?" Teri asked, her lips threatening to turn up.

"*Last night?*" Cat added, not even trying to hide her smile. "Cookie sniffing your shirt?"

"It wasn't what it sounds like. We shared—"

"Intimacy?

"Hot, sinful passion?"

"*Information,*" I managed without strangling the pair. I forced a smile when Mrs. Hagen glanced our way. She nodded once and walked with her husband toward the annex. "Long story short, we think Rachel was blackmailing the person who killed Marilyn. Marilyn also had traces of ketamine poisoning, which killed Rachel. And Dr. Thomas is on our short list of suspects, though I don't really think it's him because he loved Marilyn." I paused. "Oh, and Chad has kittens, he cooked me dinner, and he looks like a Greek god with his shirt off."

That said, I left my friends behind as I walked toward pancake breakfast, my sights set on the Salter family. I had questions I needed answered.

But Teri must have raced after me with those skinny legs. She tugged on my hair.

"*Ow.*"

"You're an awful person, Lexi Jones," she hissed. "You don't just tell your friends about a half-naked Berg and not deliver the goods."

"What is wrong with you?" Cat griped, caging me on the other side. She leaned closer and growled. "When this is done, we are *so* convening at your place and getting the scoop. All of it." She pounded her fist into her palm.

I laughed. "Ha. Fine. But you two have to let me know how your weekends went as well. Because Roger looks physically pained to be apart from you, Cat. And Randy is chatting with your parents like he's soon to be part of the family, Teri."

My friends shut up.

"Exactly. Now, you two, spread out and listen. See what you can find out about who has money in this town, and if they knew Rachel."

We entered the crowded annex with its long tables lined from one end to the other, chairs on either side for a group breakfast. The large room smelled like syrup and coffee, and the bright sunlight spilled through the upper windows and illuminated smiling faces.

I spotted my quarry—Cathy's husband.

And made my move.

Chapter Twenty-Two

I smiled at Cathy Salter, seated with her family. "Hi. I'm Lexi. I'm not sure if you remember me. Is this seat taken?" I gestured with my head at the spot across from her, next to one of her children. I held a tray of pancakes, a glass of milk, and a cup of church coffee. Bland, obviously, because anything too dark might send you straight to hell (or so I'd once heard Nadine saying about Peggy's taste in her brew.)

Cathy smiled back. "No, it's open. Please sit. Hi, Lexi. Sure, I remember you. What did you think of the service?"

The whole family looked like they should be the inserts in picture frames. Wholesome, handsome, and polite. Her husband had even, white teeth, a dark tan, and bright blue eyes that smiled at me. The teenagers invited me to sit with them as well, no artifice but genuine welcome.

And the family matriarch, Cathy Salter, a real estate beast hiding beneath a floral dress and light perfume.

I sat and said, "I thought the service was nice, but I almost fell out of my seat when Pastor Nestor raised his voice the first time."

Her daughters giggled, and her son laughed. "Dad did too."

"I did not." He turned to me. "Hello. I'm Darren. My son Brian, and my daughters Sadie and Juliette."

"Hi. Nice to meet you. I saw your pictures at your mom's office," I told them.

The kids nodded, then turned when one of their friends asked a question.

"What did you think of the service, Darren?" I asked.

Cathy had tucked into her pancakes with a groan. "I was so hungry."

I guzzled a cup of coffee, needing strength.

"I thought it was nice, if a little loud," Darren said. "I only met Marilyn a few times. For obvious reasons, we didn't associate." He nodded at Cathy. "Not a good look to be too friendly with your wife's biggest competitor. And, well, Marilyn was a little too social, if you know what I mean. She made me uncomfortable those few times we did meet."

"I'll bet," I murmured.

Cathy snorted. "You had to hand it to her. She'd do whatever she could to win."

"But you don't."

"Nope. I work my tail off, and I'm always asking questions and trying new things. But there are some lines you don't cross."

I couldn't be sure, but it sounded a lot like that had been directed at Darren.

We continued to eat and talk about the upcoming Owl Hoot, which we all looked forward to. The time between festivals always felt empty, as if our town was missing something.

Didi Harden popped next to Cathy. "Hi, Cathy. Can I talk to you for a second? I'm so sorry, but my cousin is visiting and now thinking of moving here. She fell in love with one of the properties you have listed, and—"

"Say no more." Cathy took a large swallow of orange juice and stood. "Where's your cousin?"

Didi grinned. "Come on over. I'll introduce you."

They left. The children continued to talk with their friends, ignoring their dad.

Perfect timing.

I turned to Darren casually. "So, Darren, what do you do? Real estate like Cathy?"

His son, apparently still paying attention, scoffed. "No way. My dad's Heisenburg."

Darren flushed. "I am *not* a drug dealer, Brian."

"Sure thing, Walter White," his older daughter said with a knowing look.

I was confused, not sure if they were teasing or letting out family secrets. "Walter White?"

Darren laughed, looking embarrassed. "Brian has been watching *Breaking Bad*. The main character is a science teacher turned drug dealer. I am neither. I work, *legitimately*, in pharmaceutical sales."

"That makes a lot more sense." I laughed with him, but inside, my guts were churning. Pharmaceuticals. Would he maybe have access to ketamine? I had no idea if what had killed Rachel and Marilyn had been from a recreational version of the drug or something found in a medical facility. Did Chad know about Darren's profession? He should. Had he already talked to Darren?

Ah well, in for a penny, in for a pound, as my grandma used to say. "What did you think of Marilyn, honestly? I haven't heard a lot of nice things about her."

Darren waited until his kids were occupied with each other once more then answered, "I think she wanted to be number one and would do anything to get there. I don't think she cared who she hurt in her pursuit to the top, either." He sighed. "She got a kick out of jerking Cathy around, and she did a lot of, not quite illegal, but frowned-upon practices in her business. I met her partner, Hank. Surprisingly, he's a really nice guy. I can't understand how they worked together for so long."

"I haven't met him."

"He's heading back to Maine soon. That's where he lives. He and Marilyn used to be married but figured out they made better business partners than spouses." He smiled as his wife sat back down beside him. "Unlike me and Cathy. We're much better spouses than business partners."

She huffed. "You got that right. No way I could work with you. You're too bossy."

"Right back at ya." He winked at her.

"You interrogating Walter White?" she asked.

He turned red. "Cathy, not you too."

I had to laugh. I didn't know if the pair had been honest with me, if Darren had actually had a thing with Marilyn or not, but I liked them as a couple. And I liked Cathy for being a strong, independent woman with a family she loved.

After I finished my breakfast, I rose and went to see if the cooks needed help washing dishes. As I loitered to pick up a fallen napkin, I spotted Rachel's sister, who looked just like her, standing off in a hallway with a man I assumed to be her husband. And Natalie Childers.

I took my time picking up that napkin and listened.

"Are you sure? You don't think she killed Rachel?" Rachel's sister asked between tears.

Natalie said, "No. She did threaten me, and that's why I warned you to be wary, but Cathy came up to me the other day and apologized. She realized Rachel had nothing to do with the listing Marilyn had stolen and felt super bad about taking it out on me too. There's so much going on with the investigation into SunSweet and into Rachel's death. It's a lot for everyone to handle. The police have been asking questions, but I honestly don't think Salter Realty had anything to do with Rachel's death. But that's just my opinion." Natalie sighed. "Rachel was always so nice to me. I really miss her."

"So do I," Rachel's sister whispered.

"Aw, honey. Let it out and cry. It'll be okay," her husband said.

I slowly straightened to toss away the napkin.

Natalie bumped into me as she left and apologized. She saw it was me and gave a brief smile before darting away.

I didn't want to be seen eavesdropping, so I hurried to the kitchen to see the Hagens, Alison, Stefanie, and Abe Cloutier doing dishes and being cheerful.

Without missing a beat, I turned around and made haste to my car.

And in the parking lot bumped into Mike Todesco minus Sherry. "Oh, sorry, Mike."

"No problem." He gave me his charming smile, and I had to admit he had a nice grin, pleasant features, and a sexy, manly-man kind of physique. A frame kind of between Dash's lean and toned body and Chad's large, muscular build.

"How have you been?" I asked him, striving for pleasant and a tad flirty. "I haven't seen you around town lately."

"Oh, we've been slammed at work. Dash going to jail has actually gotten us a heck of a lot busier."

"That's weird."

He propped a foot on a small boulder and leaned over his knee, like a cheesy advertisement for male cologne. "Nah.

People are people. Nosy as fu—er, as all get out. So what are you doing at church?"

"Hmm. That tells me you must come here often to know I don't."

He laughed. "Yeah. Sherry's folks like to see me praying to the Lord." He huffed. "Keeps 'em outta my hair."

"Mike, can I ask you something?" I was going to be pushy, but oh well.

"Sure. I'm always game to answer a pretty lady."

I needed to phrase this right, to compliment instead of annoy him. "Well, and don't take this the wrong way because I just love Sherry, but it seems like you guys break up a lot. And you're a really good-looking guy, and it's just . . . You're still a couple."

He nodded in understanding. "Yeah, I get asked that a lot. I'm hot, and Sherry's hot, but she's just one woman. But like, I'm a man in demand." He winked. "I have a lot of *friends*." He leaned closer. "And what Sherry doesn't know won't hurt her."

"Were you and Marilyn friends?" I asked, though I'd meant to ask about Rachel first.

He looked startled, sad, then angry. "What the hell does that mean?"

"I only ask because she dated a lot of guys. But I can't imagine her never looking at you. I mean, of the ones I know about, you're clearly the best looking. The hottest," I said, trying to think of something to calm him down. "I can't see her letting you go if she ever had you."

Mike straightened and shrugged, but I'd swear I spotted grief in his eyes. "Yeah, well, she was gorgeous. And nice." He glanced away. "She made me laugh. I genuinely liked her." He turned back to me and lowered his voice to say, "Sherry hated her. And I don't like making my fiancée cry. Marilyn was a long time ago. It's just me and Sherry now. Josie's fun and all, and I've flirted a bunch of times, sure." He grew louder. "But it's Sherry I want to make my life with."

I didn't know why he needed to broadcast it, but I agreed. "You're a lucky man. Sherry's sweet and super smart. You guys will make a lovely couple."

Sherry tapped me on the shoulder, grinning. "That's what I keep telling him."

"He can't say enough about you," I said with a smile.

She threaded her arm through his. "Time to head home. We have landscaping to do."

"She's domesticating me," Mike teased.

"It looks good on you." I watched them walk away and get into the car, where Sherry planted a long, wet one on her man. As they passed, she watched me with a blank expression though she waved.

Man, I had no interest in having a relationship if it would denigrate into jealousy and drama. Sherry and Mike deserved each other. Me? I had a picnic and a dog to get to.

Never let it be said a Jones picked love over a good barbecue.

* * *

A few hours later in the afternoon, I shared a barbecue with my uncles and Cookie at their place. Collin was hanging around with his friends, and I had dinner plans with Cat and Teri later that night, where they no doubt intended to batter me with questions about a half-naked Mt. Bachelor.

"Am I the only one who almost fell out of the pew at church earlier when Pastor Nestor started screaming about God?" I asked.

Jimmy laughed. "No. Elvis smacked his head on the bench in front of us. It was hilarious."

Elvis frowned, lifted his hair, and showed a small bruise on his forehead. "I'd leaned down to tie my shoe, and okay, I was having a tough time keeping my eyes open. Then Nestor starts screaming. I nearly knocked myself unconscious."

"Such a baby." Jimmy motioned Elvis closer, then pulled his head down and kissed his bruise.

"Aw, will you kiss my boo-boo too?" I asked sweetly.

Elvis mock-glared at me while Jimmy laughed and kissed the paper cut on my finger.

"Anything stand out to you at the service?" I asked them as Jimmy and I sat in the backyard and watched Cookie run around, then stop dead and pant under an aspen tree, dog tired.

"A lot, to be honest." Elvis flipped burgers and nodded to Jimmy. "Tell her."

"We were keeping our eyes open while listening to Berg and Roger Halston talking not as softly as they thought they were."

"Oh?"

"Yeah." He turned to me, drumming his fingers on the patio table, and gave me the dad glare. "Why exactly does Chad Berg want to know what you like and don't like to eat?"

"I . . . What?"

Elvis was trying not to smile.

Jimmy looked like a thundercloud ready to pour. "Yeah. He was asking Roger to secretly interrogate Cat for answers."

"He was?" Why? What did that mean? Was he interested in me? Like, really interested? Or was this some type of way to keep tabs on me to make sure I didn't endanger myself in the case. *How? By cooking me into a stupor?* "He and I came to a kind of truce about the case, and he's letting me give him info. But I don't trust him." I frowned. "Except he rescued two kittens he made me kitten-sit while he gathered clues yesterday, and now I can't hate him. Because, kittens."

Elvis put down his tongs. "Did you say kittens?" He looked at Jimmy, who suddenly announced a need to grab us all beers and darted inside. Elvis grinned at me. "You're welcome."

"What just happened?"

"I was hinting a few days ago that it would be nice to have a pet. Your uncle got a constipated look on his face about having animals. He loves Cookie but doesn't want to take care of anything furry full-time. Not counting your cousin."

"Ha ha."

"So I thought I'd mention the idea of pets to get him off your back."

"Oh. Thanks." I joined him at the grill and inhaled the lovely scent of roasting hot dogs and grilling burgers.

"Now tell me, what's going on with you and Mt. Bachelor?"

I chuckled. "Oh heck. I don't know. I went over Saturday night because I remembered what the note said."

"Note? Oh, the one you found at Sweet Fiction."

I nodded. "I ended up going to the Ripe Raisin to talk to Noah, because he remembered something that bothered him." When Uncle Jimmy returned, I explained what I'd learned from Noah, about the note, and why I'd gone to Chad's house.

Jimmy looked relieved. "That makes sense, I guess."

Elvis accepted the beer and took a large sip. "Ah, that hits the spot." He fiddled with the grill.

Jimmy drank, then looked at me and drank again. "Still doesn't explain why the detective wants to know what you like to eat."

Cookie came up to us, sniffing at Elvis's side. "Do not give her any meat, Uncle Elvis. You are turning my dog into a beggar."

"Sorry." He quickly withdrew the hand snaking down toward Cookie. "Can she have a bone?"

My mooching pup's eyes darkened, and her head swiveled between Elvis and me.

She gave a soft whine, and I relented. "Fine. But please, make her do something for it. She's getting spoiled."

Elvis handed his tongs over to Jimmy. "Come on, Cookie. Who's my best girl? Who wants a bone?"

They bounded inside, leaving me alone with Jimmy. He just waited, watching me.

"What?"

"Why is Berg trying to feed you?"

"It's not a big deal."

"Then why are your cheeks red?"

I scrubbed them and frowned when Jimmy chuckled. "Not nice."

"But funny." He flipped some burgers.

"I guess because he—"

"Wait," Elvis yelled from inside. "I want to hear!"

Once he joined us, I tried not to feel weird as I told them about barging in on Berg. And I knew things would only get worse when my friends interrogated me later.

But at least with my uncles, I didn't mention Berg not having a shirt or the meshing of our mouths. They expressed more interest in the kittens he'd rescued than anything, so I thanked my lucky stars I'd avoided at least one grilling.

So to speak.

Cat and Teri weren't nearly so easy.

Chapter Twenty-Three

"He had no shirt on?" Teri asked, munching on popcorn as we sat inside at my place.

Alt rock hummed through the Bluetooth speaker connected to my phone while Cat carried over the pizza she'd brought—her contribution to dinner. Mine had been drinks. Teri's was snacks.

Cookie was in heaven, once again chewing on the bone Uncle Elvis had given her. Plus, she'd nearly caught Mr. Peabody in the back. That or something else had gotten her sniffing and barking all over the yard. Probably a poor chipmunk with the nerve to be scoping out the property.

"No shirt." I nodded. "And it was a glorious sight. Mt. Bachelor in the flesh, so to speak."

"Oooh." Cat grinned and set the box of extra-cheese pizza on the coffee table. We sat around it on the floor, swapping stories. "I bet he's cut."

"Like a diamond." I sighed. "We were arguing and then sharing info about the case. And then we played with the kittens together and just talked."

"About what?" Cat asked.

"About what this town is like compared to Portland and Seattle. We both lived in big cities and prefer it here. And he likes the kittens and was surprised to really like Cookie."

"Why surprised?" Teri asked.

"Because he still thinks she's a troublemaker, but she's so smart and well-behaved too. He took her to do some police-safety class for some kids last Monday, and he said she won them all over in seconds. Plus, he's secretly—though he won't admit it—a cat person. He acts like he's just fostering those kittens, but I bet you money he keeps them."

"A sexy man who loves animals. You hit it."

"Hit what?"

"The jackpot, idiot." Cat snorted.

I glared back.

"She's right. We can tell he likes you." Teri didn't sound too happy about that. "But how can you marry and love Dash forever if you're crushing on Berg?"

"*What?*"

Teri nodded. Out of the corner of my eye, I saw Cat rolling hers.

"My mom has decided that you're as great as I always said you are, because you're helping Dash. And when I told her how awesome it would be to have you as a sister-in-law, she said she'd consider it."

Cat and I just stared at her.

"What?" She crunched more popcorn, dropped a piece, and tossed to Cookie, who gobbled it in seconds. "I think the plan makes sense."

"Teri, Dash and I aren't romantically involved."

"Well, not now, because he's in jail."

"*At all,*" I emphasized. "He's your brother. He looks at me like I'm a pest."

"I don't know," Cat said. "He's been changing around you. And you know, at least he's not the type to cheat on a girl or go behind her back on things."

Teri nodded. "He's no Mike."

That gave me pause. "Has Dash talked to Mike a lot about his behavior at the bar?"

Teri groaned. "So many times. I like the guy. Mike's funny and sweet, but man, he comes on to anyone in a dress. Or pants. I mean, if you have a set of boobs, he's honey-sticky sweet."

"Yeah." Cat handed me a slice of pizza on a plate before starting on hers. "Teri, eat your dinner," she said around a mouthful of gooey cheese.

"Yeah, because pizza is so much more nutritious than popcorn," I muttered and ate my own slice. Delicious.

"Dash is jokey and fun to be around," Teri said, "but at work he's a professional. Like, another person. He's bossy, tells Mike off, tells Noah off, heck, he's told me off."

"So he bosses Noah around too?"

She nodded.

I put my pizza down. "You know, we've been looking at Marilyn and Rachel's deaths as related to Marilyn and their real estate deals or boyfriends. But what if it all really revolves around Dash?"

Teri put her popcorn down. "What do you mean?"

"Well, what if whoever killed Rachel and Marilyn just wanted to punish Dash? I mean, they did leave Rachel's body in his backyard. Not at the bar, not by the Confection Rose."

"What about the Confection Rose?" Cat asked.

"I'll fill you in. But bear with me. This was personal. Dash is good-looking, has his share of dates, and is a pretty popular guy. Noah is funny and handsome. He dated Rachel a while ago. Then Dash comes in planning to go out with her again. And Dash dated her before. Maybe Noah was jealous and killed Rachel out of spite."

"But the blackmail note. What about that?" Cat asked.

I ignored her, on a roll. "Then Noah leaves her at Dash's and plants evidence. He knew where Dash hid his key. And he knows Dash better than most people."

Teri paled. "That's not nice to think about."

"But it could be true," Cat said. "But if Marilyn was killed just to get at Dash, that's a lot of planning."

"Premeditation, yep." I nodded. "And that would be one sick puppy to kill Marilyn and Rachel just to get at Dash. But then, how many people know exactly who Dash sleeps with? And he wasn't with Marilyn for more than a year?"

"But Noah would know." Teri looked sick. "He could have set it all up."

Cat frowned. "Now hold on. That still doesn't explain the note you found. And just what did it say anyway?"

I told them about the note, then had to backtrack when I realized I hadn't told them about the ketamine or confirmation Marilyn really had been killed. And the roses. Gah. I hadn't talked to them since seeing Dash in jail, and our brief convo at church hadn't helped.

"That's a lot you learned!" Cat gaped at me. "Wow. Talk about the case taking a weird turn."

"Right?" Teri nodded, no longer so morose. "I'm sorry, but if Rachel had seen Marilyn's murder, and if Noah meant for Marilyn to die to implicate Dash—which is still a little thin— then that implies he only killed her because she was blackmailing him. But if he'd set out to kill them both from the beginning . . ."

"I know. The Noah angle isn't that strong. Unless he hadn't meant to kill Rachel too. He liked her," I remembered. "But then she got drunk and reconnected with Dash. Maybe that's when it came to him to take her out."

"No way." Cat huffed. "That's pushing it."

I groaned. "Yeah. I think maybe we can ignore that. But if we're right about Rachel blackmailing someone to get money to start her own agency, then she had to be after someone who had money. Of our pool of suspects, I'd say that includes Dr. Thomas, Dr. Ryan, anyone who lives on Lemon Loop—"

Teri jumped in. "Including Darcy's husband, the mayor, and Pastor Nestor."

"The mayor?" I hadn't considered him a suspect.

"We really do need to talk with everyone again. I learned on Friday at work that the mayor had some deal with Marilyn that fell through, and he wasn't happy about it."

"I hadn't put Foot on the list." I was coming to hate this mystery. "Every time I think we can eliminate a suspect, we add more. Noah? Foot?"

"It would help if we could narrow down the motive," Cat said.

"Right. We don't know why anyone killed Marilyn. We think Rachel was killed because she was blackmailing whoever killed her boss. Her murder makes more sense."

"Does Berg have a lead?" Teri asked.

"If he does, he hasn't shared it with me."

"I thought you two shared a transcendental moment over kittens?" Cat grinned.

"And the mouths meeting. What about that?" Teri asked with a smirk.

Cookie watched us, gnawing on her bone.

"Okay, I'll tell you this in strictest confidence." I waited for them to agree. "Seeing him without his shirt was awe-inspiring. Sincerely. He was even handsome when he put a shirt back on. Just a T-shirt, but all those muscles! He cooked me food that tasted awesome. And we shared information like a team. Then I got to pet adorable kittens with him, and we seem to share the same taste in movies and TV."

Teri and Cat watched me like I was the most entertaining thing they'd heard in years. "And? Don't stop there," Teri warned.

"The whole time we're hanging out with the kittens, the tension is growing. And I'm feeling really attracted to him. I can't be sure, but I think he felt the same. He looked at my lips a few times like maybe he wanted to kiss me."

"Oh, this is so good." Cat's gaze never left me, even as she got herself a new piece of pizza.

"So then we started to get up from the floor, and I tripped over his foot. His foot, not mine. And I twisted so as not to hurt the kittens."

"And?" Teri asked.

"And I fell onto him and our mouths touched."

"Touched?" Cat frowned. "That's not romantic."

"It wasn't a kiss. But now he thinks I fell on purpose to kiss him. And I keep telling him it was his own fault because he has huge feet. They're like boats at the end of his long, long legs."

"But your lips touched. Hmm." Teri tapped her own lips with a finger, deep in thought.

"It wasn't a kiss, trust me. But, well, the contact lingered because my hands got caught between us on his chest, and boy, was I not ready to stop touching his pecs. That man is seriously built." I fanned my face.

"Yes! You're not totally hopeless," Cat cheered.

Teri shrugged. "Eh. This is not good for Dash. But I can't fault you on the man's body. Berg, when he's not frowning, is actually pretty handsome. And he's stacked like a fireman on crack."

"What?" Cat frowned. "Firemen don't do crack."

"Oh, you know what I mean. Fine, steroids."

"They don't do steroids either," Cat argued.

While the pair argued about firemen, bodybuilders, and work-out routines, I went over the thought of Noah as the bad guy, tucking away distracting thoughts of Detective Berg. I just couldn't make it fit, though something about Noah was rubbing me the wrong way. I should talk to him again. Then I recalled all he'd said about Mike being a screwup and Sherry's parents being rich.

"Hey, maybe it's Mike and Sherry."

My friends stopped talking. "What?" Teri asked. "Why?"

"I asked Mike about Marilyn at church, and he looked sad then angry. A little too angry that I'd accused him of being with her. Heck, he flirts with everyone at the bar. And Sherry knows it. That's why she hates Josie so much." I frowned. "I think she suspects Mike and I have slept together too."

"Mike? Come on, Lexi, have some standards." Teri shook her head at me.

"I didn't say I slept with him," I growled back. "Only that Sherry thinks I did. But I did *not*. My point is, Noah and Dash are constantly correcting Mike because of how he acts at work. And maybe he got tired of it. He slept with Marilyn and Rachel—that's a maybe on Rachel, though, I'm not sure— then . . . And that's where it falls apart. If he slept with them both, and Sherry already knew, what's the big deal? He's engaged to her. They have a house."

"That Marilyn helped them buy," Cat reminded me. "They have no beef with her."

"Ack. I know. It's just I can feel we're close to the answer, but it keeps slipping away."

"You want my take?" Teri asked. "It's one of the doctors in town with access to ketamine. Dr. Thomas works at a hospital. And Dr. Ryan—that hottie—at Sassy Pets."

"Wait a minute. There's ketamine at the vet's office?" I hadn't realized that.

"Duh." Teri looked at me as if I was a moron. "They use it to anesthetize animals. Why do you think one of its nicknames is horse tranquilizer? Because they use it on horses."

"Oh boy. Well, then we definitely have him on the list. He had a thing with Marilyn. Everyone knew that. But Uncle Jimmy once saw him outside Rachel's in the early morning, locking lips."

"That is such a bummer." Teri shook her head. "I've had a crush on him forever. And he went for Marilyn and Rachel? Ugh."

Cat nodded. "Well, there's your guy that slept with both murder victims. Besides Dash, I mean."

"There is that." I didn't like the thought of dashing Dr. Ryan being a suspect either, but he did fit the bill. And unlike Dash, he had money to pay off a blackmailer. "But why would he kill Marilyn?"

"Maybe you should ask him," Cat said. She glanced at Cookie. "Didn't I hear that someone needs to update her shots?"

Cookie stopped chewing on her bone, stared at the three of us, then took her bone and walked outside with it.

I couldn't help laughing. "Such a drama queen," I said loudly. But to my friends, I said, "Good plan. I'll get an appointment for this week, if I can. But for sure, Macaroons meeting tomorrow night at six thirty."

"We know. Stefanie sent out an SOS after church." Cat finished off her pizza. "Now, I think it's time we heard what's really going on."

"I told you guys everything." To my shame.

Cat turned on Teri. "You did, but not this one. Now, Miss Teresa Hagen, what's going on with Randy? And why are your parents—especially your mom—so chummy with him?"

Teri turned bright red.

"This I have to hear." I folded my arms over my chest. "Well? Get to it, Hagen. I haven't got all day."

Not with plans to stop a murderer before he, or she, killed again.

Chapter
Twenty-Four

"So she totally has a thing for him, and now he knows it," I told Cookie as we got in the car at two o'clock on Monday afternoon. I'd managed to get her an appointment because someone else had canceled. But at the slow rate she was moving, it might take us until Christmas to visit Sassy Pets.

I boosted her into the back seat, ignoring her grumbling, and waited for her to sit before I started up the car. We drove toward the west side of town, past a few suburban communities and a new elementary school subdivision. Sassy Pets sat on several acres, behind which Dr. Lee Ryan lived in a pretty ranch-style home. All alone.

One of the town's most eligible bachelors, Lee Ryan had been playing the field for a few years, since coming to town to set up shop, according to Teri. Who had been not-quite cyberstalking the man to learn details.

Tall, handsome, successful, with a caring mien and gentle spirit, Lee Ryan had that square jaw that made you just want to stare and tell him to do nothing more than look pretty. Then he'd talk and you'd hear all that intelligence, see his kindness with animals, and wonder to yourself what must be wrong with him that someone hadn't snapped him up by now.

Then I'd remember how awesome and single *I* was and chastise myself for thinking that way.

I had to carry Cookie from the car because she didn't want to go inside. She hung from my arms, deadweight, not even trying to play nice. "You're ridiculous, you know that?" How was I going to open the door with my arms full of furry drama?

She moaned, as if mortally injured.

"Gimme a break."

Fortunately, Evie, one of Dr. Ryan's techs, opened the door for me and stared with concern at my dog. "Oh no. Is she okay?"

"No. She has a case of the dramatics." I gave her a little shake. "Would you stop? You're embarrassing me." A glance around the waiting room showed two other people with pets waiting to be seen. Pets sitting nicely and behaving.

Cookie gave a loud sigh, then jumped out of my arms and walked to an empty seat. She sat next to it and laid her head on her paws.

"She's adorable." Evie laughed. "Would a biscuit help?"

"It might." I attached the leash to her collar, just for propriety's sake. Plus, the lady with the cat in her lap was giving me the evil eye.

Evie came back with a biscuit, which Cookie cheerily gobbled down before returning to her sad position by my side.

It took us another fifteen minutes, but we got into a back room after Evie weighed Cookie. "Oh, wow. You've dropped a few, Ms. Lovely. Looking good at a cheery thirty-seven pounds."

After being led into the back, we sat in a private room and waited for someone to come in to give Cookie her wellness exam as well as a rabies and leptospirosis vaccine.

"Now remember," I whispered, pleased she at least looked to be listening, "I need you to be super nice. I need to get Dr. Ryan to answer some questions for me. And if we're lucky, we'll see Sherry too."

Dr. Ryan had a few technicians working for him, as well as a new veterinarian to help balance his workload. He was a favorite in town and always had more business than he knew what to do with.

I figured we'd likely see him since Cookie needed a wellness check. Plus, he genuinely liked her and typically peeked in when we visited.

Sherry came in first. "Hey, ladies."

Cookie smiled and walked up to give Sherry a lick. Then she sat like a good girl, glancing from the jar of peanut butter treats to Sherry and back again.

With a laugh, Sherry gave her a treat, then moved to the iPad on the counter and typed in a few things. "Okay, so any problems? Anything the doctor should be concerned about?"

"Nope. She's pretty healthy. We're just here for our regular checkup and a few vaccines."

"I see that." Sherry looked nice, even in scrubs.

"I know I said this before, but you really look amazing with that haircut and color."

Sherry preened. "And the makeup. See how I'm doing my eyes?" She leaned closer to me.

I saw dark liner and hints of brown shadow, maybe? I'm okay when it comes to makeup, but whatever Sherry had done left a dramatic impression. "Wow. I wish I could do that."

"Well, it takes skill." She gave me an odd look. A cross between pity and scorn, if I wasn't mistaken. "And practice," she added with a broad smile.

Talk about weird vibes.

"Right." I paused while she looked over Cookie, petting and praising. Nice to the pooch at least. "You know, Sherry, I hope you don't have the wrong idea about me and Mike."

She gave a light laugh. "What do you mean?"

Should I see what I can get out of her or be nice? Hmm. Dash remained behind bars. I'd have to go with a reaction. "Well, I know Mike is pretty friendly with a lot of women in town, but it's not like that with him and me."

Sherry straightened. "What do you mean by friendly?"

I actually felt sorry for her. "You know."

"I don't think I do." She stood, stiff and angry. "My fiancé works hard, and sometimes he might act flirty to help with tips. But that doesn't mean he's available for the poor, pathetic, lonely girls in town."

Now that look—and tone—were definitely on the aggressive side.

"Exactly. He's engaged *to you*. And you're gorgeous, smart, and financially independent. Why would he want anyone else?"

She started to soften, looking confused. "Well, yeah. Right."

"I mean, Josie Letford is funny but she's nothing compared to you. And Rachel was on another level altogether. Not to mention Marilyn, who—"

"What are you talking about?" she snapped.

Cookie took a step closer to me, her eyes on Sherry.

"Mike Todesco loves me, and I love him. We have a house together. We're getting married. And soon we'll be having babies together. Marilyn was an old whore, and Rachel wasn't much better. She just thought she was hot, out for whatever she could get from people." To my dismay, tears filled her eyes. "Josie's a skank, not even worth a mention. Mike's just the best. He's mine. We love each other."

Oh boy. She wiped tears from her cheeks, and I suddenly felt awful for baiting her. "But he ended things with them. It's just you now."

She nodded and grabbed a tissue to blow her nose. "Yeah, just me." She pointed my way, still crying. "So keep your claws off him. You might be blond and pretty, but you're nothing like me. You keep away from my man." She wiped her eyes.

"I never had any intention of getting near your man," I told her, but it didn't seem as if she believed me.

Just then, Dr. Ryan knocked and opened the door, all smiles. "Hey, there. How's my favorite—Sherry? Are you okay?"

She sniffed and nodded, not looking at me. "I need a minute. I'll be right back." She hurried from the room.

Dr. Ryan shut the door behind her. "What happened?"

I sighed. "I think she's having problems with Mike."

He sighed with me. "Those two. Sherry's such a lovely person. A really hard worker. I don't know how she can tolerate—" He blinked and forced a smile. "Not my business. Not at all. Forgive me for talking out of turn."

Dang it. Teri was right. This guy looked like a male model and had Cookie melting for him, on her back and showing her belly as we spoke. He laughed and rubbed her, then stood and lifted her onto the exam table with little effort. "Well, now, Miss Cookie. Let's check you over."

He did his thing, checking out her teeth, her paws, her tail. "Her coat looks terrific, so keep feeding her what you're feeding her. Gums and teeth look good too."

I nodded. "Those toothie things are great." Treats that acted like toothpaste.

"Yep. I recommend them to all our patients."

"So, Dr. Ryan, did you find the owner of the kittens Detective Berg found?"

He looked up at me. "What's that?"

"The kittens Berg found. Did anyone report them missing?"

"Oh, no. I'm afraid the detective has his hands full with them. I have a few people willing to foster them, but he insisted he'd take care of them."

"Right." That big liar. Chad was a cat person. I *knew* it.

"So how are Lydia and Hershel? Still traveling through the Midwest?"

"Yep. My folks are still having fun and taking loads of pictures around the country." I pulled out my phone to show him the latest, and he laughed.

"They really helped me when I first arrived in town. I used to take care of all Brownie's aches and pains, the poor guy."

Brownie, my parents' deceased St. Bernard, had been a real character. "You helped them all through a tough time. Thanks."

"That's what I'm here for. I just love animals." He grinned at Cookie, who grinned back at him.

She wouldn't smile like that at a killer, would she?

"Yeah, animals are great. My parents miss having Brownie, but it's easier for them to travel without her right now." They weren't getting any younger, though they didn't like hearing it. "My mom was especially sad to hear about Marilyn and Rachel dying. Marilyn and my mom did a lot of work together in the chamber when she was alive."

"I remember that." He nodded. "Marilyn was a funny woman. Very smart and engaging."

"Did you know her well?" I asked and came closer to pet Cookie, watching the doctor for any signs he might be lying.

"We dated a while ago. A very interesting woman."

"So I've heard."

He gave me a hard look. "I can imagine what you've heard, and Marilyn wasn't like that. She was sweet and smart, and went for what she wanted. A lot of people didn't like that about her."

"Oh, no. I'm sorry if you misunderstood me." I wanted to believe his defense of her, but something about it felt lacking. "I meant I'd heard she was a real go-getter. Even some of the people who didn't like her can't help but talk about how savvy she was. I like meeting or hearing about other independent business owners." I pretended to share a secret. "I haven't told many people, but I'm thinking of buying my parents' bookshop from them. So I'm all about getting tips from successful business-women." I sighed. "Rachel was next on my list. She was right up there with Marilyn as far as being smart and professional."

A flicker in his eye, the firming of his brow. Great, I could see him reacting. But what did it mean?

"She was a great person too. Our town is losing too many of its caring members."

"Yeah." I shrugged. "But I guess when it's your time, it's your time."

His lips firmed. "Well, I don't think it was Rachel's time, not with Dash Hagen murdering her."

"Do you really think Dash did it? I heard they were planning on going out on a date this weekend. Getting back together."

"Back together?" Ha. There. He looked nonplussed. "Rachel with Dash Hagen? He's her type?"

"I don't know. I'm best friends with his sister, but I don't know Dash all that well," I said, in case he knew how tight Teri and I were. "He's nice enough. And the Ripe Raisin is the place to hang out. I saw Rachel there last week. She had just made a big sale and was so happy about it. It makes me sad to think she's gone now."

He watched me. "Did you know her well?"

"No. I mean, we talked occasionally. And I was thinking about joining the chamber of commerce."

He nodded. "I saw you there Friday night."

"Are your meetings always so . . . energetic?"

He laughed, but it sounded forced. "No. What with Marilyn dying, leaving Ed Mullins in charge, and then Rachel also passing, it's left a lot of us feeling down. I think we needed an excuse to gather and celebrate our friends, in a safe environment."

"No doubt."

Cookie licked his hand, and he softened. "Thanks, Cookie."

I smiled. "She always knows what to say. Or not say." I saw my dog canoodling with Dr. Ryan. No, he couldn't possibly be guilty of murder, could he? "I want to apologize if I made Sherry upset."

"What's that?"

"I mentioned how much I love her new haircut and makeup, and how great she is. And somehow we got to talking about Mike. She acted like she thought Mike might have been flirting with me, and I wanted to assure her he hadn't, but I'm not sure she believed me. Then Marilyn's name came up."

He frowned. "Marilyn? What does—did—she have to do with Mike?"

"No idea. Not about Marilyn. Though I thought I heard a rumor that Mike and Rachel dated."

"No," he said pretty quickly. "I don't think so."

"Oh. In any case, I didn't mean to make Sherry cry."

He shook his head. "That's on Sherry. And after she marries Mike, I won't be surprised to see her crying regularly." He bit his lip. "Sorry. That was pretty unprofessional of me to say. We're here about Cookie, not gossip."

"Doc, I watched Mike grope a woman's butt at the bar a few days ago. And it wasn't Sherry. I just think she can do so much better."

"Yeah. It's tough when the people you care for make mistakes. But the heart wants what the heart wants."

Cookie licked her lips, easing the tense atmosphere. "And Cookie's heart wants more treats," I said, causing the doctor to laugh. "Say, I have one medical question for you."

"Shoot."

"Is it safe to use ketamine on animals?"

He frowned. "Why do you ask that?"

"Oh, I was watching a documentary the other day on farming and they had some vet arguing its use on horses. Then I remembered reading about it being used as a drug with teenagers or something weird like that."

He nodded, his gaze pensive. "We sometimes use ketamine hydrochloride as a chemical restraint, like when we do surgeries, to keep our animals calm. They use ketamine in hospitals, on people, for the same reason. It can also be used to treat depression, though I've never used it that way and don't know a whole lot about that."

"Oh, okay. I was just curious."

"Well, be careful if you come across it. It can cause some bad side effects." He frowned, petting Cookie in thought.

Evie entered with a smile. "I'm here to help! Hiya, Cookie."

My dog gave her a welcome grumble and took her shots with a minimum of fuss and a little Cheez Whiz sprayed on a cracker.

We left the office and had just entered the car when Sherry knocked on my window. I rolled it down. "You okay?"

"I'm so sorry." Sherry wiped her eyes, smearing her mascara. "I didn't mean to break down, but the wedding planning and my parents are stressing me out. And then with Rachel getting killed, and we were friends . . ."

"Oh, Sherry. I'm so sorry. Look, fix your mascara before you go in." I handed her a tissue, and she used my sideview mirror to set herself to rights. "And forget everything I said. Mike is great for you. You're a strong, worthwhile person. You deserve every happiness."

"I do." She laughed. "Sorry. Every time I say that I imagine walking down the aisle."

"You're going to make a beautiful bride. You're a lot braver than I am."

"Oh?"

"Dating, getting married, buying a house together. That's a lot of commitment. I can't even commit to flavored creamer or regular creamer for my coffee."

We laughed together, then she left after apologizing again.

I drove us to the bookshop, pitying the fiasco of Sherry's pending marriage and not sure what to think of Dr. Ryan's attitude about Rachel possibly dating Mike.

Or the odd way he'd reacted to mention of ketamine.

Chapter
Twenty-Five

"Order, order," I called as the Macaroons got out of hand later that evening.

I'd already broken down everything that had happened between our last meeting and this one, and our whiteboard had been erased and rewritten on in multiple colors multiple times by multiple people. Finally, to shut everyone up and make peace, I'd handed all the colors to Darcy, since she had the neatest handwriting.

Yeah, it bothered me, because who doesn't love writing on a whiteboard with colored markers? But sometimes, sacrifices have to be made.

Our motive statement read: *M Killed, R Blackmailing Murderer.* Of everything I'd seen, heard, and understood to be true since the killings, our motive seemed to be spot-on. At least for Rachel's murder. We still had no idea why Marilyn had been killed.

"Right now, we have a host of suspects. Let's start crossing people off. Okay, Darcy. Number one."

"Cathy Salter."

Alison shook her head. "Nope. She was in Seattle when Marilyn died. Found out from a friend at the airport. So she couldn't have killed Marilyn."

"But her husband could have," Stefanie said. "I like Darren, but we can't confirm or deny his involvement with Marilyn."

"What about with Rachel?" I asked.

Elvis answered, "Nope. Darren didn't have a thing with Rachel. She wouldn't do that to a married woman. Seriously, she has no reputation for sleeping with married men. Single men, now that's another story. But even most of her exes speak well of her."

"Okay. I say we agree with that statement because everything we know and have heard about Rachel corroborates that part of her character." I looked around. Everyone nodded.

Darcy gave Rachel a pink heart by her name.

I refrained from frowning, because, really, a pink heart? "Next, we have Dr. Ken Thomas."

Alan raised his hand. "He's on top of my list. I know you and Elvis said he spoke highly of Marilyn at the chamber of commerce meeting, but I don't like him."

"Oh, why?"

Alan, one of the nicest, most laidback men I knew, liked everyone. He'd even been friends with Gil Cloutier, one of the grumpiest men on the planet.

"He's too full of himself and tried pushing me around when I went to him for a health problem a few years ago. Nothing serious. I didn't like the way he talked to me." He flushed. "Sorry, but I also know he's a big fat liar. He cheated on his wife and used to lie all the time about fake fishing trips. I hate anyone who uses fishing as a lie. It's a sacred sport."

"True enough." Kay nodded, her husband a huge fishing enthusiast.

"Also," Darcy added, "he's very wealthy. Or at least, his wife is. If he'd been having an affair with Marilyn and she threatened to tell his wife, that's motive right there. Because Morna Thomas would have left him high and dry. Their wealth is hers. And then you have Rachel blackmailing a person with means, and you have Dr. Thomas again."

"All in favor?" I saw everyone nod. "Mark him up, Darcy."

She put a circle around his name in red, then put a little devil face next to him. Oy.

We continued going down our list. Ed Mullins was pretty far down. Noah too. A few of Marilyn's exes lingered in the middle. Dr. Ryan wasn't that far down from Dr. Thomas, and of course, we had to add Mike.

"I hate to do it, because I made Sherry cry."

"Way to go." Cat grinned. "I mean, um, not cool," she added when Teri frowned at her.

"I don't care about Sherry crying," Teri said. "But you need to get real here. Sherry has access to ketamine via Dr. Ryan, and he's on our list. So we should add Sherry too."

"That makes no sense," Kay said. "Sherry is a jealous maniac, but she's also loyal. Marilyn got them a deal on their house. If the woman was sleeping with Mike, Sherry would have punched her lights out a while ago. Plus, Sherry loves Dash. I saw her kiss him on the cheek a few weekends ago for letting Mike have time off to be with her family."

"I'm afraid I agree," I said. "But I think Sherry could have gotten the ketamine *for* Mike."

"But why would Mike kill Marilyn and Rachel?" Stefanie asked, sounding annoyed. "He was bebopping with both of them. With Josie too, which spurred that fight Sherry had with her at the festival. Mike has it made. He sleeps around and Sherry pretends he doesn't. Plus, he's marrying into money. What's his angle?"

Elvis nodded. "Yeah, Stefanie's right." She grunted at him. A lot like Cookie did to me, but not now, sleeping under the table where she hoped to catch a crumb of the cake Cat had brought. "Mike's not the brightest in the bunch, but he has no reason to kill."

"That we know of," Teri said, then sighed. "No, strike him off the list."

"Are we sure?" I didn't want to but was outvoted.

"Next, Clint Ayers."

Stefanie perked up. "I never did tell you what I learned about him and Gary Conroy."

"Is that what you were going to tell me at church on Sunday?" I asked.

Stefanie frowned. "No. I don't think so. Anyhow, Clint and Gary are running some scam in Bend. Heard from my friend's brother's cousin—"

"Larry?" Alison asked.

"No, Lou. But technically, he's my friend's brother's cousin's cousin, but we shortened it for—"

"Stefanie," I interrupted before she went down the rabbit hole of relations. "What did you find out?"

"Oh, right. Well, Lou told me that Gary's in serious trouble for illegally undercutting some state-funded projects, and his past is catching up with him. Apparently, he did the same thing in California. Turns out Clint knew, and that's why he wanted to work with Gary, because they work cheap and planned to split the money they pocketed."

"Whoa." A lot of real estate troubles going on. "Does this at all tie in to Selma's Lot 49-71?"

"Yes and no." Stefanie groaned. "Sorry to say, it has nothing to do with anyone getting murdered. Clint needed Marilyn alive to keep him in the loop. With her gone, people started asking more questions and learned about his crimes."

"Okay, so we can strike their names off the list."

I watched Alison and Stefanie whispering back and forth while Elvis and Alan, and Kay and Darcy, started their own conversations. Then Cat and Teri broke off.

"Bathroom break, everyone," I declared.

Like magic, they parted, some stretching their legs, others gravitating toward the dessert table. Cookie opened one eye, watching the legs moving around her. And bingo, she darted out to snatch a piece of lemon cake that fell, munching happily.

"Uncle Elvis!"

"It wasn't me, I swear." He nodded at Alan, who flushed. "Sorry, Lexi."

"Oh, no problem." But then I saw Elvis smile at him. "Ha! It *was* you."

Teri and Cat had disappeared, probably outside. Then Cat raced in and shouted, "Incoming! Darcy, the board!"

Darcy rushed and flipped the whiteboard over, showing a framed discussion of points of view. We had listed the characters in my novel on the board, and I was prepared to talk about my suspense novel at length, should the need arise.

And in walked our need—Detective Berg in all his uniformed glory. "Ladies and gentlemen. Oh, and Lexi."

Teri snickered, saw me glaring at her, and shrugged. "What? That was funny."

"It kind of was," Cat agreed.

Berg ignored them. "Lexi, can I have a word?" He saw our whiteboard and made a weird face, like strangling a smile. "In private, please?"

"Guys, I'll be back soon."

Elvis watched us with a peculiar intensity, which made me nervous. He'd been on my side last time, but I had a feeling he'd snitch to Jimmy when he went home.

Conversation around us resumed. I walked toward Chad, expecting him to move. He didn't, and if I hadn't stopped myself, I'd have bounced off his chest.

"Say, is that cake over there?"

I rolled my eyes. "Wait here." I cut him a slice and brought him a plate with a compostable enviro-friendly spork. "Here you go."

"Thanks." He smiled, then turned and waited for me to precede him into the bookshop. He put a hand on the small of my back, guiding me toward the mini kitchenette. Once inside, he sat and consumed the dessert, barely taking the time to breathe, and said around a mouthful of cake, "This ish awshome."

I waited for him to finish before asking the obvious. "Do you know who did it?"

"No, but I wanted to let you know we narrowed in on three suspects."

"Who?"

"Right now, we have Dr. Lee Ryan and Dr. Ken Thomas at the station. Tad Oliver came to talk to me, because he thinks his wife might have done it, and the lieutenant is talking to her. I already talked to Darren Salter." Chad frowned. "I don't like that we have too many unanswered questions, not to mention a connection to the Ripe Raisin and stolen wine. Which leads me to suspect it might really be Mike Todesco we need to talk to.

But we can't find him. And his girlfriend hasn't seen him in a while either."

"Mike? Really?"

"Like I said, we don't know. But I want you to make sure you keep Cookie by your side. Don't go out alone. Or go into anyone's dark basement with someone you might think is a killer," he said dryly.

As if I needed the reminder of my last brush with murder.

"Right. Well, we were just discussing my book."

"Sure you were." He snorted before scraping the plate.

"Why don't you just lick it clean?"

So he did.

I did my best not to laugh and encourage him. Then Cookie entered and wagged her tail so hard I feared she might break it.

Chad's expression eased. "Hey, Cookie. We've got a bad guy on the loose, but we're not sure who it is. Keep an eye on Lexi, okay?"

Cookie sat and gave him a paw.

"Right. On your honor. Paw promise." He shook.

"Paw promise? What's that?"

"Dog version of a pinkie promise. The kids came up with that at our police safety class. Pretty clever."

"Uh-huh. And speaking of kids . . . How are Butterman and Angel doing?"

"Oh, the kittens are fine. Thanks for watching them."

"You mean, thanks for catching them when you threw them at me before running away?"

"I've never thrown tiny creatures in my life." He stood and glared down at me. "I live to protect and serve."

"But you do run away."

"I wouldn't call it running. More like a strategic retreat." He took his ballcap from where it had been tucked over his radio and set it on his head.

Did he know it put a shadow over his eyes, emphasizing his square jaw? Did he realize the hat made him that much more attractive? Was this a move of some kind?

I narrowed my eyes. "And just why are you trying to worm information out of my best friend?"

"Ah-ha. Halston owes me money." Chad grinned. "I knew you'd find out. That guy can't keep a secret from the tall redhead to save his life."

"For your information, it was my uncles who overheard you. Not Cat. Roger didn't tell her a thing."

"He admitted he did. Maybe your friend just didn't ask you yet."

"Ask you what?" Cat said from the doorframe, stuck there next to Teri, staring at us. "What she likes to eat? I told Roger already."

Chad gave me a look.

I flushed. "That doesn't mean he's not trustworthy."

"Oh, he's trustworthy. He's just got a soft spot for your friend. But now that I know that for sure, I can work with it."

"What does that mean?"

"That's classified information."

"Oh brother." I refused to look at my friends, who I could *feel* smiling at me. "Don't you have some criminals to catch?"

"Is that what your murder club came up with? Two suspects?"

Funny how fast one's friends could move in the presence of the law. Those goofballs deserted me.

Berg didn't look upset. Then again, he didn't look happy with me either.

"I have every right to meet with the Macaroons to discuss books."

"I know." He blew out a breath. "Look, just be careful, okay? There's something off about all this. But at least we have suspects to interrogate. Keep it quiet, and stay around your friends."

"Will do, Detective."

He walked out after saying goodbye to Cookie.

Leaving me alone in the kitchen, since she'd followed him to the front door.

We now had several suspects, but who was the one to watch?

I returned to the room to see every pair of eyes focused on me. Stefanie didn't bother to look Cookie's way when my dog sniffed at a dropped cookie under the table and ate it.

"Well? What does your new boyfriend have to say?" she blurted when I remained silent in thought.

"What? Hey, now. Detective Berg's not my boyfriend." Oh boy. I had no idea what Cat and Teri had told everyone, but Elvis looked amused for sure. And Kay kept giving me a thumbs-up.

"What did your not-boyfriend say?" Elvis asked.

"That they have taken Dr. Ryan, Dr. Thomas, and Darren Salter in for questioning. Oh, and that Tad Oliver thinks his wife may have killed Marilyn."

"Oh, right. Tad and Connie as killers. I meant to get to that," Stefanie said.

"What? Why didn't you *lead* our meeting with that?" Teri asked, shocked.

"No kidding." I glared at Stefanie. Talk about burying the lede. "Well? Details, please."

"Fine, fine." Stefanie proudly stood to say, "I distracted Connie while Alison went in and had a come-to-Jesus talk with Tad.

Apparently, he slept with Marilyn to make Connie jealous, but he hadn't thought it would work so well. He can't remember why she wasn't at home the night Marilyn died. And he thought she had a grudge against Rachel too but couldn't be sure."

"Whoa." Alan goggled. "That's a lot right there."

"No kidding," Elvis said. "Nice work, Stefanie."

"And Alison," Cat said.

"Right. Alison too."

Alison flushed with pleasure. Stefanie sat down again.

"Anything else from Detective Hot Pants?" Stefanie asked.

Teri choked on her coffee.

"Something else of interest: they're looking for Mike Todesco, so if anyone spots him, let the cops know."

"Mike's on the lam!" Alison nodded. "It fits."

"I don't know." Darcy frowned. "Mike's more a lover than a fighter." We all looked at her, and she blushed. "I don't know that from personal experience, mind you. But he never struck me as the violent type, and I've watched Sherry slap him silly after a fight."

She had a point.

"Well, the good thing is that we're getting closer. We have motive. We have a few suspects. Pretty soon, we'll have our killer. So everyone, be safe and stay together. If Detective Berg suspects we're investigating, the killer might as well." I swallowed hard. "And trust me, none of us want to be in his or her sights."

Cookie gave a soft grunt in agreement.

I nodded. "Yeah, what she said."

Chapter
Twenty-Six

By midafternoon on Tuesday, the police were still looking for Mike. It had been all over the news that any information leading to his whereabouts should be shared with the police. And it was all anyone could talk about, myself included.

"Wow. This town has become a thrilling place to visit," one of my regulars said as she checked out a pair of new cozy mysteries. "Redmond is boring by comparison."

I grinned. "We don't normally have a lot going on besides great food and drink. A festival every other weekend."

"Tell me about it. We're outside of Bend, and they're as bad."

"I haven't been to Bend in a while. I was actually planning to go to Sisters when I get a free weekend." And get my book a little more polished. Unfortunately, trying to reward myself for writing with a trip out of town hadn't done much to get my work done. I was starting to feel like a big old slacker.

"Oh, you should. You know the annual Sisters Folk Festival is at the beginning of October."

"Right. I wanted to go to that last year but got busy. I should go this year." I loved bluegrass music. Well, all kinds of music really, except gospel and easy listening. I'd never been into those genres, though I'd tried. I didn't like limiting my entertainment. But the Sisters Folk Festival was well-known for its bluegrass and blues. And cost. I'd have to make sure I could afford it.

"Make sure you do. Should be a fabulous time. I'll be there." The older woman smiled as she left, and I told myself to seriously get busy on my book.

I promised myself to at least have my first revisions handed over to an editor friend by the end of the month. And of course, to have Dash out of jail by then.

Cat yelled for me from the back room, where she'd been straightening up. I met her and realized the time.

"Yep, time to close early," she said and stacked the chairs by the side wall. "Selma's memorial is in half an hour."

I rushed back to the main store and gently urged everyone to leave, not that we had that many people left. Then I closed the store, making sure our sign that said open again tomorrow was visible. I changed into a dark, sleeveless, knee-length dress and joined Cat, who wore a dark skirt and blouse, and we hopped into the car with Cookie.

After dropping off my canine with Collin, we hustled over to the cemetery north of town.

We parked and met Teri, Randy, and Roger in his uniform. I didn't see Chad, but then he was no doubt busy interrogating half the town.

We walked out to Selma's plot and waited through the touching service. Then at the end, her daughter, tears in her eyes, invited us all to Strawberry Fields for one heck of a throw-down for Selma.

"My mom loved the lake and the fields. We want her sendoff to be a remembrance filled with joy. Hope to see you all there."

I wiped my eyes, touched by what many said about Selma, a bookworm, loving grandmother, and pain in the butt when it came to dominoes and card games. She'd been a definite personality, and she wanted what was best for her town. Confection would sadly miss her.

I also heard talk of Selma leaving everything split equally among her children, with Lot 49-71 going to the city. So no hidden motives for murder from her family.

All in all, the memorial had been a fitting end to a woman beloved by many. The party at Strawberry Fields was even better, with children laughing and the wind just cool enough to add a pleasant nip to the air, which the sun warmed perfectly.

I laughed with my friends, pleased to see them looking so happy with Roger and Randy, who fit in well with the group. I knew Roger Halston well, but I needed to get to know Randy better. Now that would be an odd twist. Randy Craig being the murderer all along.

I gave him the side-eye when he wasn't looking, but Cat caught me.

"What's up?"

"How do we know Randy isn't the killer?"

She laughed. "When would he have had the time? He's been trying to catch and hold Teri's attention since the beginning of the summer. Plus, I don't think Marilyn's his type. Rachel, maybe, but Marilyn was too aggressive for him."

"Are you kidding? He likes Teri, and she's more aggressive than a Tasmanian devil."

Small but feisty. I likened my friend to a can of soda that'd been shaken but not yet opened, the potential for all that fizz to hit you right in the face once she exploded.

"Well, that's true. But it's not Randy."

His name never had come up in any of our questions about the dead women. "How do we know?"

"Because Teri had him investigated by a private detective after their first date."

My jaw dropped. "She did not."

"She did too. She's paranoid, you know that."

I did. "But—"

"No buts. That's how I knew she really liked him. She went all-out right away."

"Wow." That took paranoid to a whole new level.

"Let's put it this way. He doesn't owe the IRS any money, he doesn't live with his folks or have any baby mommas anywhere. And he really does have a great job as an independent financial investor slash consultant."

"Just . . . wow."

Cat grinned. "I know, right? She even impressed me."

"And speaking of you, how's your baking going for Mel?" *Are you going to leave the store? Are you going to leave me?*

"It's great." Cat looked so excited. "You loved my strawberry rhubarb pie, so that's getting featured when I deliver it to her. The S'more Books, Please cookies are a Sweet Fiction only find, but I'm making those citrus scones for her too. And a few other cookie recipes."

"Can you do more book ones for us? Some creative choices?"

"Like what?"

"I don't know. How about a cozy mystery cupcake? Or a heavenly cookie for inspirational reading? Something cutesy."

"I can do that."

"Cat, you do realize this is you being a business person, right? That this is your own business starting to take off?"

"Stop it. You're freaking me out."

"I'm supportive one hundred percent. But you need to start thinking bigger. You need a kitchen to work from to create new recipes, more product."

"Oh my gosh. Product. That sounds so serious."

"It is. You're a baker and soon a business owner. Teri and I will help you set it up, though I bet Randy might have some ideas. He's a financial guy, after all."

She looked ready to pass out, so I motioned for Roger to come back.

"Hey, Lexi. Cat, you okay?" He drew her close.

She rested her head on his shoulder. "Lexi's scaring me. Make her stop."

I chuckled. "I told her she needs to take that first step and commit to her new business."

His frown cleared. "Ah. Well, yeah. I've been telling her that too, but she's taking her time."

"Because she's a wimp," Teri said and socked Cat on the arm. "Suck it up, princess, and bake."

I knew Teri had to feel like I did, that slowly, Cat was starting to pull away, making a new future. But Teri had Randy by her side, and I had Cookie. Hey, it was what it was. I could be practical and not hurt and wish the best for my friends.

Besides, Cat and Teri had just started dating their guys, yet they still found time for me. I felt a little better realizing that. Life changed. People moved on. Heck, if Sherry could open herself to marry Mike, I should be open to accepting new people into my life. New man-people.

Hmm. Had Marilyn perhaps come to this same thought? The perpetually single man-eater finally ready to settle down and focus on one special person?

Sad to think she might have tried and failed.

But what if she hadn't? What if she'd tried . . . and succeeded?

* * *

Having dressed in my fancy walking sandals, which went well with my dark dress, I had no problem asking Cat to drop me off near the police station two hours later.

"Are you sure?" she asked.

"Yeah. I'm going to talk to Berg, then walk to get Cookie. It's still light out. I'm fine."

Unfortunately, Berg was busy with suspects, and I was "not invited to hang around and bug him when he had work to do."

I sneered back at Officer Brown. "Thanks so much, Officer Brood."

"That's Brown," he corrected and waited for me to leave.

Geesh. What had happened to the nice clerk at the desk who'd been all smiles the other day?

I bumped into Roger as I left.

"Hey, what are you doing here?"

"I wanted to talk to Detective Berg, but Officer Fat Head told me not to bug him."

Roger masked a grin by coughing. "Right."

"What did she call me?" Brown asked in a loud voice.

Roger tugged me outside. "Want me to pass a message?" he asked kindly.

"Roger, you like Cat, don't you?"

He flushed. "Yes, I do."

"She really likes you too." I patted him on the arm. "Please don't screw her over."

Roger gave me his solemn oath he wouldn't, and I believed him.

"Please tell Berg that I think Marilyn wanted to settle down with the right guy. It all stems from that, I think. Tell him to focus on Marilyn, not Rachel."

"Tell him?"

"Er, tell him I *suggested* he should look at it from that angle. Who really loved Marilyn the most?"

"I'll relay the message. I'd also feel a lot better if we'd found Mike already. What can he be thinking by avoiding us? It just makes him look guilty."

"I know." I had a bad feeling he might just be as guilty as he looked. Everything added up to Mike being the bad guy. Poor Sherry. After she'd sacrificed so much for him. Like her self-worth.

I shook my head. "Okay, I'm off. The bookshop is closed, so I'm giving myself permission to enjoy the rest of the day."

"That service was really nice. Selma lived a good life."

"She really did." Feeling teary, I left him with a smile and forced myself not to cry. I didn't know why I felt sad. Selma had lived a great life, and she'd finally gone to join her husband in heaven or wherever they landed.

Man, I felt mopey and hated myself for it. So I made myself enjoy downtown, grabbing a new blouse from Honey Threads, a small clutch of flowers from J&D Floral, and a homemade raspberry pop tart from Cookie Crumbles. After devouring it, I wondered if Cat would consider making some for the shop. Because, *yum*.

I wandered home, the sunlight playing over my face, the breeze whisking the edge of the dress against my knees. My hair flew freely, and for once I stopped to smell the roses.

"You. I have a bone to pick with you."

Oh boy, did I stop at the wrong house.

I glanced up to see a mulish Ed Mullins bearing down on me from his front porch as I sniffed his red roses from the sidewalk.

"Hi, Ed."

"Don't 'hi' me, Miss Jones."

I didn't even try to hide my rolling eyes.

"What is the meaning of telling Detective Berg that I'm a prime suspect in his murder inquiry?"

"Excuse me?"

"It's all over town that you and the detective are an item. He listens to you. And you've always tried to get rid of me. Well, now you're nearly there, aren't you?"

I wanted to ask if he was off his meds, but that sounded insensitive, even in my own mind, so I kept that to myself. "What are you talking about?"

"I've been voted out of the interim chair position at the chamber."

"I'm sorry." Was I though? Not really.

"Yes. Apparently, my character is in question."

"No kidding? Who's in charge then?"

"For now, until we have a vote, Tad Oliver."

"Really? Because everyone knows he slept with Marilyn Freeman. And I thought his wife had no alibi for the murder and was considered a suspect."

Ed goggled. "Connie Oliver?"

"Well, she was angry that Tad slept with Marilyn, and she was always talking about Marilyn. Heck, my friend overheard her a few nights ago in the Ripe Raisin being glad Marilyn had died."

"Oh ho." Ed looked thrilled at the news. "Which friend?"

"What?"

"Which friend overheard that?"

"Teri Hagen, but—"

Ed yanked out his phone and called someone. "Nestor? It's me. We need to reconvene to discuss interim chair. It can't be Tad. He cheated on his wife with Marilyn, and get this, Connie is a suspect in the murders!"

Uh-oh. I probably shouldn't have shared that. "Well, not really, but maybe, I'm not—"

Ed talked over me, and the bits I did catch were enlightening.

Screw Officer Brown. I had to talk to Chad. Stat!

Chapter
Twenty-Seven

I found him in the courtyard of Eats 'n' Treats because he'd taken his dinner break there, wanting out of the office.

The many people eating and waiting for their meals watched as I plunked down across from him. "Why haven't you called?"

Chad looked around, put his sandwich down, and leaned back with his arms crossed over his chest. Despite not knowing what reaction he was aiming for, I felt neither amused nor intimidated.

"Excuse me?"

"I have *information*," I bit out and added in a quieter voice, "Connie Oliver has an alibi. She was talking to Nestor, confiding in him about her husband, when Marilyn was killed that Thursday night. And while she was, Ed was with Tad. Then Connie went right home to her husband after that. She and Tad can't be guilty."

He frowned. "I know."

"But . . . You know?"

"Ms. Jones," he said in an alarmingly loud voice. "You are not welcome to speculate on the investigation. It's none of your business, and I'm not sure why you think I'd be interested."

Confused and mortified, I had to ask myself why I'd thought he and I might actually end up getting along. Even though he did love kittens. Heck, everyone loved kittens. I'm sure serial killers liked kittens. But in the end, they were still serial killers.

"Now, for the last time, would you please stop harassing me? I'm here to protect and serve, but I'm having a tough time doing that on an empty stomach."

If that wasn't bad enough, Mel bustled over to scold me like a two-year-old. "I'm so sorry, Detective. Lexi, honey, why don't you leave him alone? He's been super busy lately with the cases he's working."

"You're an ass." I rose, saw the shocked faces around me, and hurried to say, "Not you, Mel. You, Detective Berg. Fine. You've already arrested the wrong man once. Do it your way and keep going down the wrong path." I marched away, nearly knocking Sherry and Evie down. "Sorry," I muttered and kept going.

Behind me, I heard Sherry say, "You go, girl."

"Men suck," Evie added.

What a super huge jerk. He'd told me to help him. I had vital information he blew off as inconsequential. "I know," he'd said. Well, had he bothered to tell *me* that? No. How was I to know what he already knew? I was no mind reader.

Fuming and needing a break, I walked to the Ripe Raisin. The hour hadn't reached full dark yet, so the place was just filling up. I sat at the end of the bar and hung my bag of goodies on a hook under the counter. "Noah, I need something strong."

He nodded. "How about a cocktail just for you?"

"Yes, please. And make it sweet."

A few moments later, he brought me a lemon fizz that was delicious, a mix of sour and sweet and it relaxed me in no time. I chatted with a few tourists who sat at the bar next to me before moving on. Then I nicely but firmly persuaded a younger guy that I wasn't up for a date.

He left just as Noah pushed a new lemon fizz my way. "What's wrong?"

"You're busy. I don't want to bug you."

"Not at all. Jen and Josie have everything running just fine."

I saw a tall brunette capably handling the bar and decided what the heck. I needed a friendly voice. "Berg's a jerk."

"Um, I know. He's my cousin."

"I mean, he embarrassed me in front of everyone at Eats 'n' Treats. How hard would it have been for him to tell me to go away? Quietly, I mean."

"That's Chad. I don't know how his tiny brain works." Noah paused. "But I do know he means well. He's socially awkward sometimes, but he's not mean-spirited." Noah looked me over. "I think he likes you."

"So that berating was the equivalent of a little boy pulling a little girl's hair?"

Noah tugged a strand off my shoulder, and we both laughed.

"It's nice to see you smile. You've looked so down lately," I told him.

He shrugged. "My best friend's in jail for something he didn't do. How would you feel?"

"Yeah." I studied him. "Noah, what do you really think about Dash? He's bossy, gets women to come to him way too easily, and is a pain to work with, especially when he thinks he's right."

"Yes, yes, and yes."

"How does that not irritate you? I mean, he went out with Rachel. And you went out with Rachel."

Noah leaned on the bar. "Let me tell you. I met Dash in third grade. He tried to steal my Oreos. I punched him right in the face. But when the teacher caught me, he never ratted me out. We bonded over cookies and Susie Hobbes, our mutual third grade crush. He has literally given me the shirt off his back. When Laura dumped me my sophomore year of college, he was the guy who let me crab about her constantly. And when my dad passed, he and the Hagens were there for me and Mom.

"Dash is a standup guy in so many ways. And yeah, he can be a know-it-all and way too bossy sometimes, but he's my best friend. I know he's innocent, the same way I know my cousin would never deliberately hurt you. Dash will be cleared of all charges. Chad will make sure of it. Don't give up on either of them, Lexi."

And to think I'd doubted Noah's innocence, mentally accusing him of maybe killing Rachel in a fit of jealousy over her and Dash. I was *so* glad I'd never asked if he'd done it.

"Thanks, Noah. I'm sorry. I'm just down, I guess. Your cousin is pissing me off, and I'm upset Dash is still in jail."

"His bail hearing is tomorrow."

"I hope he gets it."

"Me too."

I finished my second and last lemon fizz, then asked for water.

Josie came over to deliver it since a group came in asking for the manager. Frankly, I didn't know how Noah didn't murder obnoxious customers.

"Rough day?" Josie asked.

"Yeah. How about you?"

"Same. I missed Selma Livingston's funeral. Bummer, because I'd wanted to go. I heard it was really nice."

"It was."

Josie looked me over. "That's a good funeral dress. Cute and respectful yet stylish."

"Yeah, and it was on sale when I bought it."

She grinned. "Even better." She wiped the bar in front of her. "Did you hear that Marilyn Freeman's service was also today? Her ex made it a private affair though, so only a handful of people could go. I guess he didn't want a spectacle, especially since I heard they had to do an autopsy on her body. Gross."

"Sad."

Josie shrugged. "You know, I feel kind of bad for her. Marilyn had style, looks, and money. But in the end, she was all alone. Her ex-husband is seeing to her affairs. Her family is supposedly distant, and she had no boyfriend or lover to see her off. No kids either. That's awful. I'm single, but I have my mom and sister here. And I'm setting my sights on a new guy."

"Who, can I ask?" The lemon fizzy started to make me dizzy. Wait, lemon fizz. Hey, I'd rhymed. I chuckled. Gosh, I was such a lightweight.

"You know that cop who's always with Roger Halston?"

I grimaced. "Officer Brown? But he's a grade-A jerk."

Josie laughed. "Oh, but honey, bad boys make the best boyfriends."

Meh. Bad boys or idiot men. Both made for bad bedfellows, in my opinion.

Having done what I'd set out to do—relax and get over ballistic Berg's bad behavior—I left Noah a huge tip after settling my bill and walked toward my uncles' house, just a little farther past the bar to Lemon Loop.

But I hadn't counted on getting jumped as I passed the alley between the bar and Cinnamon Avenue.

A hand covered my mouth and steel arms wrapped around my waist, tugging me off my feet with ease.

I was so scared and stunned I put up no fight at all. *Idiot.* I started to struggle but stopped when I recognized Mike's voice.

"Shh. Lexi, it's me. Mike. I swear, I won't hurt you. I just want to talk. Please, believe me. Here. I'm setting you down. Look."

Mike gently put me on my feet, and I wavered, done in by two lemon fizzes and an adrenaline rush.

"Dang it."

"I'm so sorry." He moved as if to help steady me then jerked away. "I don't want to scare you any more than I already did. I'm so sorry," he said again, and I forced myself to relax.

"What the heck, Mike? Don't you know that everyone's looking for you?"

"Why do you think I'm hiding in an alley?" He paced.

Grimy jeans, a dark T-shirt, weary eyes, and an unsmiling face. Mike was stressed for sure. He never looked less than his best, even after a long shift at the bar.

"Look, I didn't kill Marilyn or Rachel. I swear."

"O-kay."

He ran a hand through his hair. "Everyone thinks I did it, but I didn't. Hell, I loved Marilyn."

"Mike, tell me everything. No judgment. I'll listen." *And then I'll tell Berg, to his face, what a moronic, sexist tool of a man he really is when I announce the killer.*

After listening to Mike ramble about how much he loved Sherry for five minutes, I forced him to sit with me on an abandoned bench at the end of the alley, what used to be called Smoker's Alley before the city had banned outdoor smoking within twenty-five feet of any Confection business property.

"Lexi, I don't know what to do." Oh man. There were tears in his eyes.

"It's okay, Mike. Tell me. Did you and Marilyn have a relationship?"

"We did." Mike sighed. "Sherry's my girl. Has been for years. We hooked up in high school and have kind of always been on and off again, you know? I saw other girls. She knew it then, knows it still. It's how I'm wired. But Marilyn, she was something different."

"How?"

"She met me in the bar months ago. Oh, I'd seen her before with a different guy almost every other week. But you know, I respect a woman who knows what she wants and isn't afraid to take it. She was fine. Smart. Rich." He grinned, but it was a grin tinged with grief. "I'd never felt anything like I felt with her. It wasn't just sex either. I've done that. A lot. But Marilyn made me feel good inside. Like I was worth something."

"Sherry doesn't make you feel that?"

"She tries, but she's too much a daddy's girl. She does whatever her parents tell her to, except when it comes to me. She loves me. I know that. But she always tries to get me to change so her parents will like me more. Marilyn didn't want me to change. She liked me for me. And I liked her." He paused. "I loved her."

"Were you the man she'd fallen for?"

"Yeah. I knew she had a lot of exes. Not as many as everyone said, but if she saw a guy she liked, she went after him. And men loved her. It wasn't just me. If you knew her, you'd understand her magic."

I nodded for him to continue.

"We grew closer, and Marilyn told me she loved me. That she'd never said it before. I didn't know what to think. I mean, it was what I'd wanted. But Marilyn and I . . . I had Sherry. Hell, Marilyn helped us buy a house under the asking price. And it should have gone for a lot more. But she loved me, and she wanted me happy."

"She sounds like she was a loving woman." Who didn't care that Mike had been engaged at the time of their relationship, but hey, I'd said no judgments.

"She was." Mike sighed. "The last time I saw her, I brought a bottle of wine she'd been dying over. The Ripe Raisin had ordered it for some schmuck, but he didn't deserve it. So I snatched it and took it to Marilyn's. But after we drank, we fought. She wanted me to break it off with Sherry. But Lexi, I love Sherry. I mean, I loved Marilyn too, but she didn't get it. Sherry's my girl."

And Marilyn had threatened to tell Sherry everything.

And there. Mike's motive for killing Marilyn.

"I didn't know what to do. I was in love with two women and didn't want to hurt either one. So I left. I told Marilyn I'd call her the next day, that I needed time to think it over. She told me not to take too long." His eyes welled. "I left her. And I never saw her again after that."

"Did Sherry know?"

He stared at me wide-eyed. "Are you kidding? She'd have gone ballistic. But Marilyn had told me a few weeks ago she thought someone was watching her. That maybe one of her exes wasn't happy she'd told him no."

"But you didn't know who that was."

"No. I wish I did, just so she wouldn't have been so scared the last few weeks. Unless she'd been imagining it or lying for attention. I don't know." He dropped his head into his hands. "I really loved her. I miss her so much."

I expected him to wipe more tears, but when he raised his head, his eyes looked dry. Mike appeared composed. Had he been putting on act or just gotten himself together?

"Anyway, I found out the next day she'd had a heart attack. It was like fate kicked me in the teeth. I wasn't meant for Marilyn. I should have felt better about things. But I didn't. Sherry could tell, but I told her it was just work. She believed me. And we're that much closer to getting married and living happily ever after."

"Mike, I don't understand. What you said makes plenty of sense. Why not go to the police and tell them all this? They think you killed her."

"She died of a heart attack."

"No, she died of an overdose that led to a heart attack."

"She killed herself?" He looked stricken.

"I heard one of the officers say she was poisoned."

"*What?*"

"Yeah." I patted him on the arm. "I'm sorry to tell you. But I think maybe it was one of the men she'd known before you. Are you sure she never mentioned who might be watching her?"

"No. But if it was poison . . ." He scowled. "That bastard. I bet I know who it was." Mike stood and looked at me as if seeing me for the first time. "I have to go."

"Wait."

He stopped.

"What about Rachel?"

"What about her?"

"You didn't kill her, did you?"

"Why would I kill her? We never said more than a few words to each other." He didn't look sorry about Rachel, not like he had about Marilyn. Hmm.

"So you never had a relationship with her?"

"With Rachel I'm-Too-Good-for-This-Town Nevis? Hell, no." He rushed from the alley and disappeared.

I reached for my bag only to realize I'd left it in the bar. Shoot. I hurried back inside and found it sitting where I'd left it, along with my flowers and blouse. I should call Berg about this. But no, he'd irritated me so much that even after two lemon fizzes I wanted to belt him one.

So I called Roger instead. Let him talk to Iceberg. I had a dog to gather and a bed to crash into.

Chapter
Twenty-Eight

The banging on my door would not stop. And neither would Cookie's barking.

"Okay, already." I managed to pry one eyelid open to see it had reached one in the morning. I threw a ratty robe over my overlarge T-shirt and stumbled to the front door.

Cookie sat in front of it, smiling and wagging her tail.

I saw Detective Dunderhead through the door-lite, the shape of his head and the ever-present line of his frown impossible to mistake.

"What?"

"Let me in. I need to talk to you."

"Sod off." I smiled. I'd been wanting to use that British phrase for a long time, since first getting hooked on British mysteries.

"Lexi, open this door," he growled.

Cookie growled back.

"Tell her, Cookie," Berg ordered.

My doofus of a dog turned and growled at *me*.

"Hey, I feed you. Remember that."

She blinked, looked at the door, then at me, and trotted to Mr. Leggy on the floor, where she flopped and watched the humans' live entertainment.

To Berg I said with as much disdain as I could infuse into my voice, "You're a cretin who intentionally yelled at me—like I'm your freakin' kid—in front of the people I work with and live with in this town. Tell me why I should let you into my house."

"I'm sorry," he enunciated, slowly. "I had my reasons."

"Well? What are they?"

He sighed so loudly I heard him through the door. "Can I please come in so you can yell at me face to face? In private?"

"What should I care about privacy? You obviously don't care about mine."

"Because it's one in the morning and your neighbors might not want to be woken up."

Shoot. There was that. I unlocked and opened the door but refused to let him inside past the hallway. "Stay right there. Apologize." I really wanted to add "on your knees, peasant."

"I'm sorry. I'm very, very sorry I was rude, but I did it to protect you."

"That is just terrible. Worst apology I've ever heard. How about I punch you in the face for your own good? How about that?" I snapped.

He bit his lip and turned away.

I growled, "And if you are laughing at me, I will kick you so hard you'll never sit again. Or have children."

He turned back, his face expressionless. "I'm truly sorry I hurt your feelings."

"You didn't hurt my feelings. You embarrassed me."

"Again, I apologize. Can I explain?"

"It's *may I* explain, and yeah. Get to it."

He nodded, dressed in a wrinkled polo and slacks. Berg noticed me looking and said, "The LT wanted me in plain clothes to do the interviews. Thought it looked more intimidating than the Confection PD uniform I normally wear around town."

"Whatever." I had been curious.

"Look, when you tracked me down at Eats 'n' Treats, I was tired and famished and the center of attention. You came near me, acting like we were buddies, and I felt all those eyes, some of which might have belonged to our murderer. So I pretended you had nothing to do with me or the investigation to keep you apart. To keep you safe."

"Bull crap."

"It's true." He held a hand over his heart. "I swear."

"That's so stupid I just can't . . ." I punched him in the chest. Hard.

He didn't move, though I thought he might have given a little huff. But my hand hurt.

"Feel better?"

"No," I said, feeling miserable. And tired.

He sighed and walked around me, returning with ice wrapped in a dish towel. "Come on."

We sat at my dining table, and he apologized again. "After you left, I felt like a real heel. And then Mel tore into me."

"What? After she told me to leave you alone?"

"Yeah. Said I treated you badly and should apologize. But then people started whispering. And soon word was you had no influence on the investigation and that the Gil Cloutier murder was a one-off."

"Oh, good, I guess. Though Ed Mullins thought I was the one putting ideas into your head to accuse him. But then, you already knew that."

He had the grace to look ashamed. "Yeah. But everything you just learned from Mike. That's new. Roger told me." He looked me over. "You okay?"

"I'm fine. I was scared to death when he yanked me off the street. Mike's really strong."

Berg's eyes narrowed. "He'll pay for that."

"I don't know what to think of his non-confession." I shifted the ice on my knuckles. "He says he loved Marilyn. He seemed like he did. But he loves Sherry too and sleeps around on her. I think Mike really loves himself."

"He admitted he was the last to see her and that he brought that stolen bottle of wine. So why wasn't it at Marilyn's when we arrived? The cleaning person didn't take it. The glasses were clean and dry. I think Mike poisoned her and took the bottle with him. Then Rachel saw and tried to blackmail him."

"He was pretty adamant that he had no love lost for Rachel."

"Hmm."

"Mike also seemed pretty sure of the murderer."

"Or he said that to put you off."

"I considered that too. I'm not sure. He seemed upset about Marilyn's murder but not devastated. And he didn't turn himself in even after I told him how guilty he looks."

"That bothers me too. After his assault on you, though, now we can—"

"It wasn't an assault." I felt foolish calling it that.

"He put his hands on you and scared you. Call it what you want. I want this guy behind bars. Now. We're looking for him."

"Good luck finding him in the dark."

"I know." He sighed and moved the ice off my hand, studying my fingers. He took my hand in his and moved the digits. "Anything hurt?"

"No." But my stomach was doing somersaults. "Are you wearing Kevlar or what?"

He smiled. "I'm strong. You have small hands." He turned them over. "Graceful hands."

He looked at me.

I looked at him.

We shared a moment of steamy silence, and his gaze slipped to my lips.

Then his radio squawked and made us both jump.

He took the call and stood. "I have to head back. They think they found him out by Strawberry Fields."

"You should really check Sherry's parents' house. I bet he's hiding there."

"We have people on it. Don't worry. We'll get him."

"Great. But if he's not the murderer, you're still at square one."

"Maybe." He pulled me into his arms and hugged me.

I froze, not sure where to put my hands.

He set me apart and grinned down at me. "You have bed-head and you're still pretty." He walked away. "Cookie, keep an eye out. No one in or out unless she says so."

Cookie grunted.

Berg chuckled. "Lock up after me," he said in the open doorway.

"Blah blah, I heard you," I said grumpily, feeling weird after hugging Adonis. But I locked the door after he left.

I hightailed it back to bed and warned Cookie to bite the man next time if he arrived when the sun refused to shine. But she used that selective hearing that tended to flare up and ignored me. Typical.

I slid between my sheets and dreamed about Berg locking me up in jail, then joining me in our solitary bunk. Right before Marilyn's shadowy murderer did us both in.

* * *

By the time the store opened and we had a nice stream of people after lunch, Cat and I had shared what we thought Mike's revelations really meant.

Cat nodded. "He did it. I feel it. But it would be really cool if Marilyn or Rachel's spirits stuck around to let us know who did them in. Just like *Ghost Hunters*."

Cat and her spooky nonsense.

"Does Roger know yet about your haunted fetish?"

"I thought I'd break him in over Halloween."

"The Owl Hoot. Are we doing it?"

"Yes. Sweet Fiction always has a booth. I'll provide the treats."

"Yes, you will." I grinned at her. "Come up with a name yet for your new business?"

"Stop pressuring me! You people are giving me high blood pressure."

"Well, if that's the case, then by all means, don't take any ketamine." I paused, knowing my joke had been in poor humor. "Cat, what if Mike knew who killed Marilyn because he put two and two together?"

"Um, that's four. I put it together too, and I have no clue who you're talking about."

"Well, we know you can find ketamine at a hospital or veterinary clinic. And we have two doctors under suspicion. But when I spoke to Dr. Lee Ryan about it at Cookie's vet appointment, he acted weird."

She pounced. "Weird how?"

"I don't know. I could be projecting."

"You mean, putting your own weirdness onto others?"

"Thanks so much for explaining away my delusions."

She grinned. "Don't mention it."

Before I could say any more, Roger burst into the shop with a big grin for Cat. He walked up to us and said quietly, "We caught Mike Todesco earlier this morning outside Dr. Ken Thomas's home, lying in wait."

"So it was Thomas, not Ryan? Huh."

Roger frowned at me. "What?"

"I thought Dr. Ryan had to be the guilty party. Sherry, Mike's girlfriend, works for Dr. Ryan. And I once overheard Mike jealous of the guy. I just assumed Dr. Ryan would be the one Mike went for."

"Well, Mike is sobbing like a baby, claiming he did it and he's sorry. He refused to confess at first, but when we had him on the missing wine bottle, blaming Dash, his boss, for it all since his boss nearly fired him a time or two, and then stealing the ketamine from his girlfriend by using her key to the office—which we found in her house with his prints on it—he folded." Roger sighed. "It was actually pretty sad."

"Oh man. There goes Sherry's big dream wedding." Cat sighed.

"Why are *you* so upset?" I asked.

"She wanted me to bake the cake."

"Oh, bummer." I didn't like any of this. "Roger, I just . . . I get Mike killing Marilyn, but why Rachel?"

"She saw him kill Marilyn."

"Wait. She did?" Now Cat was frowning.

"We think she saw him leave Marilyn's house with the wine bottle in hand, taking the evidence with him. She needed money for her new business that she couldn't get from the bank. It all fits."

"Yeah, it does." So why was I still bothered?

Roger kissed Cat on the cheek. "Good news for Dash, right? His bail hearing today shouldn't take any time. The DA is dropping all charges."

Relieved, I hugged Cat, then a blushing Roger. "Thanks. I'm calling Teri right now."

"Ah, I'm thinking the DA might let her know before you do. But if you do let her know, just tell her to keep it to herself. I'm not supposed to say anything yet. It's not concrete, and Mike hasn't officially written out a statement, but he verbally, on camera, told us everything."

I watched him leave, on the phone with Teri.

All my doubts left me when she nearly blew my eardrum out with her scream of joy.

Cookie gave a soft yip under the counter and went back to sleep.

"Well, Cat," I said, "you might not be baking a wedding cake, but I'll hire you to bake a cake for Dash to celebrate his getting out of jail."

"No problem." She grinned. "That one's on the house."

Chapter
Twenty-Nine

Early Thursday evening, the party was in full swing at the Hagen house. Inina and Ben lived out near my parents on a few acres of land in a big, fancy house with plenty of room for revelry. They'd started around three, but I hadn't arrived until just now at five, closing the bookshop early.

They had a pool and patio that fit dozens comfortably, and I threaded through the cheerful faces gathered to celebrate Dash's homecoming. He looked tired but happy.

"Lexi," he called as I neared. Cookie beat me to him, jumping into his arms and licking him all over, to the amusement of everyone nearby. He set Cookie down before giving me a hug that took me off my feet. "I'm so glad the nightmare's over," he murmured before setting me down and kissing me on the cheek. "Thanks so much."

"You know, the Macaroons were pretty good this time around, but we have Mike's guilty conscience to thank for getting you out so soon. He confessed."

"I can't believe it was him. I mean, it makes sense why he chose me. He could have easily overheard me tell Noah where the rent-a-key was. He didn't like me dating both women. Not that I talked about them or anything, but he might have seen or heard me mention them. And then there was the fact that he was on thin ice after two poor performance reviews. The guy screwed around on his phone or with women all the time. I almost fired him a few times, but he'd beg me to give him another chance. He needed the money for him and Sherry."

"So sad." Cat shook her head, standing arm in arm with Teri next to us. "I saw Sherry earlier today, and she looked terrible."

"Wouldn't you?" Teri said. "But still, I hope Mike gets what's coming to him. He was happy enough to blame my brother for murder. Geez."

"Happy thoughts," I reminded her. "Your brother is free, and you'll be back to work helping him at the bar soon enough."

"Eh, I didn't miss that." She grinned at Dash. "Although Noah is much nicer to work for than you are."

"Hey."

Noah perked up, holding a beer. "Someone call my name?" He danced over to us and grabbed Dash in a bear hug. "Brother, I'm glad you're out, but we were getting so much business having a criminal as one of our owners. I hope it stays steady."

"Glad to know my being in the slammer was good for something." They laughed and joked.

I smiled at my uncles in the pool. I also saw half the CGC milling around, exclaiming over Mrs. Hagen's flowers while she gave them a tour. Mr. Hagen stood with a bunch of chamber folks talking about fishing and good beer.

Teri and Cat moved closer, petting Cookie. "Ah, life is back to normal once more," Teri said.

"Oh? I don't see Randy or Roger," I said.

Cat blushed but had the nerve to add, "And we don't see Chad."

"Stop it. We're just friends."

Teri frowned. "What did you do to your hand?"

"I hit something hard," I muttered. "Now why don't we check out the amazing cake I heard is the centerpiece of the party?"

Cat beamed. "It's so cool. Ugly, but so tasty. I put a little toy prisoner in it somewhere, like they do at Mardi Gras with their King cakes and the baby."

"What?"

"During Mardi Gras, they bake a brown sugar and cinnamon yeast cake and hide a tiny plastic baby when they bake it. I hid a tiny toy prisoner. Whoever finds the prisoner gets a prize."

"Now that's clever."

Before I could see the cake, my phone buzzed. I saw Sassy Pets and moved aside to take the call. "One minute guys. I'll join you."

I answered, "Hello?"

"Oh, hey, Lexi." Evie sounded busy. "I'm so sorry to bother you, but would you be able to come in really quick?"

"I'm kind of at Dash's party," I said.

"Well, that's part of it. We all feel so bad about him being accused, so we got him a present but won't be able to drop it off in time." Someone else murmured in the background, then Evie said, "Could you swing by and pick it up for us? It would mean a lot to Sherry. She's having such a tough time."

"Poor Sherry."

Evie sounded rushed when she added, "And when you come get it, you can pick up the credit card you left here after Cookie's appointment."

"Oh wow. You're kidding. I left that there?" I lived in constant fear of losing a credit or bank card. And the one I'd used there had a direct link to my bank. "You guys are still open?"

"Yeah. We have appointments until eight tonight. It's not too busy, but we have a steady revolving door. Come on by." She sounded overly perky for a late afternoon at work.

"I'll be right there. Thanks." I went in search of my friends. "Hey, guys, I'm running over to Sassy Pets real quick. I left my debit card there on Monday. Evie called to tell me."

"That's a little weird they waited until now." Cat frowned.

"Well, Evie also wanted me to pick up a present they all got for Dash, feeling bad about what happened. Especially because it was Sherry's Mike that made such a hassle."

Teri's eyes softened. "Oh, poor Sherry. Come on. Let's go."

"No. You stay here. I'll take Cookie. She loves Dr. Ryan. Besides, I just got back in your mom's good graces. If I skate out of here with her precious daughter at her precious son's welcome home party, she'll cut me off again. And I'll get the glaring stare of death. I can't handle that kind of evil, Teri."

She laughed. "Stop. My mom's not that bad."

Cat just looked at her and shook her head. "Go," she told me. "We'll cover for you. But if you're not back in half an hour, we'll come and drag you back."

"Fair enough." I whistled for Cookie. "Want to go see Dr. Ryan?"

Cookie gave a low groan of excitement, and we hurried out to the car. Except we were low on gas, darn it. I stopped by Filler Up, filled the tank, and sped merrily toward the vet's office.

"No shots, just treats." I laughed, overjoyed that my friend was safe and freed and the guilty party in jail. Where he belonged.

Cookie actually barked, sharing my mood, and we grooved to old school 80s rock on our way to Sassy Pets. A few cars were in the lot, and I left the car unlocked, the windows down, as Cookie and I went inside.

I went to hold the door open for a man with his hands full of two schnauzer puppies.

"Thanks."

I nodded and walked toward the empty front desk with Cookie.

No one around.

"Hello?"

"Hold on. I'm coming," Evie called, sounding a little manic. They must have been busier than they seemed.

I saw the tower of treats with Dash's name scrawled on yellow ribbon. "Aw, Cookie. Look what they got for Dash."

A huge box of gourmet chocolates, cookies, crackers, fancy candy, and caramel popcorn, and all wrapped in swaggy paper. "He's going to love this." Dash and his sweet tooth. I was already wondering how to talk him out of the popcorn when Sherry, dressed in her scrubs, walked up to me and Cookie.

"Hey, Sherry." I hadn't expected to see her there. "How are you?"

She blinked teary eyes but smiled. "I'm good as can be. I know Mike's innocent. I have hope."

I didn't want to shatter her illusions. Hey, if the girl couldn't see him cheating on her plain as day, what made me think she'd accept the notion of her lovebug as a murderer?

"I'm sure you're right. I hope for the best for you two."

"Thanks. You've always been so nice."

I didn't know what to say to that. "Um, Evie mentioned you guys had my credit card?" I craned my neck to look for her. Hadn't she called out just a few moments ago?

"Oh, yeah. But we had a problem running it. It might be the machine though. Dr. Ryan sometimes has us use the one in back if the one in front is busted. So it might be back there." Sherry started walking, so Cookie and I followed her. "Have you ever been behind the curtain?"

I felt so bad for the woman, trying to act normal and together. So I did the same. "No. Are we getting the tour?"

"Might as well before our next patient arrives." We passed a room with Evie in it. She seemed to be frowning at something on the exam table. Not lice or worms, hopefully. Ew, I was squicking myself out.

We continued to the back.

Sherry nodded to an office off the back laboratory. "Out that hallway is a line of in-patient housing, as we call it. Or cages." I could see through the lab's glass windows to the cats and dogs lying in cages, some with IVs hooked to them. "And that room back there is where we do surgeries. In here we run some lab work and can do minor stitchwork on the table." Two long metal tables took up the center of the room. "That wash basin is for a flea dip or bath." She smiled at Cookie. "But not for you."

Cookie took a step back then nosed her way over to Dr. Ryan's door. Knowing she'd be fine, I let her go.

"Oh, there it is." I saw the card on the floor by the machine she'd been talking about. But as I bent to pick it up, I felt a sting in my neck and jerked away, only to see Sherry behind me holding a hypodermic needle.

"Well aren't you spry?" She laughed. "I didn't get it all in."

"Wh-what?" I watched her watching me, and after a few seconds, started to feel a little fuzzy.

Then I heard something large fall from down the hall, back where Evie had been.

"Don't worry. She's not dead." Sherry looked worried. "She won't be unless Dr. Ryan kills her too."

"What?"

Dr. Ryan? Why had Sherry stabbed me with . . . that? What the heck was going on?

Cookie barked like a crazy dog, scratching like crazy at Ryan's door while coming back to me to nip at Sherry.

She danced out of Cookie's way and glared. "Hey, behave. I'm not hurting her. I'm trying to help her."

"What?"

Pounding from the doctor's door sounded overly loud. I felt dissociated from my body, giggly, floating outside myself, then okay. "Sherry, what's going on?"

"You'll be okay. I'll protect you," she said and helped me to lean against a medical table. "Dr. Ryan killed Marilyn. Rachel saw, so he killed her too. I found out, so he set up Mike to take the fall. And Mike confessed because he knows if he doesn't, Dr. Ryan will kill me too."

"Sherry." I gasped, overcome, scared, yet not. "We need to call the police. They can help."

"I hope so." She nodded. "I'm going to go check on Evie. Take this to protect yourself." She handed me a pair of long scissors and a scalpel. "Surgical tools. Sorry, I don't have anything sharper or longer. But they'll do the trick. Just stick him before he sticks you." She squeezed my hand. "I'll be back."

I stumbled as I turned and felt another prick at my neck, then Cookie was there, barking her head off and whining by my side. "I don't feel so hot."

I heard banging, and Cookie barked. The banging stopped. "Let me out!" A pause. "Lexi? Is that you? Cookie? Hurry before she comes back."

I heard something about hurrying and remembered what Sherry had told me about Dr. Ryan killing Marilyn. "Y-you killed them."

"I did. No, I didn't." He didn't sound too sure of himself.

Cookie licked me again. I tried to focus. Something . . . Wait. Sherry had injected me with something. Something that made it hard to think.

"Hurry," he yelled, and started banging again.

Cookie dragged me by the arm toward Dr. Ryan's door. I tried the handle, but it wouldn't open.

"Use the key," he said, not looking so good. Through the large window of his door, I saw blood on his scalp and hazy eyes. "Cookie, get the key."

Cookie looked from me to Dr. Ryan and whined. "The key," I said to her, trying to keep my balance. I had a clear thought. *Sherry, you witch. You did this.* Then I was gone again, trippy dippy.

I heard Sherry yelling at me and Dr. Ryan, blaming us for this mess. "You just had to come snooping, asking questions," she said to me. I closed my eyes for a second, then opened them to find myself dragged into Dr. Ryan's office. He lay on the floor, looking bruised and less than his normal ideal.

I stirred to a sitting position and started laughing. Dancing cartoon Cookies chased each other over his head.

"Come closer and I might hurt you," he warned.

"Huh?"

"You, Lexi. Stay back. Please."

"So you *are* trying to kill me. Sherry, help!"

But Sherry had left again. "Cookie?" I called. I heard her snarling and snapping, her mean growl that she'd used the last time I'd been in danger. Uh-oh. Not good.

"Is, ah . . ." I tried hard to concentrate, but Dr. Ryan's smile got really, really wide. Like, inhumanly wide, and his teeth grew super sharp. "You look like a human shark."

"You look like a naked mermaid." He slapped himself. "Oh wow. I am not a fan of ketamine."

That should have made sense but didn't. Not exactly. "Where's my dog?"

"Playing hero with the evil sea witch. Oy. Ignore me. I can't think." He laughed.

A nice laugh. I laughed with him.

And then I realized we were all alone in a small room with a flickering overhead light. One that looked like heaven, then hell, then heaven again.

It was just me and Dr. Ryan.

And the scalpel and scissors still in my hands.

Chapter Thirty

I slashed out with the scalpel and heard swearing. Not my swearing, but deep manly swearing. "Sorry. Did I cut you?"

"Yes, thanks." Then laughter. "I am *soooo* not happy about this." Dr. Ryan giggled. "It doesn't hurt, but I know it should."

"Huh." I looked at my arm and cut it. "You're right. I'm bleeding. A lot, actually. Doesn't hurt!" I laughed with him, and Sherry came back, entering the office to stare down at us.

Dr. Ryan and I yelled, "Sherry!"

She smiled at us. "This is nice. This is the way it should end for you." Sherry leaned down and slapped me. "Can't feel that, can you?"

"Nope." I slapped her back, and she reeled.

"I deserved that, I suppose."

I frowned. "That shouldn't hurt."

"I'm always hurt."

"Oh, Sherry." I started to cry. "You're too nice to feel bad."

She sighed. "So are you. Maybe you can live, and we'll take Evie out instead. But someone needs to see how evil Dr. Ryan really is."

I wanted to remember this later, because Sherry had been such a peach. While she stared at him and kept babbling about his love affair with Marilyn, I fumbled to get my phone out of my pocket and hit my record button. Then I hid the phone near the trash can on the floor so I could surprise Sherry with it later.

"Wait. Dr. Ryan killed Marilyn?" I asked loudly and laughed again, because that sounded silly.

"No. I liked her a lot. I loved Rachel." He sighed. "Sherry killed them all. With the ketamine she stole. I knew it when you said it."

"What did I say?" I frowned, having a tough time remembering. Was I frowning? I felt my face. "I can't for the life of me remember."

"You came in with Cookie and kept asking me about Marilyn and Rachel. Then you asked me about ketamine. And I told you it had side effects. And I knew . . ."

"That ketamine can affect the heart," Sherry said. "He wanted to know what happened to the spare key that he keeps in his desk for the meds. And the other key, for the office. It was like he knew."

"I knew you were magic," Dr. Ryan said with a laugh. He coughed. "No. Magical, yes, but mean. Mad."

"Killer mad!" I exclaimed.

"Yes." He and I high-fived, and I watched blood drip down my arm. So pretty.

Wait. That was my bad arm all good again!

"Sherry, it's not broken." I looked at my weak arm, surprised to no longer see the cast. "You did it. I'm healed!"

I jolted up and hugged her.

"Damn it! Now I have blood on me. Lexi, stop or you're going to die."

I gasped. "I'll bleed out! Hurry, Doc. Hold me." I kneeled next to Dr. Ryan and put his large hand over my cut that still didn't hurt.

Sherry groaned. "You two are super annoying."

"You know who's annoying? Detective Berg."

Sherry snickered. "That's true."

"But he's pretty cute. I mean, he's not great at kissing." I puckered up. "Who can kiss when you do this?" I made fish lips, which Dr. Ryan thought was hysterical. So he started making them.

"Look, Sherry, we're fish."

"Dead fish," she corrected and sighed. "Evie won't have much longer, sadly. And by the time the cops get here, it'll be too late for you too. Overdoses of ketamine. He killed you and Evie, then himself. Thankfully, I survived."

Dr. Ryan and I started clapping.

"She's pretty good," I said. "Wait. Where's Cookie?"

"Your dumb dog pushed through the window in the office. Can you believe that? She ran away. Probably hit by a car by now."

I should have cried, but my dog is super smart. "No way. She can fly. Look." I pointed to the cartoon canines flying over Dr. Ryan's head. Then they floated over to Sherry's head.

"No one else is coming." Sherry sounded sad. "We're all just going to go to sleep now."

Sleep sounded good. I looked at Dr. Ryan, but he was staring at his hands. "Oh, I don't feel so good."

I felt just fine. And then I yawned. I thought I heard my name. But probably not. So I went to sleep and felt like I floated through space and time to land on Berg's face for that fish-faced kiss that wasn't so disgusting the more times we did it.

* * *

"Okay, there you are. Wake up."

That slap hurt a little. "Ow. Stop it."

"She's good. She's back. Oh, God."

That sounded like Cat.

"She's bleeding. Cat, hand me some gauze."

A long wet tongue scraped the side of my face. "Did you just lick me?" I asked the muscular detective propping me to sit up.

"That would be super dog." He looked at Cookie and smiled. "She was running so fast she passed me going the other way. I had to turn on the siren to get her to stop."

"What?"

"Hey, lady, do I know you?" I heard Dr. Ryan ask. Then a few choice swear words. "Where's Sherry?"

"Right here," Cat said, though I couldn't see much past Chad's chest in my face. "We found Evie in the other room."

"She's unresponsive. We have a unit and ambulance on the way."

"Ketamine overdose, likely," Dr. Ryan said. "Sherry really wanted her to die."

"Sherry did this?" Chad asked, wrapping my arm. "Because the note next to her body says you did it."

"Nah." I patted his chest. "Sherry killed everybody." Which wasn't funny but I found it hilarious. "I made her a movie about it."

"She's higher than a kite," Cat said.

"I can see that."

"Cookie," I sang, "Cookieeeee."

I heard howling and laughter. Dr. Ryan was cracking up.

"Finally." Cat sighed. "I hear the ambulance."

Dr. Ryan started giving them instructions on where to find mermaids, but I wanted to sleep. So I did.

* * *

When I woke up in the hospital, I had a mini freak-out. "What the heck? What happened? Who died? Where's Cookie?"

"You're all good," Teri told me. Next to her sat Dash and Cat. And Cookie, curled up at the foot of my hospital bed. Huh. How about that?

The door opened, and Detective Berg and Officer Halston walked in. Roger winked at Cat, who blushed, then asked, "How are you feeling, Lexi?"

"I have no idea. What the heck happened?" I yawned and saw a bandage on my forearm. I touched it and felt the burn. "Ow."

"She's back." Chad wiped a hand over his face. "Tell me what you remember."

"I was going to the party. To Dash's party." I frowned. "Cat made a King cake as a welcome home cake. I couldn't wait to see it, then nothing." I scowled at my arm. "What the heck?" I turned to Dash. "Why are you here?"

He looked worried. "We cut the party short. Cat got worried when you were gone for so long, since you said to give you a half hour. She was on the way to Sassy Pets when Detective Berg screamed past her heading toward the vet. Then he slammed on his brakes and hit the sirens when a certain dog flew past him going the opposite way."

Cat nodded. "I watched the car door open and Cookie get in. Then I followed them to the vet. Cookie was maybe half a mile from the vet's when he got her. We found everyone unconscious, you and Dr. Ryan bleeding, and it was scary as heck."

"It was." Berg nodded. "Evie is still out, but they're monitoring her closely in a quiet room. Sherry Resnick wanted her dead and for Dr. Ryan to take the fall. That would make Mike look innocent and give them the happily ever after she wanted for them."

"And me?" I couldn't remember a thing after arriving at Dash's party.

"She wanted you gone too. With you and Evie dead, and her looking like a victim, Lee Ryan would go down for all the murders. The link being the ketamine. Sherry would wake up and accuse the doc. She was counting on being the only one to wake. But if you did happen to survive, you'd have no memory of what occurred.

"There's a reason they call it a date rape drug," Teri said with disgust. "It fogs your memory, can cause hallucinations sometimes."

"Huh." I wanted to yank the bandage off my arm but didn't. "So how do you even know this, because I can't remember much. Did Dr. Ryan tell you?"

"He's a little foggy too. He remembered some, but not all. It was you who told me what I needed to know." Berg still looked annoyed.

Roger, however, kept trying not to laugh.

"What am I missing?"

Berg cleared his throat, and Roger grew serious. "You managed to record her confession and your attempted murders. Sherry is guilty to her bones. I'm just glad Cookie led us to save you. She saved the day again."

"Yes." I smiled and petted her. "But I knew something was off from the beginning. Mike confessing was too easy, especially after how adamant he was that he had loved Marilyn. He was covering for Sherry."

"Yes. I intend to get the whole story from him as soon as Sherry wakes to tell her side. We'll see what they have to say." He stroked Cookie's head and nodded. "I just wanted to check on you. Halston, let's go."

Roger followed him. The door shut, and the four of us—
five, counting Cookie—just looked at one another.

"What are you idiots doing here?" I asked, feeling groggy
again. "Go party. Cookie and I are going to sleep." I closed my
eyes. "Welcome home, Dash."

"Yeah, see you soon, Lexi." I felt the press of his lips on my
forehead. Then they were gone.

And I had the best sleep I'd had in ages. Just me and my dog.

* * *

The next afternoon, after my uncles pampered me and then
drove me home after insisting I call if I needed *anything,* I had
just entered the house and taken a few steps down the hallway
when I heard someone knock. I paused, just wanting to rest.
Maybe if I remained quiet they'd go away.

Then came the incessant banging. When I saw the perpetra-
tor, I groaned and opened the door. Cookie growled her approval
then left in search of Mr. Leggy.

"Come on, Detective. What are you citing me for now?"

He looked furious yet didn't make a move toward me, standing in my open doorway.

I frowned. "What's wrong?"

"How do you feel?"

"Fine, actually. Never better . . . except for this cut. It stings."

He nodded, stalked toward me, then hauled me close for a
kiss that knocked my socks off.

When he pulled back, I think my eyes had crossed, and I
could do nothing but pant and stare up at him as I clutched his
shirt in my hands.

With a satisfied grunt, he gently pulled away, walked out,
and shut the door after him.

"What the ever-loving"—I filled in a bunch of cuss words—
"was *that?*"

Cookie just looked at me, then walked around the house
with Mr. Leggy in her mouth. Apparently, the human species
was doomed to remain a mystery to my wise and noble canine
companion.

I opened the patio door and watched her drop Mr. Leggy in
favor of Mr. Peabody, the pair ranting at each other. Something
I hadn't missed during my short hospital stay.

Then I laid down on the couch for a short nap, thinking
about Chad's kiss, and fell asleep smiling.

* * *

Five hours later, my friends arrived with snacks and drinks. But
I stuck to water and bland pretzels, thanks very much.

"You're now officially a legend among the Macaroons," Cat said.
"Stefanie told me to tell you we want full details on Monday night
for book club. *Thor: Ages of Thunder* is going to have to wait."

I laughed. "What I can remember? Sure. Not much." I
wasn't lying.

But my friends wore wide grins that told me I wasn't exactly
in on the joke.

"What?"

They burst into laughter upon seeing me look so confused.

"You have to hear it to understand." Cat placed my phone on
the table and played a recording.

Afterward, I stared at them blankly, my cheeks red-hot.
"That's me giggling with Dr. Ryan. Making fish sounds. I said
Berg isn't a good kisser." Where the heck had *that* come from? I
swear, if I hadn't recognized my voice, I'd never have believed
that was me.

"Yep." Dash kicked back and laced his hands behind his head. Cookie, that traitor, jumped up on his lap and fixated on the bowl of crackers near him, licking him to remind him of her love. And the crackers, so close. "That recording makes up for the eight days I spent in a jail cell, I tell you. The look on his face when he heard it was priceless." They all burst out laughing, and I had to join in.

"That's terrible." And not true at all, as I well knew now. "Wow. I was really high."

"What was it like?" Teri asked.

"I can't remember much, but I do remember feeling really out of control, like, not a part of what was going on. And the aftereffects suck. Short-term memory loss, feeling woozy. And of course, not feeling pain while I cut myself, which I feel right now. Not great."

"Yeah, I can't see how anyone would want to do that stuff for fun." Cat shook her head and went to the kitchen to grab a covered platter. "Why lose yourself in drugs when you can lose yourself in . . . cake!" She pulled out a cake she'd baked that looked smaller than Dash's but just as tasty. "I call it the Can't Kiss Cake. There's a plastic fish somewhere in there. Whoever finds it gets a prize."

We laughed and celebrated the end to a crazy case.

"So it really was Sherry," I said as the night wound down.

Teri nodded. "Apparently, from what Berg and Roger have told us, Sherry found out about Marilyn and tampered with the wine. We don't know if she meant to kill them both or not, but I'm thinking not, because she does love Mike, and she knows he hates wine. Either way, she wasn't worried about all the ketamine she'd injected into the bottle, unbeknownst to Mike. He only drank a little with Marilyn before he left. Sherry was outside waiting for Marilyn to die—because that stuff seriously affected her heart. After giving it some time, Sherry went inside Marilyn's, washed up after herself, and took the bottle with her."

Dash took over. "But Rachel, who'd been stalking Marilyn, trying to get some dirt on her she could use to fund her new business, saw Sherry leave with the bottle. When Rachel learned Marilyn had died, she put two and two together and decided to blackmail Sherry."

"Because Sherry's parents have money." I nodded, it all finally making sense. "But why blame Dash?"

Dash said, "I can answer that. I used to ride Mike pretty hard, and she didn't like it. The guy was a constant slacker and screwup, yet she thought he deserved a raise? Gimme a break. She also knew I'd dated both Marilyn and Rachel. Mike shared everything with her, right down to the place where I hide my key. So she, without Mike's help, killed Rachel by drugging her, then set her up in my yard. Apparently, Rachel was taking too long to die, so Sherry bashed her in the head with a hammer. That wasn't part of the plan though, and she freaked."

"Overthought things and made it more complicated, if you ask me," Teri said.

"I'm still confused." I frowned. "What was with the towel and the panties?"

Dash sighed. "When Sherry clocked Rachel in the back of the head, Rachel bled all over her and the ground. Sherry panicked and started cleaning up. Changed her mind, then dumped Rachel in that lounger and propped her in it like a doll. But she had a bloody towel she didn't know what to do with and dumped it in my house—while I was sleeping—with the panties. Then she snuck away, went home, and acted like she had nothing to do with it."

"Creepy." Cat shuddered.

Dash shook his head. "Mastermind or insane criminal. I can't decide which. Sherry wasn't making much sense with her confession, from what I heard."

Cat nodded. "Roger said she started babbling. I think she was trying to re-create a mystery she'd seen on TV. But the only parts she got right were wiping away her prints, hiding the murder weapon, and planting the towel and panties to back up a story about Rachel and Dash being intimate and him killing her."

Dash snorted. "She should have kept it simple. Anyway, she was happy enough to let me take the fall. Fast-forward to your vet visit, when Dr. Ryan found out ketamine and that key were both missing—after talking to you, Lexi. He questioned his staff, and all clues pointed to Sherry."

Teri added, "Sherry made Evie call you after giving her a small dose of ketamine. Oh—the Tower of Treats was real, by the way." Teri flashed a smile. "Everyone loves my brother, and they felt bad, including Dr. Ryan, for believing he could have done it. You forgetting your credit card on Monday was the cherry on Sherry's cake."

Cat said, "Sherry'd already locked Dr. Ryan in his office, and after Evie lured you in, Sherry injected her with a second dose of ketamine. I can't believe Sherry was willing to kill Evie and you. That's messed up. And think about it. After she poisoned Rachel, she bashed her head in to hurry her death. She was really clever at some points and really stupid at others. How sick do you have to be to go to so much trouble to frame an innocent man? To kill two people for *love*?"

"She was jealous of everyone." I couldn't believe it either. "So what do you think will happen to Mike?"

"He confessed to a crime he didn't commit. They can charge him with interfering in a police investigation, is my guess," Teri said. "But I'm betting they won't. His whole life got turned upside down by the woman he loved most."

"Yeah, he loved her so much he slept with other people," Dash muttered.

"That." I agreed. Mike's idea of love and commitment needed serious work. "But another case solved by the Scooby gang." I smiled at Cookie. "One thing though. Why was Berg on his way to the vet's? I know Cat went to check on me. How did he know to go?"

Cat answered. "Roger told me something Mike said made him curious. I think he had more questions for Dr. Ryan, then they got a very strange call from Evie before she lost consciousness. Fortunately, Evie's going to be okay. Everyone is, really, except for Sherry. That girl is bound for a rough life."

"One she deserves."

Cookie grumbled.

"Exactly," I said. "Now, Cat, how about cutting that cake?"

Chapter
Thirty-One

Saturday morning, I was out watering my garden. Abe had come by to check on me, and I had him sample my pink lemonade, which he claimed tasted worlds better than his. I gave him a short rundown of the previous day's events—at his request—and he whistled.

"You really are a crime solver."

"Well, you could say I attract trouble, I guess."

He laughed.

I pointed to the tall man walking up my driveway. "Yeah, see? Trouble. Capital T."

In a good mood, Abe laughed and walked back to his place. "Funny. Later, Lexi."

Shoot. I'd been meaning to ask him to come to our next Macaroons meeting. I'd have to remember to ask him the next time I saw him.

Cookie raced to Chad and sat, her tail wagging. He crouched to pet her, gave her a large baked bone-shaped biscuit, then straightened to walk to me.

He watched me watering my flowers for a few seconds while Cookie crunched her treat. Dang it, but he looked fine. Off duty, I guessed, in shorts and a sweatshirt to combat the cooling temps.

"How are you feeling?"

"Good." I smiled.

He smiled back, his grin turning sly. "Just good? Not hot and bothered by that amazing kiss?"

My cheeks felt blazing-hot.

"Good. You have no idea how much heat I've taken from the entire precinct for that recording. Not a good kisser? Please."

"Oh man. Everyone heard it?"

"It's evidence." He didn't seem bothered. If anything, his eyes shone with mirth. "So I hear you like Indian food, pizza, salads, and healthy fare. But you're partial to sweets."

"Huh?" I turned off the water. "What are you talking about?"

"The date I owe you. I'm planning on steaks with a nice side salad, fresh beets, maybe corn on the cob, and the dessert of your choosing."

"Date? What are you talking about?" I tried to look genuinely puzzled to mess with him.

He frowned. "You know. Our dinner date."

"I'm sorry. I'm not following." I let myself appear bashful. "Honestly, I feel stupid. I keep forgetting things. I think it might be the ketamine.'"

He looked concerned. For a moment. "You're pulling my leg."

"I'm not sure. What's your name again?" I grinned.

He laughed. "You really are a pain."

"I am. But you know it. Just like everyone knows what a bad kisser you are." I had to laugh at that.

He chuckled. "They might think that now, but we'll prove them wrong, won't we?" He turned and hummed as he walked away. "I'll pick you and Cookie up tonight at six."

"Wait. What?"

"And prepare to pucker up, Miss Trouble."

I swear he hummed the *Scooby-Doo* theme song.

Cookie and I watched him leave, then looked at each other.

A big old grin stretched my mouth wide. "Well, you heard him. Let's go see what we're going to wear tonight."

She picked up what was left of her biscuit, nudged Humperdink, the good-luck garden gnome, and preceded me inside.

Acknowledgments

I'd like to acknowledge my agent, Nicole Resciniti, and the wonderful folks at Crooked Lane for making this book possible. Special thanks to Cathy Malk for her in-depth information about real estate and Stefanie de Gruyter for her knowledge about the law. And a huge shout-out to my beta readers, Sarah and Michele, for taking the time to give me great feedback. You're always appreciated.